I0705286

This is a work of fiction. References to real people, events, establishments, organizations, or locales are intended only to provide a sense of authenticity and are used fictitiously. All other characters, and all incidents and dialogue are drawn from the author's imagination and are not to be construed as real.

Chasing Shadows

Printed in the United States of America. For information, address
Acorn Publishing, LLC
3943 Irvine Blvd. Ste. 218, Irvine, CA 92602

www.acornpublishingllc.com

Interior design by Kat Ross
Cover design by Damonza

ISBN-13: 979-8-88528-125-6 (hardcover)
ISBN-13: 979-8-88528-124-9 (paperback)
Library of Congress Control Number: 2025900303

CHASING SHADOWS

A.C. ADAMS

Helping talented writers publish exceptional books

Author's Note

Chasing Shadows was inspired by the search to uncover my father's secrets. When he vanished, leaving an inscrutable message that revealed he had a new life and must never see his children again, my world was turned upside down. He was a brilliant university professor and a caring parent—almost a super dad who bought me and my siblings a horse, encouraged our interests, and took us camping at all the National Parks. I idolized him and needed to understand why he would leave us. Hoping to discover the truth, I embarked on an international search with my husband and writing partner, Anthony Leigh Adams. What we learned about his hidden past changed everything I thought I knew about my family history. Although we interviewed many of my father's friends and colleagues, his labyrinthine life was a Gordian knot that was impossible to unravel fully. To protect our sources, their names have been changed, and we took creative license with several of the locations, but many of the events of his life and the details of our search are true.

We hope you enjoy *Chasing Shadows*.

—Christina Adams

Chapter 1
Voices from the Past

Dr. Aidan Ryan felt the fateful ticking of the clock set in motion years ago, and although filled with dread, he embraced the momentous change rushing toward him like an unstoppable freight train.

On a foggy June morning, he strode across the campus of El Encanto College, briefcase in hand, dressed in a navy-blue linen sports coat, a collarless white shirt, and khakis. At sixty, the tall and dynamic history professor possessed a charisma that led strangers to believe he was famous. He wasn't, but he looked the part and carried himself with the gait and vitality of a much younger man, outpacing his students on walkways and racing up campus stairs, leaving them in the dust.

A cool breeze blew through his blond hair streaked with silver as he passed the Spanish Colonial buildings of the esteemed private institution in San Diego, perched on a bluff overlooking the Pacific Ocean where perfect sets of waves crashed against the rugged cliffs.

Dr. Ryan passed through a courtyard shaded by towering Italian cypress trees and under a topiary arch, into a quiet place he referred to as Magistral Garden because it reminded him of a miniature version of his favorite park in Italy.

After settling on a stone bench beside a colorful Mexican tiled fountain, he opened his case, pulled out his lecture notes, and then began writing. Moments later, he heard approaching footsteps and turned to see his daughter Sofia. The young woman—a luminous, willowy blonde, as skittish and timid as a fawn—was wearing white jeans, a purple sweater, and knee-high suede moccasins with fringe around the cuffs.

"You left early this morning, but I got your note," she said. "What did you want to talk about?"

He patted the bench, inviting her to sit. "I have a few things to discuss and thought it would be nice to chat in our special place."

Sofia sat next to him and studied his face with concern. "Are you all right? You haven't seemed like yourself lately."

Aidan could tell by the look in her emerald-green eyes she sensed his distress, and he forced a smile. "Nonsense. I'm fine."

Clearly, she wasn't convinced. "What's wrong? I can tell something's bothering you."

"You know me too well." He glanced at her apologetically. "Once again, my work is taking center stage, and I'll be out of town on your birthday."

"Is that all? You had me worried. Where are you going this time?"

"London. I'll be lecturing at a conference. The keynote speaker broke his hip, and they begged me to fill in at the last minute."

"Then take me with you. I can finally use my passport, and it'll be the best birthday present ever."

"Sorry, angel. You know that's not possible. I never mix business with my personal affairs."

"Can't you break your own rules once in a while?" she asked.

"No, but I have an early birthday gift for you that I hope will make up for my absence." Aidan reached into his coat pocket and pulled out a small blue box tied with a white satin ribbon.

Her eyes lit up as he handed it to her. "They say good things come in small packages." Sofia untied the bow and opened the box. Inside, on a square of blue velvet, rested an ornate silver ring. There was something soulful about the delicate piece that tugged at her heart. She ran her finger across the embossed symbols. "Is this an Irish friendship ring?"

"Yes. The heart signifies love, the crown stands for loyalty, and the clasped hands represent friendship."

Noticing there was lettering inside the band, she held it up to the light and read the faint inscription. *May God be with you.* Since her father wasn't religious, the sentiment surprised her. "It's beautiful. Thanks, Dad."

"My brother gave it to me when I was a child. I thought you might like it."

"Are you kidding? I love it." Moved, she slipped the ring on her finger. "This makes me feel more connected to my uncle. Please, won't you tell me more about him?"

Aidan's face darkened. "I've told you all you need to know about my family."

"But they're my family too."

"You know better than to ask about them. This discussion is over," he stated with finality.

She twisted a tendril of her long, golden hair as she hesitated. "My psychology professor said that talking about personal trauma is good for you."

"You don't know what's good for me. And an introductory

course in psychology doesn't make you an expert on how I deal with grief." His voice was as sharp as a scalpel.

Wounded, Sofia responded softly. "I was hoping you might finally be ready to share."

"Someday I may tell you about them, but not now."

"As if that will ever happen," she muttered. Arguing with her father was futile.

Aidan softened his tone. "Now, please, let's discuss something more pleasant, like your graduation present."

"All right. What is it?" she asked.

"It's a secret. Meet me after class, and I'll show you."

Sofia was excited. "Did you finally buy me a VW Bug?"

"No. The car I gave you for your high school graduation is still in mint condition."

"Okay. Now, I'm really curious."

"I think you'll find it's worth the wait. Well, I must prepare for my lecture."

"Can't wait to see what you have up your sleeve." Sofia got up and walked away.

When she was gone, Aidan closed his steel-gray eyes, straining to conceal the inner turmoil behind his stoic demeanor. To still his mind, he took deep breaths and concentrated on relaxing every muscle in his body and slowing his heart rate. After a few minutes, the soothing sound of water flowing in the fountain calmed him, but his equanimity vanished when he heard a familiar gruff voice.

"Hello, old friend," a man said.

Recognizing the distinctive Irish accent, Aidan opened his eyes and scowled at the intruder sitting on a bench across from him. Jack McLoughlin sported the wry grin of a self-satisfied con man. His pale freckled skin and icy-blue eyes were chilling. Ginger hair, slick with pomade, crowned his broad, thick skull and a fighter's physique bulged through his tight red shirt.

Aidan had detested him for years, and although in his late sixties, he looked even more menacing than when he was younger. "Jack! What are you doing here?"

"The time has come to fulfill your agreement, and the boss wanted to confirm you're still on track."

"Don't insult me. I'm quite clear about my responsibilities."

"Not so sure about that," Jack said. "You've been unreliable in the past."

"You have no business being here."

"Actually, it is my business to keep an eye on you. Just saw your lovely daughter. She's a pretty young thing, almost as bewitching as the mother."

Aidan lunged at Jack with lightning speed, then hurled him to the ground. "Sofia and Ella are off limits! Stay away from them, or you'll regret it," he warned, looming over him.

Unperturbed, Jack rose and dusted off his pants. He clenched Aidan's shoulder with his powerful hand and squinted at him with cold fury. "If anyone else had done that, I'd slit their throat. Lucky for you you're the boss's pet."

Aidan shoved his hand aside. "Tell him I'll be there. Now, get the hell out of here."

"Be careful, mate. Stress leads to an early grave." Jack strolled away, whistling a carefree tune.

Aidan followed him, then thought better of it, and stopped dead in his tracks, his heart pounding. He was straddling two incompatible worlds, but the die was cast and there was no turning back.

Chapter 2
Patterns of Control

The June gloom had burned off, and the afternoon was warm and clear as Aidan and Sofia headed toward the faculty parking lot. While making their way through the campus, she fixed her eyes on the adobe brick path, trying to pluck up her courage.

"Dad, there's something I need to talk to you about."

"Of course. What's on your mind?"

"I really don't want Ella to come tomorrow. Can you please uninvite her?"

"Absolutely not. And stop being so selfish."

"I'm not selfish. She's never cared about me, so why should she come to my graduation?"

"Because she's your mother, that's why. You sound like a broken record. Don't ask me again."

"I guess it doesn't matter anyway. She'll probably be a no-show," Sofia said.

"You should give her a chance to make amends."

"She doesn't deserve it, and I'm not ready to forgive her."

"Don't be closed-minded. As Alexander Pope said, 'To err is human; to forgive, divine.'"

Sofia didn't want to admit he was right and tamped down her feelings as they walked along in silence. When they reached the car, he opened the passenger door of his new silver Mercedes sedan. She got in, buckled up, and then sank into the plush leather seat.

Aidan started the car. "Before we leave, I need you to close your eyes en route to your graduation present."

"Dad, that's silly. Just tell me where we're going."

"Come on, humor your old man."

The plan seemed ridiculous, but she agreed. "Okay, if it makes you happy."

As they pulled away, he popped a cassette of Puccini's opera *Gianni Schicchi* into the car's audio system and the celestial soprano voice of the Italian diva Gemma Ricci soared as they drove to the mystery destination. Her father was a passionate devotee of opera, and Sofia knew better than to disturb him while he was listening to his music, which was a transcendent experience for him.

She tried to relax and enjoy the ride, but it was impossible. Tomorrow night, she would have to face her mother, which she dreaded. At long last, she was starting to feel in balance, and allowing Ella back into her life would disrupt everything.

Before long, Aidan slowed the car, pulled to the right, and parked.

"Can I open my eyes now?" she asked.

He stopped the music and shut off the engine. "Yes, let there be light."

Sofia opened her eyes and discovered they were on a quiet street in front of a small house near Mission Bay. "Are we visiting someone?"

"Come along and you'll see."

They got out of the car and walked to the door of a charming Spanish-style cottage in Crown Point, a bayside neighborhood with homes built in the 1940s. Aidan stared at her with an enigmatic smile.

"I don't understand. Where's my present?" she asked.

"You're looking at it. You've always loved the beach, so I bought this property for you." He took a key out of his pocket and handed it to her.

Sofia felt faint and disoriented. "Why didn't you ask me? I don't want to move out!"

"You've been mollycoddled your entire life, and it's time to stand on your own two feet."

Her face reddened. "Just because you're my father, you don't have the right to decide for me!"

"It absolutely is my right," he said with an intensity that rattled her.

Despite his extravagant gift, she felt manipulated. "But I love the ranch. And there's no place for Gaia here."

"That's no problem. You can visit your horse whenever you wish."

"Are you mad at me?" she asked. "It seems like you're forcing me out."

"Nonsense. You should be delighted. Most people your age would be."

"Well, I'm not the least bit delighted." Her father was the one person she thought she could trust. *How dare he blindside me like this?*

Aidan gently touched her cheek. "Don't be melodramatic. I thought you'd enjoy having your own place. You'll be free to do whatever you want and invite friends over any time."

"You know I don't have any close friends."

"Then it's time to make some. You need to learn how to get along with other people. I won't live forever, you know."

Her pulse quickened. "Dad, you're scaring me. Are you sick?"

"No, I'm perfectly healthy. For your own good, you need to be independent."

Sofia brooded and crossed her arms defiantly. Springing this huge life change on her out of the blue was infuriating and she fought the urge to yell at him. "Why are you so controlling?"

"I don't mean to be. I only want what's best for you."

"But this is all so sudden."

"It's not sudden," he said. "Look in the mirror. You're not a child anymore."

Sofia was taken aback. She wasn't used to thinking of herself as an adult; it snuck up on her when she wasn't looking and the thought of it was daunting.

"Please, won't you at least have a look inside?" he asked, crestfallen.

She relented. "Okay, but I won't like it."

"Give it a chance." Aidan nudged her forward.

Resigned, she unlocked the door and entered, followed by her father. The two-bedroom house was warm and inviting, and although Sofia didn't want to like it, she had to agree it was attractive. Sunlight streamed through the picture windows overlooking pristine Sail Bay. The furnished cottage had a royal blue velvet sofa, carved wooden lamps, and a glass dining table with four white rattan chairs. On an entertainment console across from the sofa, there was a large color television, record player, and radio. The fully stocked kitchen, which opened to the living room, had countertops decorated with red, blue, and yellow Talavera tiles.

She looked around in astonishment. "This must have cost a fortune! How can you afford it?"

"Years of scrimping and saving, but it's an investment in

your future. Beach front real estate in San Diego will always be valuable."

Sofia felt a pang of contrition. "I don't mean to be ungrateful, but I wish we'd discussed it. Maybe I'm not ready to be on my own yet."

"I'm attempting to prepare you for success, and you lack a plan." Aidan gave her a hard look. "It would be wise to get a part-time job while studying for your master's degree and teaching credential."

His advice instantly raised her hackles. "Seems like you have my life all figured out for me! Shouldn't it be my choice?"

"What is your choice?" He looked at her impatiently. "I'd love to hear all about it."

Sofia paused, trying to come up with a brilliant answer, but drew a blank. "I'm not sure yet."

"That's what I thought. You need to understand, your options are limited."

"Thanks for the vote of confidence." Sofia was crushed. Despite her best efforts, she always fell short of his expectations.

As if addressing a class, Aidan slipped into his professorial voice. "If you can find the courage, delve deep, discover your true nature, and choose a path that makes the world a better place. In the immortal words of Socrates, 'The unexamined life is not worth living.'"

"I'm not your student and I don't need to hear one of your lectures." She sighed in frustration. "It's not as easy for me as it was for you."

"You seem to lack clarity, so I'm suggesting a viable path."

"A path created by you." She looked away, unable to meet his gaze.

Aidan spoke in a soothing tone. "Not at all, angel. You must chart your own course. My intention was to inspire you."

Sofia's anger slowly subsided. For years, she'd been anxious and fearful, but it wasn't her father's fault. She took a deep breath and faced him. "Sorry I reacted so badly. I really appreciate your amazing gift."

"You've earned it. You're the class valedictorian and my number one daughter."

"I thought I was your only daughter."

"As far as I know," he said with a wink. "Fortunately, I don't fly out until Wednesday, so I can help you move in. I'll rent a truck to bring your things over, and we'll pick up any supplies you need. What do you say?"

"Can't I move in when you get back?"

"No, the electricity and water will be off at the ranch, and workers are coming to do the upgrades while I'm away. So, we need to get you settled now."

"But what about Gaia?" she asked.

"Don't worry. She'll be boarded at Hilltop Stables until the work is completed."

"As usual, you have everything planned."

"Of course. Perfection is in the details." Aidan gave her a long hug, his eyes shimmering with unwept tears.

When he released her, Sofia looked at him with concern. "Dad, why are you so emotional?"

"It's hard to believe my little girl has finally grown up."

Since it was a fait accompli, Sofia resolved to accept her new reality and reluctantly forgave him for pushing her out of the nest. "Well, I guess I better start packing."

Chapter 3
Crossroads

Morning mist blanketed the wild chaparral on Ryan Ranch, the bucolic ten-acre estate where Aidan and Sofia lived in Alpine, nestled in the Cuyamaca Mountains of San Diego County. At the heart of the property was a sprawling home that looked like it grew right out of the rich, chocolate brown earth. Large smooth boulders surrounded the bottom half of the exterior walls, cedar shingles encased the rest, and a natural slate roof topped the attractive residence.

Sofia had slept uneasily, drenched in murky dreams, until the morning sun streaming through the windows awakened her. Her spacious bedroom—the same one she'd had her entire life—was painted a sky-blue color she loved and overflowed with art and keepsakes. She could hardly believe that within a few days she would no longer live there.

Nestled under a white quilted comforter, she looked around at the many treasures her father had brought her from his travels around the world. On a shelf there was a set of hand-carved rosewood elephants from India and an exotic mask collection hung on the wall, each a memento from a country he had visited while on sabbatical.

Built-in bookcases with hundreds of meticulously categorized record albums, history books, and literature, revealed her orderly nature and eclectic tastes, from Bach to Steely Dan and Homer to Vonnegut. On a teakwood desk was a family photo album, and a framed picture of Sofia with her brother Liam, a handsome boy with curly blond hair and an irresistible smile. They were eight years old, posing in front of a sandcastle they built at Ocean Beach. The twins could read each other's minds, finish each other's sentences, and were best friends. But it was deeper than that. After Liam's sudden death, half of her died too, never to return. The loss was unbearable. It felt like all the color had drained out of her life, and she was living in black and white—a walking shadow without hope or joy. Her energy vanished as she sank into a bleak pit of despair which she was still climbing out of.

As Sofia dressed, she couldn't stop thinking about Liam and a strange sense of unease welled up in her. If he were alive, he'd be by her side and graduating from college with her. They'd been inseparable, and her world imploded after his death. Her parents' marriage fell apart, and her mother moved out. Except for her father, there was no one in her life she was really close to and now she would live alone for the first time in her life. Since her horse always lifted her spirits, she decided to go for a ride. She ran downstairs, ate a quick breakfast of granola and strawberries, downed a cup of creamy coffee then headed outside.

The morning was cool and clear as Sofia led Gaia out of the barn. She held the reins of the twelve-year-old Palomino, which she'd named after the Greek goddess of the Earth. The magnificent mare had a flowing blonde mane and tail, and her stunning golden coat glistened in the sunlight. They passed a grove of blooming orange and lemon trees, and Sofia inhaled the sweet fragrance. She loved the ranch and would miss living there, but at least she could visit anytime.

On her way to the trailhead, Sofia approached Aidan who was lounging on a wooden swing suspended from the long portico that covered the front deck. On either side of the steps leading to the porch, clay planters with agaves stood like guards, their blue spikes reaching toward the cloudless sky.

Sofia paused in front of him and saw he was reading the play *Titus Andronicus*. She couldn't understand why her father loved such a bloody revenge tragedy, but he was obsessed with all of Shakespeare's works. Engrossed in his reading, he didn't notice her arrival.

"Good morning, Dad. Titus again?"

Annoyed, Aidan looked up at her. "You know I don't like to be interrupted when I'm reading."

"Sorry, didn't mean to bother you. I'm going for a ride."

"Have you finished writing your speech?" he asked.

"Of course. I'm all set."

"Good. I'll see you later." Aidan went back to his book.

Sofia swung into the saddle, and Gaia galloped toward the riding trails that meandered through the ranch. As the wind whipped through her hair, Sofia shook off her melancholy and, after an exhilarating ride, stopped by a stream to give Gaia a drink. She dismounted, stretched out on the grass shaded by a canopy of gnarled old oaks, and closed her eyes. The smooth rocks tumbled musically in the creek as the tributary wound its way down from the mountains.

As she listened to the babbling brook and the wind rustling through the leaves, Sofia thought about her future, and a wave of insecurity washed over her. Tonight was her college graduation and in less than a week, she'd be twenty-one. It was time to choose a path, but which one? She was at a crossroads, and felt unformed, like malleable clay unfired in a kiln. The easiest thing would be to get her master's and doctorate degrees and pursue a career as a professor, like her father. But although she wanted to emulate him, she wasn't sure she'd enjoy teaching. Public speaking intimidated her and dealing with departmental politics seemed nerve-racking. Maybe she should go on a grand adventure before committing to a long-term plan. Unfortunately, she was afraid of flying and traveling alone.

The more she contemplated her future, the more elusive it became, like a dream that slips away. Sofia closed her eyes, attempting to calm her thoughts, but was startled by drops of water splashing on her face. She giggled when she saw Gaia looking down at her, inches away, her muzzle wet from drinking in the stream.

"Silly girl. Are you ready to go home?" Sofia stood and stroked the white diamond pattern that adorned the horse's face. She mounted Gaia and with a gentle squeeze of her legs, the mare knew where to go and galloped away.

On the way back to the house, she thought about her graduation. It would be stressful enough to speak in front of a crowd of people, and the possibility of seeing her mother only added to her anguish. They hadn't spoken in ages and the divorce had been ugly. After watching how it changed Ella, Sofia vowed to never get married or have children. She preferred spending time alone in nature, sitting under a tree, and reading books. Nature, solitude, and Gaia were her best companions.

As they approached the house, the scent of burning hickory filled the air and smoke curled from their chimney made of stacked boulders that seemed to defy gravity. Gaia slowed to a trot, whinnied, and tossed her head playfully.

Sofia stopped in front of Aidan, who was waiting on the porch swing, already dressed for the night in a suit and tie, holding his daily tumbler of Connemara whiskey on the rocks.

"Hey, Dad," Sofia said and dismounted her horse.

He tapped his watch. "Have you decided not to attend your graduation?"

"Of course not. I'll be ready in time."

"Well, you better get a move on. It's getting late."

"I've never been late in my life."

"Good. Let's not develop any bad habits."

"You're my father, so I don't think that's possible." Sofia walked Gaia to the barn, then headed into the house.

Chapter 4
Slings and Arrows

Elysian Plaza, at the center of the campus, was the gathering place for all the important outdoor events at El Encanto College. Filigreed wrought-iron lamps cast a golden light on the pathways extending off the courtyard like the tentacles of an octopus. The plaza hummed with activity as families and friends of the graduates, dressed in formal attire, mingled, and chatted. Above the brightly lit stage, the school colors were proudly represented by a purple banner with gold letters proclaiming *Congratulations, Graduating Class, 1978!*

Befitting the auspicious occasion, the sunset behind the stage was dramatic. Fiery red and orange clouds splashed across the sky as the fading light of the sun sparkled like diamonds on the ocean.

Dean Locke, a commanding figure in a blue suit and red bow tie, tapped the microphone and cleared his throat. "Welcome, ladies and gentlemen. Our graduation ceremony is about to begin. Please take your seats."

The audience settled into the chairs positioned throughout the plaza.

Sofia, in a cap and gown, sat onstage behind the podium, next to the other honors students and special guests. Eyes downcast, with her hands neatly folded in her lap, she was eager for the ceremony to be over. Rituals and crowds always made her uncomfortable, but tonight was especially difficult, and her stomach churned with anxiety.

As the dean droned on in a stentorian voice about the value of a liberal arts education that emphasized analytical skills and a strong moral compass, she wished she were anywhere else. Even getting a root canal would be preferable. Although she tried to tune him out for what seemed like an ice age, she snapped to attention when she heard the words, "Please welcome our class valedictorian, Sofia Ryan."

The audience burst into applause as she approached the microphone, clutching a small sheet of notes in her sweaty palm. Sofia looked out at the enormous gathering and spotted Aidan sitting in the front row, solemnly watching her. Next to him was a chair with a "reserved" sign on it which he had saved for her mother, but as anticipated, she was a no-show.

His presence should have calmed her, but with so many people looking at her under the bright lights, her mouth turned dry. She nervously glanced at her notes, then spoke softly. "Thank you and congratulations to the graduating class of 1978."

"Louder!" a few voices called from the back of the plaza.

She took a sip of water and got closer to the microphone. "We've all worked hard to get here, and thanks to our outstanding education, we have the tools to achieve our highest potential. So now, as we take our place in a challenging world, it's incumbent upon us to share our knowledge and skills with humanity and do our best to serve others."

Sofia stared at her mother's empty chair and crumpled her

notes. "I prepared a speech, but rather than bore you with lofty platitudes, I think what really matters is to acknowledge the people who have supported us throughout our lives. So, I'd like to thank my father, Dr. Aidan Ryan, who's taught World History at El Encanto for over twenty years and has guided me through, in the words of his favorite author, William Shakespeare, 'the slings and arrows of outrageous fortune.' I've always tried to live up to his high standards of honesty, integrity, and compassion. He's my inspiration, and I know his teaching has inspired many of you as well."

She gestured to Aidan, and the audience cheered. Several students enthusiastically chanted, "Ryan, Ryan, Ryan!" He stood, motioned for them to hush, then sat down.

When the crowd fell silent, Sofia continued, "Thank you for the privilege of being class valedictorian. I'll do my best to live up to this honor." Relieved to escape the spotlight, she hurried back to her seat. The dean took the podium and brought the proceedings back to order. Sofia felt self-conscious, as if under a magnifying glass, and quietly observed the rest of the graduation with detachment.

At last, the ceremony was over, and she had regained her composure. As the audience applauded the graduates, she tossed her cap in the air with the rest of her peers, then left the stage to see her father, who was waiting for her.

Sofia ran up to him. "Sorry for messing up my speech, Dad."

"I don't mean to criticize you, angel, but what you said about me was quite inappropriate. A graduation ceremony isn't the time nor the place for such an overt display of filial affection."

"I didn't mean to embarrass you," she said, dispirited. "But everything I said was true."

"Plenty of people would disagree."

"Then they don't know you like I do." Sofia pointed at the seat reserved for her mother. "I hate to rub it in, but I told you she wouldn't come."

"It shouldn't bother me, but I'm disappointed that Ella didn't support you tonight. It's the least she could do."

The mention of her name touched a nerve. "I want nothing to do with Mom. She doesn't exist for me anymore."

Aidan gazed at her reproachfully. "You're too hard on your mother."

"Let's not talk about her, okay?"

"As you wish. Are you excited about the graduation party?"

Sofia twisted her hair, apprehensively. "Honestly, I wish I hadn't agreed to go."

"Don't be absurd. You must commemorate this important milestone."

"But there's so much work to do to get ready for the move."

"We'll start packing first thing tomorrow morning. Now, try to have fun for once." He hugged her, walked away, and disappeared into the crowd.

As Sofia left Elysian Plaza and headed toward the parking lot, she got the creepy feeling someone was following her. She looked over her shoulder and several yards behind her was a burly man who seemed to be fixated on her. He wore a black baseball cap which obscured his features, but his energy frightened her. Her heart pounded and she picked up her pace. When she glanced back a short time later, he had vanished into the sea of parents and well-wishers.

By the time she reached her powder blue Ford Pinto, Sofia had convinced herself she was imagining things, and the party might be a good distraction. She opened the door, unzipped her black graduation gown, revealing a royal purple sleeveless silk mini dress underneath, and then tossed the gown into the back seat. Slipping off her black flats, she put on the purple heels she bought for the occasion. The ensemble felt like an uncomfortable costume, but she hoped it would help her fit in.

After locking the car, she made her way toward sorority row, which adjoined the campus. She wobbled in her stilettos as she walked and wondered why so many women worshipped such impractical footwear. Hopefully, she wouldn't fall on her ass and humiliate herself at the party.

When she approached the two-story brick sorority house, she heard the monotonous thumping beat of disco, which she detested. Through the open doors, flashing lights shone on dozens of giddy graduates gyrating wildly to the blaring music. More wallflower than party animal, she couldn't bring herself to enter the madhouse of forced revelry.

Sofia wanted to go home, but her father would grill her with questions about why she left the gathering early and she was tired of being judged by him. So, to kill time and burn off steam, she took off her high heels and ran until she reached a wild space at the edge of the campus. She fell panting on the deep grass and stared up at the strawberry moon, which hung huge and low in the sky, as the wetness of the ground soaked into her dress. *What's wrong with me? Why can't I be like other girls and enjoy a stupid party?*

Startled by a sudden rustling sound, Sofia realized she might get attacked by a maniac, and no one would know where to find her. She jumped up and raced back to the parking lot. As she ran, the warm evening air dried her dress. After arriving at her car, she sat behind the wheel, breathless. In the rearview mirror, she thought she saw a man snapping a photo of her, but when she turned around to get a better look, he was gone. Was she being paranoid, or was someone really following her?

Either way, she'd had all the so-called fun she could stand for the night.

***

22

Jack emerged from behind a white van, flashed a lascivious grin and watched Sofia drive away.

Chapter 5
Chrysalis

The next five days were a blur of activity as Aidan helped Sofia move into her beach house. They found places for her art and books, filled the refrigerator with groceries, bought household supplies, and stored the rest of her belongings in the garage. Her resentment for her father had turned into gratitude. His gift was incredibly generous, and she chastised herself for being neurotic.

Aidan would be dropping by soon on his way to the airport, and almost everything was in place. She loved organizing and decorating to music and Pink Floyd's album, *The Dark Side of the Moon*, was the ideal soundtrack. As Sofia hung her clothes in the bedroom closet, the doorbell rang. She tossed the garments on the bed, turned down the volume on the record player, and rushed to the door.

It was her father, carrying a large pizza box and a bottle of Dom Perignon. He looked around, impressed. "You've made a lot of progress."

"It should all be finished before you get back."

"Splendid. Shall we toast to your new home and twenty-first birthday?"

"Sounds perfect."

"It's a gorgeous day. Let's sit outside," he said.

Sofia carried two plates and champagne flutes from the kitchen and followed him through the French doors that led to a brick patio with a wooden lattice pergola covered in fragrant pink jasmine vines. There were clay pots with an array of colorful succulents, and the view overlooking the bay was magical.

They settled at a white wrought-iron table. Aidan popped the champagne cork and filled the two crystal glasses. "To your future. You're a remarkable young woman, and I'm confident you'll make the right choices. Cheers!"

"Cheers!" Sofia took a sip, then opened the pizza box and was pleased to see it had her favorite toppings—mushrooms, artichokes, and olives. They each grabbed a slice.

While sipping champagne and eating pizza, they watched the sailboats glide on the water, which was as reflective as a mirror.

"It's already beginning to feel like home." She smiled sheepishly. "Sorry I was so grouchy."

"I understand, angel. Change is hard for everyone, but we must learn to embrace it."

"You're right. To quote a smart-ass college professor I know, 'Without change, there's no growth.'"

Aiden swatted her, playfully. "Now who's being a smart-ass. Do you have plans for your birthday?"

"Not yet," Sofia said. "But I'll figure something out."

"Maybe you should invite some classmates over."

"I might do that."

After a second slice of pizza, Aidan checked his watch. "I need to dash to catch my plane."

Sofia accompanied him to his car. "Will you have time to see a show while you're in London?"

"Probably not. I'll be lecturing all day, and they've scheduled events every night."

"Too bad. I know how much you love the Royal Opera."

They arrived at his Mercedes and hugged goodbye.

"I'll miss you," Sofia said. "I can't believe I'm living on my own."

"You'll get used to it soon enough." He took her hand and kissed it. "But be mindful. The world is filled with Homo Ignoramuses who will try to take advantage of you."

"As you've always said, apes in trousers. Don't worry, I'll be careful."

"Good. I've taught you well." Aidan pulled the keys out of his pocket, got in his car, and closed the door.

Sofia gave him a kiss through the open window. "Have a safe trip. I'll see you next week."

"It will be here before you know it." He started the engine. "I love you."

"Well, you're stuck with me, so you better love me!" Sofia waved goodbye and he departed.

When she went inside, she was acutely aware that the house, which had been bustling with activity, was suddenly still and silent. This would be her first night alone in her new home, and it was intimidating.

Chapter 6
Home at Last

Sofia drove along a country road lined with jacaranda trees ablaze with purple blossoms. The windows were down, and the gentle breeze blew through her long golden hair. Beside her in the passenger seat sat a bag of groceries. As a special treat, she had brought the ingredients to make crab benedict, a dish her father loved. She couldn't wait to see him and had a million things to discuss with him. Although he frequently traveled abroad for work, this time felt different. After her mother moved out when Sofia was eleven, Maria from Hilltop Stables would stay at the ranch to look after her. But now, she was truly on her own, and to her surprise, it felt good to be independent.

The last week had gone by in a flash. On her birthday, she made a chocolate cake with fresh raspberries and whipped cream on top. She considered inviting some classmates over to show them her new place, but since she had so little in common with them, being alone sounded better.

After devouring her entire birthday cake, Sofia embarked on a long walk around the bay to burn off the calories and explore her new neighborhood. Many people her age were at the beach, playing volleyball, tossing frisbees, and having fun. Maybe her father was right; it would be nice to have some friends, but she couldn't muster the courage to introduce herself to strangers. She wished she could be more like Aidan. He was always self-assured and knew exactly what to do, but he cast an enormous shadow. By her age, he was fluent in several languages, had graduated from college, and earned a master's degree. He often reminded her it wasn't a competition, but in comparison, she felt like a socially awkward under-achiever.

Sometimes Sofia felt like she didn't belong on Earth and was born here by mistake, which was probably why it was so hard for her to make friends. Most people loved to participate in group activities or identify with sports teams, clubs, religions, and political parties, but she wasn't a joiner and preferred peace and quiet.

Despite being a loner and having a mother who was never there for her, Sofia felt extremely lucky. How many girls had a father who gave them a house after graduating from college? His support had strings attached, like getting straight A's, but all in all, she had nothing to complain about and her life was pretty awesome.

Sofia turned on the car radio, and one of her favorite songs, "Home at Last" by Steely Dan, was playing. She sang along while driving down the winding road to her childhood home and a wave of nostalgia washed over her when she arrived at the ranch and parked on the gravel path in front of the house. Most of Sofia's memories were from here, and they would always hold a singular place in her heart.

Grabbing the sack of groceries, she walked to the porch, unlocked the door, and quietly entered. She stepped into the dark living room and then opened the drapes. Her stomach dropped as she gaped at the empty room in disbelief. All the furniture had vanished. *Had the workers robbed them?*

She hurried into the kitchen, put her bag on the table, and looked around. All the counters were bare, no butcher block knife set, no toaster, no coffee machine, no recipe books. The drawers and cabinets were empty, with no silverware or plates. And the refrigerator, which was normally bursting at the seams with a variety of food and drinks, had been cleared out. A shiver ran down her spine.

"Dad!" she called and rushed down the hallway. She threw open his bedroom door and stared at the barren room. There was no furniture, no clothes in the closet, nothing! Fear gripped her.

"Hello? Dad?" Her voice echoed in the empty house as she searched the rest of the rooms. Unrelenting panic seized her when she realized her father was nowhere to be found. Stripped of all personal belongings, the property seemed strangely unfamiliar, as if their lives and memories had been scrubbed from the premises. She trembled, and tears streamed down her face.

Sofia hurried outside and saw the porch swing rocking eerily back and forth in the wind, as if the ghost of Aidan was haunting his favorite spot. "Dad, where are you?" she whispered to herself.

Frantically, she ran to the barn, her heart pounding, hardly able to believe what was happening. She unlocked the door and stepped inside. The empty barn, which used to be one of her most cherished places, seemed cold and lifeless. She felt trapped in a living nightmare. Through her tears, she saw a duffle bag inside Gaia's stall. She slid open the zipper and discovered it was stuffed with numerous rolls of crisp, one-hundred-dollar bills. Sofia looked up and spotted an envelope with her name on it, in Aidan's handwriting, pinned to the back wall of Gaia's stall. She took it down and read the note silently, her hands shaking.

Dearest Sofia,
I knew you would come to see Gaia and wanted to make sure you'd find this note. I'm sorry my departure was so sudden, but it was unavoidable. Unfortunately, I can't explain why I left in a way you would understand. All my personal and business affairs are in order, and your horse is being taken care of at Hilltop Stables. The cash in the duffle bag should tide you over for a few years until you establish your career.

Please forgive me for any sorrow this may cause you. My actions are irreversible, so don't try to find me. I have a new life now and must never see you again. Hopefully, you will learn to be at peace with my decision. I will always love you and although she won't believe it, I love your mother too. Tell her I regret all the bitterness between us.
Your ever well-wisher, Dad

Sofia's mind reeled, and her legs could no longer hold her upright. Overcome by nausea, she collapsed on the ground and vomited. Wracked with chills and vertigo, she tried to get up, but everything went black, and she passed out.

Chapter 7
Gordian Knot

Emerging from an abyss of swirling darkness, Sofia came to consciousness. She thought she was awakening from a bad dream; then the stark reality shook her like an earthquake. When she opened her eyes, the sickening smell of bile filled her nostrils, and rough straw scratched her cheek. Her father's devastating note was still clutched in her hand. The weight of her grief and loss momentarily immobilized her as she lay there, trying to make sense of what had happened.

She stood unsteadily, shoved the note into the duffel bag filled with cash and walked to the barn sink where she washed up. The cool water revived her somewhat, and she dried her face with a towel draped over Gaia's stall. Conflicting emotions vied for dominance, filling her with a sense of hopelessness, dread, and rage. It was the ultimate betrayal.

Why did he do this to me?

There was no explanation for his behavior, but ruminating wouldn't help; it was time to take action. She grabbed the duffel bag and rushed out of the barn. What was Aidan's "new life" that he mentioned in his note, and what was he hiding? And how could a college professor have so much money? She had always been curious about how he maintained their lavish lifestyle, but he attributed it to his successful investments, and she naively believed him. It turns out she shouldn't have been so trusting.

Sofia stowed the duffel bag in the trunk of her Pinto, hopped in, and sped away. While driving to Hilltop Stables, she considered her next steps, but the path forward appeared formidable, chaotic, and terrifying. The future was a Gordian knot, and she had no idea how to unravel it.

When she arrived at the stables, she sat anxiously in her car and tried to collect her thoughts. Although the owners, Gusmaro and Maria González, were friends, how could she explain what had happened? It would be too humiliating. Besides, what would she say, that her father abandoned her with no plausible explanation? Despite the overwhelming sadness that engulfed her, she masked her pain and got out of the vehicle.

Sofia gazed at the familiar property, with its riding corral, trails, and fresh produce stand under the shade of an old pepper tree, its drooping branches covered with aromatic pink peppercorns. She and her brother first learned to ride here when they were six. The stables had always been enjoyable; but not today, and it made her angry. It was another joy her father had stolen from her, and she knew it wouldn't be the last.

She approached Gusmaro, a slim, gregarious man in his fifties who was working at the busy fruit and vegetable stand, and forced a smile, "*Hola, tío!*"

He stepped away from a customer and greeted her enthusiastically. "Sofia, *bienvenidas!* Congratulations on your graduation and your new casita. Your papa told us you're a beach girl now!"

"Thanks! I came to visit Gaia. Which stall is she in?"

"Three. Maria's in the office. I'll tell her you're here. She'd kill me if she didn't get to see you."

"I'd love to see her too." Sofia walked into the stables. Before she got her own horse, she came here every day after school to ride. She shared a close bond with Maria, and even after her father bought Gaia for her, she would stop by often to visit. They enjoyed chatting, and Maria would send her home with a bag of fruits, vegetables, and homemade green chili and cheese tamales.

When she entered the stall, her heart sank. Traumatized from being taken from her home, the horse whinnied and scratched the ground in distress with her front hoof.

Sofia stroked Gaia. "I'm so sorry, baby." She kissed the white diamond on her forehead. "It's all going to be okay. Things will be back to normal soon."

As she soothed her horse, she realized her words were meaningless. Would anything ever be normal again? She wasn't even sure what normal was anymore. Her brave facade cracked, and she sobbed, her tears wetting the horse's blond mane. Gaia pushed her muzzle against Sofia to comfort her.

"*Mi cariño*! Are you all right?" Maria asked as she entered the stall.

Sofia turned around and greeted her with a feigned smile. "Yes, I'm fine."

The petite woman stroked her hair affectionately. She was as warm as a summer afternoon, with a long chestnut braid down her back. "Why the sad face?"

Sofia wiped away her tears. "Boy trouble, but I'd rather not talk about it right now." She pretended to be embarrassed.

"You know I'm a good listener, if you ever need me."

"Thanks so much. By the way, have you seen my father recently?"

"He stopped by about a week ago to tell us you moved to

the beach. And since you wouldn't be at the ranch to care for Gaia, he wanted to board her here from now on."

"Did he say anything else?"

"There was nothing else, sweetheart. Is your papa okay?" she asked.

"Yes, I need to speak with him, and he's out of the country on one of his trips." She took a slip of paper out of her purse and handed it to Maria. "Here's my new number. Please call me when he contacts you. He's a workaholic and always loses track of time. You'll probably hear from him before I do."

"I'll call the minute he contacts me. Are you going for a ride?"

"Not right now, but I'll be back soon," Sofia said.

"It's so good to chat with you. I hope we can have a longer visit next time, but I should help Gusmaro. We're really busy today." Maria gave her a kiss on the cheek and left.

Sofia knew the only friend she had to confide in was her horse. She petted Gaia's velvety soft nose and spoke to her. "I can't let him go. Even though that's what he said he wanted, I don't believe it. He must be in trouble. What should I do, Gaia? Should I try to find him?"

Her faithful friend nickered and lifted her left leg, which was her way of saying yes.

"Agreed. I'll come and visit you as soon as possible. I love you." She hugged the mare, then rushed out of the stables.

Chapter 8
Aidan's Journal

When Sofia arrived at El Encanto College, she was laser focused, and hurried toward her father's office. Nothing seemed to have changed—the bronze plaque with his name, *DR. AIDAN RYAN*, was still on the wall. She flung open the door, and almost bumped into a man mopping the floor.

"Excuse me," she said, scanning the room. The desk and shelves were devoid of Aidan's books and personal items, including the crystal butterfly she'd given him last year for his birthday.

The janitor, his gray hair pulled back in a ponytail, looked up at Sofia, annoyed. "Slow down, young lady. You almost knocked me to high heaven."

"Sorry, I didn't know anyone was here. Have you seen Dr. Ryan?"

"Nope. I heard he retired. Check with administration."

"Where did his things go?"

He leaned on his mop handle. "Why so many questions? What's it to you?"

"Dr. Ryan is my father, and he asked me to pick up his belongings."

"I was told he wanted everything he left behind sent to the incinerator."

"The incinerator?" Sofia asked, alarmed.

"Yep. A custodian wheeled his stuff down there a few minutes ago. If you hurry, you might catch him."

"Okay, thanks," she said and walked out.

Sofia approached the college waste disposal facility with its large outdoor refuse burner and was relieved to see many of her father's files and belongings piled high on a rolling cart. Fortunately, she'd arrived in time to retrieve some of them.

A portly custodian with a buzz haircut culled through the things on the cart and tossed papers into the flames. He lifted the crystal butterfly up to the light and smiled. When he started to slip it into the pocket of his overalls, Sofia ran up to him and grabbed it.

"Stop!" she demanded.

The man froze. "Who are you?"

"I'm Dr. Ryan's daughter, and I'm here to retrieve his personal items. There's been a mistake."

"Sorry, miss. I was just doing my job, but I thought the butterfly was too pretty to burn."

"You have no right to take anything!"

He looked mortified. "Please don't tell anyone. I don't mean no harm."

She took the handle of the cart. "Not to worry. It's our little secret."

"Thank you, miss."

As Sofia pushed the cart with Aidan's possessions down the path toward Magistral Garden, the pain of his deceit weighed heavily on her. She slipped under the topiary arch that led to the quiet haven that was their favorite meeting place. Her life had been totally upended, but she hoped that something in his papers would help her understand his actions.

She sat on a bench and sorted through the items. He wouldn't have wanted his possessions burned if he didn't have something to hide. But she'd salvaged some of them, and the minor victory emboldened her. Hopefully, she would find some useful information. Most of the papers were old student essays, which she left on the cart, but underneath the piles of documents, there was a worn leather satchel she'd never seen before.

Curious, she thumbed through the contents and pulled out a red journal with cryptic pages in Aidan's handwriting. The notations seemed random, but knowing his meticulous personality, she doubted if anything was truly random. He had written many of the entries in Italian, Latin, French, and some languages she didn't recognize. She pored over the sprawling diary, which was filled with quotes from famous writers and philosophers. Dozens of drawings caught her eye, which was surprising, as she was unaware that her dad had any artistic ability.

In one compartment, she discovered a few letters from people she'd never heard of. Unfortunately, there were no addresses or contact information. There were also several photos, including one of Aidan as a child, standing next to two boys, which must have been taken before he came to America. Written on the back were the names Aidan, William, and Finn. She guessed the oldest boy was Aidan's brother, William. The other boy was playing a guitar and looked to be about the same age as her father.

Another picture showed Aidan in a tuxedo, posing at a campus event with Dr. Walter Lawrence, the former chair of the history department at El Encanto College. She hadn't thought about her dad's colleague for a long time, but they were friends, so perhaps he could shed some light on his disappearance. However, she had no idea how to reach him.

It was an excellent find. Sofia planned to study all the materials later, but first, she needed to speak to someone at the administration office. She packed the journal, letters, photos, and crystal butterfly into the satchel and dashed out of the garden, leaving the cart and its discarded contents behind.

While hurrying toward the administration building, she formulated a plan to get information about her father. After considering several scenarios, she decided not to disclose his disappearance or the note. If she told the truth, it might backfire. Although she had always valued honesty above all else and felt bad about lying to the custodians, she had to admit it had been productive. Despite her ethical qualms, she would need every arrow in her quiver to discover the truth about her father. Nothing was totally black or white, and everything was more nuanced than it appeared. A paradoxical line from Shakespeare's Hamlet came to mind. *"There is nothing either good or bad but thinking makes it so,"* and she understood the text in a whole new way.

When she entered the office, Mrs. Weems, a round-faced woman with large eyes, who always reminded Sofia of an owl, looked up from the reception desk. "So nice to see you, dear."

Sofia had met the punctilious lady several times over the years, and she'd always been nice to her. "Hi, Mrs. Weems. My father's office is being cleaned out. Do you know what's going on?"

"He retired. It was quite unexpected. You didn't know?"

Sofia shook her head. "I recently moved into my own place. My dad is out of the country, and I haven't been able to reach him. Did he leave an address or phone number?"

"No. We only have your mother's address. It's where he wanted his pension checks sent. Why don't you ask her?"

"I will." Sofia hesitated then came up with a story. "But she's out of town too."

"Oh my. I wish I could help."

"There is something you could help with. I've been wanting to get back in touch with my dad's friend, Dr. Walter Lawrence. Do you have his phone number?"

"Sorry. We're not supposed to share personal information on our faculty."

"I don't want to get you in trouble, but can you please make an exception?"

Mrs. Weems looked to see if anyone was listening. "Hold on, I'll be right back." She walked over to a file cabinet and returned holding a folded piece of paper, which she handed to Sofia. "All I have is his address. Don't mention it to anyone."

"I won't. Thank you so much. I really appreciate it," Sofia said and departed.

As she headed toward her car, her mind went into overdrive, hoping to make sense of the chaos that had become her life. *Did my father go insane? Impossible. He's the most rational man on earth. Does he have a fatal illness? Unlikely. He seemed perfectly healthy. Did someone force him to leave? Possibly. But who and why?*

Chapter 9
When Truth Lies

S ofia slumped in the front seat of her car parked on the college campus, trying to imagine why her father abandoned her. She couldn't conceive of an explanation and was so frustrated she wanted to scream. With no other leads, she took the Thomas Brothers map out of the glove compartment, got directions to Dr. Lawrence's home, then headed north on the freeway.

Before retiring from El Encanto, he was the respected chair of the History Department and shared her father's love of music. The professor played saxophone in a jazz band and used to attend concerts at the San Diego Opera and Symphony with Aidan. They were more than work colleagues. Dr. Lawrence seemed like a true friend.

When she reached the Hidden Meadows neighborhood in Escondido, Sofia recalled the day her father brought her to his house. She was twelve years old and had fun playing with his pet tortoises and exploring the succulent garden. They snacked on tortilla chips and guacamole while sitting under the shade of the avocado tree that provided the fruit for the tasty green dip.

She listened attentively as the men passionately debated a wide variety of issues and was intimidated by Dr. Lawrence's dynamic personality.

As Sofia neared his neighborhood, her conviction to speak with the distinguished professor faltered. Her heart raced, and she pulled to the side of the road and stopped the car. Would he even remember her or refuse to talk with her? She felt like a fool and took deep breaths, trying to calm down. The slightest conflict usually unnerved her, as she was not a bold person, especially around authority figures, but if she wanted to find her father, there was no escaping the rough journey ahead. Nothing would be easy anymore, so despite her fear of confrontation, she continued driving toward his home.

Upon arrival, Sofia parked in front of the old adobe pueblo-style house and walked onto the porch which had a rustic burl wood table and chairs covered by an awning draped in scarlet trumpet vines. She rang the bell beside the red wooden door and heard a dog barking loudly from inside. A moment later, Dr. Lawrence, a reed thin man in his seventies, stepped out and a smile stretched across his tanned face, crinkling the corners of his brown eyes.

"Sofia Ryan," he said. "What a pleasant surprise!"

He was as tall as she remembered, but his hair had turned white, and his ubiquitous suit had been replaced with jeans and a sports shirt. His warm welcome melted her fears. "How did you recognize me? The last time I saw you, I was only twelve."

"Your father showed me more photos of you than I can count. It's a pleasure to see you again."

"It's nice to see you too, Dr. Lawrence."

"Please, call me Walter."

"Do you have a few minutes to chat?"

"Of course, but we better sit outside. I just adopted an

overly rambunctious puppy and he'll be all over you." He gestured to the chairs on the porch. "Make yourself comfortable."

"Thank you." She pulled up a chair.

He sat next to her. "Are you still in college?"

"I just graduated."

"Congratulations. What was your major?" he asked.

"World history and English literature."

"A double major. Your father must be proud."

"Actually, that's why I came to visit. I wanted to talk to you about him."

"So, what's up with Aidan these days?"

"Well . . . He retired."

"Good for him. He can finally relax and travel the world unincumbered by the pressures of academia. Tell him to give me a call. I'd love to catch up. It's been too long."

Unable to conceal her anguish any longer, the truth tumbled out. "Actually, he didn't just retire, he disappeared, and I don't know where he is." Saying it out loud made it real, and tears came to her eyes.

"Don't worry. He's so obsessive; I'll bet he's off doing research on some arcane subject and lost track of everything else."

"I wish that were true, but he left a note that made it quite clear he wanted nothing more to do with me."

Walter was nonplussed. "That's hard to believe. You meant the world to Aidan."

"It's bewildering. Why would he do this?" she asked, choking up.

He put a comforting hand on her shoulder. "I'm sorry for what you're going through, but I'm sure everything will be okay."

"I hope so." Sofia wiped away her tears. "Since you've been

friends for years, I thought you might have some information that might help me find him."

"I'd love to help, but I can't imagine where he could have gone." Walter shook his head. "This is so unlike him."

"Is it possible that someone at the college forced him to retire?"

"No, he had tenure and is one of the most respected historians we've ever had. They couldn't force him to leave."

"Did any of his colleagues have issues with him?" she asked.

"Not really. He had strong opinions and locked horns with other scholars over the years, but big egos come with the territory. And when something ticked him off, he had an explosive temper."

"That's for sure," Sofia said. "Can you think of anyone else I should talk to?"

"Not offhand. If something comes to mind, how can I reach you?" he asked.

She handed him a slip of paper. "Here's my number."

Walter put it in his shirt pocket. "I assume you've already spoken with his sister?"

Sofia felt like she'd been hit by a truck. "Uh, no, not yet." She didn't know her father had a sister, much less one that might still be alive, and tried to conceal her shock.

"I met Margaret Grace a few times when she visited Aidan on campus, and they seemed quite close."

"It's been a while, and we've been out of touch," she said, trying to maintain her composure. "Do you happen to have her phone number?"

"No. I don't really know her, but I remember she was from the Boston area. Whatever's going on, I think Aidan will return soon with a good explanation."

"Thanks for your time, Walter." Sofia pushed her chair back and stood.

"I wish you all the best. And please, keep me posted." He waved goodbye and walked back into his house.

Sofia got in her car and lowered her aching head, her arms crossed protectively over her chest. She felt betrayed all over again. It was now obvious she couldn't trust anything her parents said and needed to question everything.

What little she knew about her family history came from them, and their stories played like a movie in her mind. Supposedly, when Aidan's parents and siblings died in Ireland—an event he refused to discuss—he came to Boston to live with his Uncle Seamus, a bachelor with no children. Seamus passed away while her father was in college, leaving him without any living relatives, which was clearly not true.

After graduating from Emerson, Aidan claimed he was hired to teach at his alma mater, where he met Ella, a student who had immigrated from Italy. Her mother said that she was orphaned when her family died during the bombing of Sicily, and a Catholic charity sponsored her journey to America to study art. The shared experience of losing their families brought them together and was one of the few things they had in common.

Sofia felt an emptiness throughout her life because she had no extended family, which always made her sad. *Why did my father lie about his sister, and what else was he hiding? Did my mother lie about her past, too?* She didn't know what to believe anymore, and her sense of self crumbled.

Chapter 10
Shattered

Sofia arrived at her beach house that night, overwhelmed by the events of the day. After pulling her car into the garage, she sat quietly for a while. It was dark except for moonlight shining through the high clerestory windows lining the left and right walls. Although she'd discovered a few intriguing details about her family, learning the whole truth seemed impossible, and she felt alone with no one to turn to. Even though her father told her not to look for him, he'd left enough money for her to continue her search. She'd spend every penny to find him, if that's what it took. There was absolutely no way she would allow him to get away with deserting her with no explanation.

She pounded the steering wheel, then got out of the car, grabbed Aidan's satchel and the duffel bag, and carried them into the house. Sofia hid the money under her bed, then headed straight for the kitchen. Drained, she felt disoriented and severed from her roots like seaweed ripped from its anchoring rocks deep in the ocean.

A glass of wine sounded like an excellent remedy to soothe

her frayed nerves. She opened the refrigerator and pulled out a bottle of Prosecco, then got a champagne flute from the cabinet. As she was about to pour the sparkling wine, she stared at the crystal glass, incensed. The last time she'd used it was the day her father left for his so-called lecture in London. The more she thought about it, the angrier she got.

What a farce! How could he have deluded me so completely? He knew he was leaving and wanted me out of his way... And was so manipulative he even picked out my fucking champagne glasses! Furious, she threw the flute in the trash can, shattering it to pieces. Grabbing the bottle of Prosecco, she stormed out of the kitchen.

Sofia sprawled on the sofa and took a swig of the wine. On the end table, there was a framed picture of her and her brother posing with their sandcastle at the beach, and the image hit her like a gut punch. If only Liam was with her now. Together, they were twice as smart and twice as brave. It was a frozen fragment of her childhood, which seemed totally normal until his sudden death.

The photo triggered a stream of memories that rushed through her mind as if an inner dam had burst. As a kid, she thought they were a perfect family, but there must have been subtle signs she was unaware of. Now her father, the one person she thought she could count on, had betrayed her. He'd been acting strange and moody lately. *Why didn't I see this coming?*

Remembering the 8-millimeter film projector and home movies stored in the garage, she brought them into the living room, loaded a reel, and projected the film on the wall across from the couch.

The first flickering images were of her as a tiny agile girl, twirling a Hula-Hoop while standing in the palm of Aidan's large hand. As she watched, transfixed, her eyes stung with bitter tears. She loved her father more than anything in the world, and thought he loved her too.

Then, there was a flash of white, and the screen lit up with Sofia and Liam carving their initials into the trunk of the majestic oak tree in the ranch garden. Seeing her brother warmed her heart, as she remembered the innumerable times they'd enjoyed climbing into the tree's broad canopy.

The film continued with images of Aidan teaching her and Liam to surf at Pacific Beach . . . Ella beaming after winning a prize at a local art show for one of her paintings . . . Sofia and Liam in front of a lighted Christmas tree at Balboa Park's Organ Pavilion, surrounded by Santa and live reindeer from the San Diego Zoo.

When the reel ended, Sofia turned off the projector. She hadn't seen the family movies in years, and the experience was a poignant reminder of how fragile life is and how quickly everything one loves can be ripped away.

It was too upsetting to watch more home movies, and although she tried to find clues, she couldn't perceive any cracks in her parents' relationship that would foretell their imminent dissolution. Aidan seemed contented, as did Ella, whose face was bright with a genuine smile and warm green eyes. Obviously, they were in love once and the family was happy.

Why did it all end so badly?

Sofia had always sided with her father, who seemed like the only one trying to hold them together after Liam's death, but now she questioned her assumption. He lied about his sister and if he could abandon his own daughter with no explanation, he was a cruel and selfish narcissist.

She picked up Aidan's crumpled note from the coffee table, smoothed it out and reread what he'd written about Ella.

I will always love you and although she won't believe it, I love your mother too. Tell her I regret all the bitterness between us...

There had to be more to their story, and she wondered what was really behind her parents' divorce. Although she dreaded it, speaking with Ella might be the only way to get some clarity, but the prospect of facing her was unnerving. Sofia wished it were different, but her mother wasn't in her life anymore, and she didn't know if she could open her heart to her ever again. She thought Ella wallowed in self-pity, blamed others for her problems, and was incapable of loving her. But what if Aidan was a master manipulator who twisted her perception of her mother?

Lost in a storm of confusion, Sofia downed the last drop of wine, then stumbled into her bedroom and collapsed on the bed. Unable to tolerate the despair any longer, she placed a pillow over her head, hoping to shut out her thoughts. Finally, exhaustion overcame her, and she drifted into the world of dreams.

Chapter 11
Free Fall

Yosemite National Park—1970

The majestic granite face of Half Dome glowed in the summer sun, and towering Ponderosa pines cast shade over verdant valleys sprinkled with purple, white, and yellow wildflowers. High in the clear blue sky, a red-tailed hawk screeched and circled above the canyon as it glided toward the top of Vernal Fall, landing gracefully on a tree branch above the Merced River.

Aidan and Sofia stood on one of the huge flat boulders overlooking the river where he was teaching her to fish. A skinny twelve-year-old, Sofia was dressed in white shorts, a blue T-shirt, and white sneakers. Her father, wearing a matching outfit with a floppy fishing hat, put a worm on the hook, and then helped her cast the line into the water.

After a moment of silence, she said, "It feels weird, Dad. You used to do this with Liam."

He put his arm around her shoulder, tenderly. "He'd want you to take his place as my first mate."

Sofia thought about it. "You're right. It's nice to be in Yosemite, but it's not the same without him."

"I miss him too, angel."

"We used to have so much fun. We'd ride a log down the river and pretend we were explorers."

"Maybe you and I can do that."

"No, you're too big for a log ride!" Sofia poked his belly.

"That's true. I'd probably sink it."

She giggled. "We'll come up with a new adventure for you and me."

"I know how close you were, but perhaps Liam was needed in heaven."

"It's not fair . . . I need him too."

"Unfortunately, life isn't always fair," Aidan said.

There was a tug on her fishing line.

"I got one!" Sofia reeled in the wriggling fish.

"Good job. Now we'll return him to his home." Aidan took the rainbow trout off the hook and dropped it back into the water.

"I'm starving. Can we have lunch now?" Sofia asked.

"Yes. Let's get back to your mother. I'm sure she's ready for lunch too."

They packed up and headed toward their picnic spot. As they approached the grassy meadow, they saw Ella lying on a blanket next to an empty wine bottle, her face buried in her folded arms. Aidan sent Sofia away, saying he needed to speak privately with her mother for a few minutes. She pretended to leave but hid behind a tree and eavesdropped on her parents.

Aidan settled next to Ella, who turned to him, her eyes red from crying. "I wish we hadn't come. It reminds me of what I've lost."

"Get it together," Aidan demanded. "We've all lost him. You're not the only one who's suffering."

Ella sat up, brushed the leaves from her white blouse and jeans and faced him. "God is punishing me."

"God wouldn't waste his time on you. You never should have been driving."

"It wasn't my fault! The man was drunk and speeding!"

"I'm not so sure." Aidan picked up the empty wine bottle and tossed it in a trash bag.

"You always blame me for everything."

"Let's be civil, Ella, for our daughter's sake."

The animosity between them was palpable and Sofia wondered if her parents would ever stop fighting. It seemed like since Liam died, that was all they ever did. As her mother and father began unpacking the food in silent resentment, Sofia remained out of sight, and pacified herself by twisting her hair, while waiting for the right moment to join them.

When the peanut butter sandwiches, celery stalks, and potato chips were laid out on paper plates, Sofia returned and sat on the blanket. Not a word was spoken as the family ate lunch. The harmonious sounds of the flowing river and singing birds did nothing to ease the tension between them. Conflicted, Sofia wasn't sure whose side she should take. She nibbled on the sandwich and chips but was too distraught to finish her meal.

Looking up impatiently, she asked, "Can I go play now?"

Ella glanced at her. "But you barely ate."

"I'm full." Sofia pushed her plate away.

"You can go, but stay nearby," Aidan said.

She hurried to the water's edge, wanting to get as far away from her parents as possible. In the distance, she could hear them arguing as she clambered up the enormous boulders. Settling on a flat rock, she watched as the turbulent river funneled through a narrow gorge, exploding into mist, and falling like rain onto the massive vertical sheet of granite known as the Silver Apron. The gigantic formation looked like a perilous waterslide that slammed into a cluster of boulders, churning like a blender before spilling into Emerald Pool and cascading over the thundering waterfall.

Sofia climbed higher to get a better view and was relieved to be alone. As she looked out at the magnificent valley, the sound of falling rocks startled her, and she whirled around. An intense, muscular man with red hair and pale, freckled skin sat on a ledge behind her, peering through binoculars.

"Hey, mister, what are you looking at?"

He lowered the binoculars and squinted at her with icy blue eyes. "Hello, Sofia." His gruff voice had an accent she'd never heard.

"You talk funny. And how do you know my name?"

"A lucky guess," he said.

The man's menacing gaze frightened her, and she wanted to run away. "I'd better go now." Sofia scampered down the boulders and slipped on the moss-covered granite, screaming as she fell onto the Silver Apron and began sliding toward the cluster of boulders that loomed in front of her.

Aidan and Ella jolted to attention when they heard their daughter cry out.

"Oh my God!" Ella shouted as she stood and saw Sofia being swept downstream.

Aidan sprang to his feet and raced to her aid. Running into the rushing river and struggling across the slippery granite, he managed to get ahead of Sofia and used his body as a buffer between her and the rocks. He dropped to his knees and slid backward in the raging water, holding her out of harm's way as the current hurled them ferociously into the boulders. Aidan took the blow and howled in pain but held on tight to his daughter.

Ella was frantic as she helped them climb onto the riverbank. Traumatized, they fell to the ground. She examined Sofia, who seemed uninjured. "Are you all right? You could have been killed!"

"I'm sorry, Mom. I was talking to a man, and he scared me."

"What? You shouldn't talk to strangers!" Aidan said.

"But he knew my name. He's over there." Sofia gestured toward the boulders above the Silver Apron.

Aidan and Ella looked where she was pointing and saw no one.

"Never do that again," he said. "Most people can't be trusted."

Ella glared at him with sudden realization. "It must have been one of the men you've been meeting with. They're making our lives a living hell."

"My work is none of your concern and this has nothing to do with my associates!" Aidan tried to stand, then slumped back down with an excruciating cry. He had injured his hip from the impact and scraped his knees and shins raw, streaking his white shorts with blood.

Terrified, Sofia touched her father's legs. "Dad, you're bleeding!"

"Sofia, stay here. I'll get help." Ella hiked down the steep trail toward the Ranger's station to report the accident.

After an agonizing wait, Sofia and Aidan heard the whirring blades of an approaching helicopter. They looked up and saw Ella in the cabin, directing the pilot to their location. The chopper landed in a nearby clearing, and the crew helped Sofia aboard. The trauma team rushed to Aidan, placed him on a stretcher, and loaded him into the helicopter.

As they took off, Sofia held on to her mother tightly. She had never flown before, and the journey terrified her as the wind buffeted the chopper on its flight between the canyon walls to the Park Hospital.

Chapter 12
A Tangled Web

Sofia awoke with a start, weary from a restless night's sleep. She hadn't thought about her family's trip to Yosemite in years, but the unsettling dream was now vividly burned into her conscious mind. She stepped out of bed, showered and threw on jeans and a navy-blue sweatshirt. After making a cup of coffee, she headed out to her patio.

As she sat at the table, sipping coffee, Sofia wiped the tears from her eyes, wishing she could as easily wipe away the memory of her father. But no matter how hard she tried, it was impossible to stop thinking about how he'd deceived her. She wanted to hate Aidan, but despite his betrayal, she still loved him and, worst of all, everything reminded her of him.

A thick layer of fog rolling in from the ocean covered the bay like an impenetrable blanket concealing what was underneath, but the sea would reveal itself when the sun burned off the mist. Light destroys all that's hidden, and although Sofia was in the dark, entangled in a web of lies, beneath the darkness was the truth, but she feared uncovering it would be daunting.

The morning slipped by as she searched through her father's journal. Most of the entries were philosophical musings that seemed irrelevant to her search, but then she came across an interesting postcard tucked between the pages, dated January 2, 1967. A rainbow-colored psychedelic third eye stared at her from the front of the card. The message was from someone named Kieran, with no last name listed, at an address in Medford, Massachusetts. She turned it over and read the handwritten note:

Happy New Year, Aidan,
It's been too long, brother! If you want to blow your
mind, come visit me anytime.
Trippin' from another dimension, Kieran.

Sofia looked up Medford on a map and learned it was near Boston. Dr. Lawrence said Margaret Grace was from there too. Aidan lied about his sister, so could he also have a brother he never told her about? Since her parents met in Boston, Ella might have met Kieran or Margaret Grace. She might even know something about her father's disappearance.

Although she had tried to avoid it, confronting her mother seemed like the next logical step. It had been years since Sofia had seen her, and the last time didn't end well. They were cruel to each other, and their hostility had become a seemingly unbridgeable chasm. So, despite a gnawing feeling of apprehension in her gut, she resolved to pay her a visit.

Chapter 13
Ella

Ella lived in Little Italy, one of the oldest neighborhoods in San Diego. It was known for its artisan shops, farmers' markets, and Italian restaurants. The houses built in the 1920s were painted in vibrant colors, including sea green, brick red, and canary yellow.

Before its decline in the 1960s, a thriving tuna industry employed many of the residents, but due to overfishing and foreign competition, the business collapsed. Despite the economic downturn, the community was slowly rebounding and becoming a popular destination for dining and shopping.

At the open-air market, vendors sold fresh fruits and vegetables. There was also a cornucopia of homemade delicacies, including pasta in a remarkable variety of shapes and sizes, as well as scrumptious desserts, like cannoli and tiramisu. As locals and tourists crowded the square, Italian, English and Spanish conversations floated on the breeze, adding to the international flavor of the bazaar.

Ella, in a sleeveless white cotton dress trimmed with light blue satin ribbon, moved quietly among the stalls, selecting food for the day. Although a natural beauty with delicate features and thick golden-brown hair swaying just above her graceful neck, there was something vulnerable about her. She had the aura of a wild bird yearning to be free, her wings clipped by life's disappointments. As always, she stopped at the Italian newsstand and bought a magazine to remind her of her homeland.

After shopping, she headed to her apartment, which was only steps away in an old Victorian-style house, converted into individual residences. Since the divorce, Ella spent most of her time alone and rarely left the boundaries of her neighborhood. She often thought about returning to Italy, but she still harbored the hope that someday she might have a relationship with her daughter and wanted to live close enough to make the dream a reality.

When she arrived at her sparsely furnished one-bedroom home, a fluffy calico cat met her at the door, meowed, and nuzzled her legs. The adorable, tri-colored feline had dramatic markings. Ella adopted the stray when she was a kitten and named her Luna because the cat's face reminded her of the two sides of the moon, half white, and half black with a vertical butterscotch stripe down her nose.

"Hi, baby. I brought you something special."

She set the groceries on the table and the cat jumped up and put her head inside the cloth shopping bag.

"You always want to be first." Ella reached into the bag and pulled out a container of freshly cooked tuna in olive oil. Luna sat and watched as she cut the fish into little bite-size pieces and placed the treat on a plate in front of her. As the cat ate with delight, Ella unpacked the rest of her groceries, then brewed espresso and made steamed milk.

The instant she settled on the couch with her cafe latte, Luna curled up on her lap and purred. While Ella sipped her coffee, she stroked the cat's silky fur and thought about the flower paintings on the walls and pottery pieces on the kitchen counter. The patterns and colors were so vivid and joyous, like her life was when she created them years ago.

Now, the Italian magazines and the love she shared with Luna were her only respite from the dreary routine that had become her reality. Every day thrummed with the same monotonous rhythm: shop, eat, pray, sleep . . . shop, eat, pray, sleep . . . again and again in an endless cycle, where nothing changed except the lines on her face.

Chapter 14
Turning Point

Sofia trudged up the stairs to Ella's apartment on the top floor, and with each step her mouth became drier and the tightness in her chest intensified. As she hesitated in front of the door, she chastised herself for being afraid to talk to her own mother. It wasn't like she was entering a lion's den, but she couldn't shake the feelings that coursed through her body. She rolled her shoulders back and took a long deep breath to gather her courage before knocking.

A little window in the door opened, and Ella's wary green eyes peered out. "Hello, stranger, what a surprise," she said, and opened the door. "Please, come in."

"Hello, Mom." Sofia walked in and looked around. Her mother seemed to live in a time warp, as virtually nothing had changed in the years since her last visit.

Ella led her daughter to the gray leather couch, and Luna jumped up and sat between them, eyeing Sofia with suspicion.

"Sorry I didn't go to your graduation. I couldn't bear to be around your father."

Sofia glanced at the cat. "Luna's really grown," she said, changing the subject.

"Yes, she's a big girl now. Would you like to join me for lunch? I have some beautiful tomatoes from the farmers' market. I could make pasta."

"No, thanks. Maybe some other time."

"I hope there will be another time." Ella shifted uncomfortably in her seat.

Sofia reached out to pet the feline, who flinched and scurried into the bedroom. "Sorry. I didn't mean to startle her."

"She's very sensitive and knows when someone is upset. Are you all right?" Ella asked.

Sofia tried to steady her nerves before bringing up Aidan. "I need to show you something." She pulled out his note and handed it to her.

Ella silently read it. "So, he's finally done it."

"Done what?"

"Left you . . . just like he left me." She passed the note back to her daughter.

"Do you know where he is?" Sofia asked.

"Of course not. And I'm glad he's gone. He was a horrible husband and father."

Sofia instinctively jumped to his defense. "Until now, he was a perfect father."

"You really don't know him like I do." Ella bristled and took a sip of her cafe latte.

"Mom, I dreamed about our trip to Yosemite last night—the time I fell into the Silver Apron."

"Oh, god. That was terrible."

"And I remembered something."

Ella winced. "Let's not talk about it."

"Please, it's important to me. You said the men Dad was

meeting with were making our lives a living hell. Which men were you referring to?"

"I never said that."

"You did."

"It was a dream, Sofia." She looked down and focused on the swirls of milk in her drink.

"No, it really happened. The dream made me remember."

"You must be confused. I don't know why your father left, but it had nothing to do with me or our trip to Yosemite."

"Come on, you must know something!"

Ella met her gaze. "I don't know anything! Until he called out of the blue and invited me to your graduation, we hadn't spoken in years."

"The college said they were sending his pension checks to you, so I thought you might still be in touch."

"No, but he made me his beneficiary, so if the checks keep coming, he can do whatever the hell he wants."

"That's all you care about, his money?" Sofia asked petulantly.

"It's the first kind thing he's done for me in years, but you've always taken his side. For your sake, I hope one day you'll realize how much he deceived both of us."

"Then enlighten me. How did he deceive us?"

"You wouldn't understand." Ella got up. "I think it's time for you to leave now."

Convinced her mother was concealing something, Sofia tried to tamp down her anger as she stood and faced her. "I just have one more question. When you lived in Boston, did you ever meet Dad's sister, Margaret Grace?"

"How could I? His entire family died in Ireland before I met Aidan."

"That's what he told me too, but it's not true. I spoke with Dr. Lawrence, and he met Margaret Grace several times."

"He must be mistaken," Ella snapped.

"I don't think so. He told me they met when she came to visit Dad at the college."

"Dr. Lawrence is an old man. He must be getting senile."

"Let's not argue. Maybe you can help me with something else." Sofia pulled the postcard from Kieran out of her purse and showed it to her. "Do you know this man?"

Ella waved it away and her face flushed. "Never heard of him."

"You're so transparent. I can tell you're lying," Sofia said.

"You need to accept it. Like Aidan said in his note, he doesn't want to be found. Believe me, we're both better off without him."

"I'm sorry you had the world's most toxic divorce, but it's not my fault."

"Please go. I have nothing more to say to you." Ella walked to the door.

Sofia followed her. "He wouldn't leave me unless someone forced him to."

"No one forces him to do anything," Ella said. "He always does what's in his own self-interest."

"If you know where he is, please tell me," Sofia pleaded.

"You're wasting your time. He doesn't care about you any more than he cared about me."

"Well, I know you never cared about me," Sofia said, accusingly.

"That's not true!" Brokenhearted, Ella spoke haltingly. "I've always loved you . . . you never gave me a chance." She opened the door. "Your father's the one who's incapable of love . . . but I guess you'll have to learn that on your own."

"I can't accept that," Sofia said as she stepped outside.

"I'm warning you, don't search for him. You may not like

what you find." Ella closed the door, leaving her daughter alone on the landing.

As she headed down the stairs, Sofia felt shaken, but the meeting with Ella had fueled her resolve. Regardless of the outcome, and no matter how difficult, she vowed to learn the truth and nothing, and no one, was going to stop her.

Chapter 15
Worlds Apart

Ella waited behind her closed door and listened to Sofia's footsteps descending the stairs. She wished their visit had been different, but as always, it ended in a fight, and she doubted if her daughter would or could ever love her. She felt cursed. Both of her children had been cruelly stolen from her; one by death and the other by Aidan's deceit. With a heavy heart, she lifted a white lace headscarf off the coat rack by the door, put it on, and left the apartment.

As she walked toward Our Lady of the Rosary Catholic Church, Ella wondered what else God wanted from her and if there was anything she could do to gain His mercy. The church, known as the Jewel of Little Italy, had been a beacon of light for its mostly Italian parishioners since 1925; for Ella, it was a sanctuary.

She entered the empty chapel, knelt at the altar, lit red votive candles as an offering, and bowed her head in silent prayer. Shafts of sunlight filtered through the stained-glass windows, casting colors on her white dress. After making the sign of the cross, she stood up, walked to a pew, and sat down. She sighed, closed her eyes, and rested her head in her hands.

I wish I had never met him. I thought he was my salvation, but he was my downfall.

Ella was lost in her remembrances when she heard footsteps approaching. She looked up and saw Father Bandini, a young Italian priest, with warm brown eyes and a caring smile.

"Sorry, I didn't mean to disturb you. May I sit?" he asked.

"Yes, Father."

He sat next to her. "You seem distressed, Ella. Are you all right?"

"I had a fight with my daughter."

"I thought you weren't in touch," he said.

"She stopped by unexpectedly and after today, I'm sure she hates me."

"With God's grace you will find a way to make peace with her. Would you like to discuss it?"

"Not now."

"I understand." He stood and touched her head as a blessing. "When you're ready, I'm always here for you."

"Thank you, Father."

"You must pray for a reconciliation. And don't give up hope."

"Yes, I will pray," Ella said. As the priest departed, she bowed her head. *Please God, protect my girl.*

Chapter 16
Ride a Rhinoceros

Sofia, her hair pulled back in a ponytail, sat at the dining room table with a typewriter, telephone, maps, and an open pizza box with a missing slice as she reviewed the letters from Aidan's satchel. She had read all of them repeatedly but found nothing helpful.

After much research, all the clues pointed to Massachusetts. Her parents claimed they attended Emerson College in Boston. According to Dr. Lawrence, her aunt lived there, and Kieran's address was in nearby Medford.

She called the telephone operator in Boston to see if there was a number for Aidan's sister, Margaret Grace Ryan, but there wasn't. Maybe she was unlisted, had moved, went by her married name, or passed away. Sofia had no way of knowing.

Kieran was her only other lead. On the postcard, he referred to Aidan as his brother. Were they biological brothers or just close friends? Sofia asked the operator about a listing for Kieran Ryan, but none existed.

When she spoke with the Emerson College Registrar's office, she learned that both her mother and father would need to send written requests before any personal information could be released. Sofia knew how to forge her parents' signatures so she could easily draft the letters, but she didn't want to wait weeks for the mail.

Frustrated, she pushed everything aside. The late afternoon sun filtering through the slats of the patio cover above the picture window created a lattice of light and shadow on her chest, and she noticed the pattern—*like the bars of a prison cell.*

Sofia grabbed another piece of pizza and pondered her next move. As she nibbled on the slice, she picked up the latest issue of the San Diego Zoo magazine, ZOONOOZ. On the cover was a photo of a rare southern white rhinoceros. While gazing at the charismatic creature, a proverb she'd read years ago by an Indian swami popped into her mind.

If you want to achieve the impossible, ride a rhinoceros.
If you fail, no one will fault you, and if you succeed,
you'll attain your dreams on the wildest ride of your life.

This was the answer to her predicament. Her goal seemed impossible, but to succeed, she needed to risk everything and jump off a cliff. Although she wasn't sure if any of the stories Aidan and Ella told her were true, and despite her fear of flying, she decided to go to Boston. Hopefully, the trip would shed light on some of her parents' secrets.

Sofia typed and signed the permission letters allowing her access to their college records, then put her father's journal, along with the photos, back into the satchel, and rushed into the bedroom to pack. She shoved clothes, toiletries, and her father's bag into a large olive-green backpack, then opened the desk drawer to get her wallet. Noticing her passport, she wondered if she should bring it. Aidan insisted she apply for it when she turned eighteen, saying someday she'd want to travel internationally and would need it. She hated to give him credit for anything, but since there was no way of knowing where her search would lead, she took it.

Reaching under the bed, she grabbed the duffel bag, removed two rolls of one-hundred-dollar bills, and returned the bag to its hiding place. After putting the money and passport in her purse, she called for a Yellow Cab.

When Sofia arrived and got out of the taxi, the sun was setting over the San Diego International Airport with its view of the city skyline and harbor. She tossed the backpack over her shoulders and stared at the entrance. Her pulse raced as she steeled herself for the trip. Ever since the helicopter flight in Yosemite, she'd suffered from the fear of flying. Once she'd accepted the worst-case scenario and made peace with crashing and burning, she could finally enter the terminal.

As she stood in line to buy a ticket, Sofia thought about her brother's sudden passing, and realized that death usually sneaks up on people when they least expect it. So, by being prepared for annihilation during the journey, she couldn't be blindsided and would probably survive with the added protection of a Bloody Mary. And now that she was twenty-one, she planned to order one . . . or two.

Upon reaching the front of the line at the ticket counter, a stout middle-aged woman dressed in a red, white, and blue uniform motioned for her to come forward.

"Welcome to National Airlines. How may I help you?"

"I need the first flight to Boston," Sofia said.

"We have availability tonight on the red eye at 10:50. The cost is $158, including taxes. Does that work for you?"

"Yes. That's perfect." Sofia pulled the cash out of her purse and paid the ticket agent.

"Do you prefer an aisle or window seat?"

"Window please. It's my first time on an airplane." She felt queasy. "Is it as scary as a helicopter?"

"Not at all. It's a piece of cake." The agent handed her a ticket.

"Since it's a long time until the flight, do you know where I can wait?" Sofia asked.

"You can grab a bite at the Airman's Lounge. It's close to A-5, your departure gate. Top of the escalator and to the right. We'll begin boarding at 10:00."

Sofia thanked her and headed up the escalator, stopping at a kiosk to buy a *National Geographic* magazine to read while she waited. When she arrived at the lounge, she was happy to see it was almost empty. There were wooden tables and chairs in the center of the dimly lit restaurant, and brown Naugahyde booths lined the walls. Behind the bar, neon signs advertised a variety of beers and a chalkboard touting the daily specials, including chicken pot pie and carrot cake.

She selected a booth in back and ordered chicken pot pie and a Bloody Mary. As Sofia sipped her drink, she tried to relax before her flight, but it didn't work. So, she ordered another Bloody Mary and took several deep breaths, which only made her head spin.

After reading her magazine cover to cover, Sofia checked her watch and realized it was time to board the plane. As she headed toward the gate, her heart pounded, and she tucked her cold hands into her pockets. Horrific visions of plummeting to her fiery doom seized her, and she panicked. She thought about cancelling her trip and going home, but the swami's words about riding a rhinoceros to achieve the impossible—or in her case, riding an airplane—resonated like a mantra and she resolved to overcome her fear and go through with her plan.

Chapter 17
Kieran

Early the next morning, Sofia's flight landed at Logan International Airport in Boston. The journey had not been as terrifying as anticipated and, after another spicy Bloody Mary on the plane, she'd quickly fallen asleep and only woke up when the wheels hit the tarmac. Nevertheless, she was relieved to be on terra firma.

Aidan always kept her on a tight leash, micromanaging her every desire, but now she was cast out of her comfort zone. Although anxious, she also felt exhilarated, as if awakening from a long hibernation.

Since it was probably too early to check into a hotel, Medford would be the first stop on her search. After that, she'd go to Emerson College. At the Hertz Car Rental counter, her first thought was to rent a Ford Pinto, which she was familiar with, but she'd always wanted a VW Bug. Aidan refused to buy her one because he said they were unsafe, but from now on, she would make her own decisions and selected a blue Volkswagen Beetle.

As she drove through the city, she marveled at how

different Boston was from San Diego. Some of the historic buildings dated from the 1600s and the streets were shaded by red maple, ash, and elm trees. Although this was where her father grew up, she knew practically nothing about his early life. Whenever she asked, he would be evasive and change the subject. She chalked it up to his traumatic childhood, but evidently, his deception was his way of hiding the truth from her and now she resented him for it.

Soon, she arrived in Medford, which was only eight miles away, at the address where Kieran lived eleven years ago. Hopefully, he was still there. She got out of the car and beheld the dramatic, pyramid-shaped structure made of redwood. The unusual home was on a hill above Mystic River. Along the shore, people were taking morning walks as row boats glided on the calm water.

Sofia heard the melodious sound of wind chimes as she approached the front porch. A rainbow-colored sign above the glass door read *KIERAN'S THIRD EYE EMPORIUM*.

The third eye logo looked a lot like the drawing on the postcard. At last, something might go her way.

When she reached the door, an impish man with long flowing white hair, dressed in a complementary white cotton tunic and yogi pants, stepped out. He greeted her with a cosmic twinkle in his eye. "Good morning, goddess. Have you come for chakra balancing?"

"No."

"Past life regression?"

"No, sorry."

"Ah, you're here for karma cleansing."

"Not really. Are you Kieran?"

"The one and only. Namaste." He bowed his head and held his hands together in prayer.

"My name is Sofia, and I think we might be related. I found

a postcard you sent to my dad, Aidan Ryan, where you referred to him as your brother." She showed him the card.

Kieran studied it with glee. "Aidan Ryan! You're damn right we're brothers. Just from a different mother, and father for that matter. We were best buds when we were kids. Well, what a thrill."

Sofia found it hard to believe this eccentric character in yogi pants had been a friend of her straightlaced dad. "Do you have a minute to talk?"

"Of course. Come right in!" He welcomed her inside and patted her affectionately on the back.

Kieran's home was a veritable hippie pad, with futons and cushions scattered on the floor. Japanese koto music played softly, and ribbons of sandalwood smoke wafted from an incense burner next to a lava lamp. On the walls hung striking paintings of Buddhist and Hindu gods and goddesses and surrealistic images that looked like a synthesis of Salvador Dali and Paul Gauguin. Sofia scanned the canvases. To her amazement, one of them was a small portrait of a couple that resembled a young Aidan and Ella.

She walked over to the painting and her eyes widened. "Are those my parents?"

"Yep. I created that masterpiece as a wedding gift, but I never got around to mailing it. If you give me their address, I'd love to send it to them."

"Unfortunately, they're divorced, and my father is missing."

"Missing? What happened?"

"I don't know. I came to Boston to try and find him."

"I wish I could help you, but we've been out of touch for ages."

Sofia's hopes were dashed. "Thanks for your time. Sorry to have bothered you."

"It's no bother," Kieran said and gestured to a futon covered with a colorful Madras blanket. "Please, have a seat. It's not every day Aidan's daughter shows up on my doorstep."

"Thank you." Sofia sank onto the soft futon. "If you don't mind my asking, why didn't you stay in touch? Did you have a falling out?"

"Not at all." He sat on a cushion across from her. "We just got busy with our lives. You're still young, but you'll understand some day. At my age, the years fly by in a flash."

Sofia leaned back on a pillow and relaxed. "What was my father like when you were kids?"

"He was funny, always playing practical jokes. In high school, we were on the sailing and rowing teams together. We were close, but sometimes there was friction because his parents didn't like me."

Sofia stared at him incredulously. "But I thought his parents died before he came to America."

Kieran chuckled. "If so, they were very well preserved."

"Do you think they're still alive?"

"It's possible . . . but they'd probably be in their eighties by now."

"Did you ever meet his sister?"

"No. She was a few years older than us. But he told me she married a bigshot lawyer in Boston. I remember because we planned a weekend camping trip, and he had to cancel to go to their wedding."

"What about his uncle Seamus?"

"He never mentioned an uncle. Honestly, I don't know what's happened to any of his family."

"I wonder why he lied to me about them?"

"No telling. But I got the feeling his folks didn't approve of him bringing home a wife from Italy, so maybe he wanted nothing to do with them."

"This is so strange. He told me he met my mother in Boston when they were at Emerson College."

"Really? He didn't go to Emerson. When he graduated from high school, his parents sent him to a private college in Europe, and I didn't see him again until he showed up years later with Ella."

Sofia sighed. "I guess he lied about that too."

"Maybe he was trying to protect you from his crazy family."

"Were they really that awful?"

"They were to me. In our senior year, they forbid us to be friends."

"Why would they do that?"

"I think I was a little wild for them, and they believed I was a bad influence on Aidan."

"They had no right to interfere with your friendship."

"It all blew over, and I was thrilled when he brought Ella here to meet me. At the time, your parents seemed head over heels in love. Too bad it didn't work out for them."

"They had nothing in common, so it's really not surprising."

"Actually, they had a lot in common. They both loved to dance and cook. And you couldn't stop Ella from breaking into song after a couple of drinks. Aidan adored her, and she was the life of every party. We had a blast skinny-dipping in the river at midnight, and Ella was always the first one in."

"I can't imagine her doing any of that. She's a devout Catholic."

He grinned. "Well, the Romans invented orgies, and she loved to party."

"You wouldn't recognize her today," Sofia said. "She's depressed and hardly ever leaves her apartment."

"That's too bad. Sounds like she's had some hard times."

"She has." Sofia glanced at the painting of her parents. "Did my dad ever tell you why they moved to San Diego?"

"I can take credit for that. An old friend of my family used to be the Dean at El Encanto College, and they were looking for professors. I recommended Aidan. He flew out for an interview, and they hired him on the spot."

"I really appreciate you telling me all this. It sounds like my parents were a lot more fun when they were young." Sofia pulled a small notepad out of her purse, jotted her contact information on a page, and handed it to him. "If you hear from him, please let me know."

"Your wish is my command."

"Thanks."

"Despite their issues, it seems like your parents raised a groovy daughter."

She smiled at him gratefully, glad to have met a friend of her father's. "You're very sweet to say that. Well, I better be going." Sofia stood and headed toward the door.

Kieran followed her. "Good luck finding your dad!" He gave her a bear hug.

"Thanks so much for everything." She stepped onto the porch.

Kieran called after her. "Hey, wait a second. There's something I forgot to mention that might be helpful." Sofia turned and faced him. "Did you know your father's last name used to be Malone?"

Sofia could hardly believe her ears. "Malone? I had no idea!"

"Yep, he changed it to Ryan when they got married. Said he wanted a fresh start."

She paused, trying to take in the revelation. "Thanks for telling me. Do you know his parents' first names?"

"Beats me. Aidan called them Ma and Da."

"Ma and Da?" she asked.

Keiran nodded. "That's what all Irish kids call their parents."

Sofia felt lightheaded and grabbed the railing.

"You look dizzy. Are you okay?" he asked.

"I'll be fine. I just need a moment."

Kieran pulled a clear quartz crystal from his pocket and placed it in her palm. "Your aura tells me you have some dark karma to work through. The purity of this crystal destroys all negative energy around it and will lighten your journey."

"Thank you, Kieran."

"Peace and love, goddess. Namaste."

Sofia walked to her car in a daze. The life she thought she knew had evaporated and she couldn't fathom why her parents concocted such an elaborate fiction. The ground beneath her feet was shifting and she had nothing to hold on to. *Will my life ever be in balance again?*

Chapter 18
What's in a Name?

Now that Sofia had learned her parents didn't attend Emerson College, it was pointless going there, so tracking down her father's relatives would be her next priority. At least now she knew their real last name. But first, she would need a place to stay.

As she drove from Medford to the north end of Boston, she entered an Italian neighborhood, which reminded her of an east coast version of her mother's community in San Diego. She spotted The Harlequin, an inviting hotel in a three-story red brick building. On its facade, several columns of bay windows framed in a green copper verdigris protruded from the top two floors. A vacancy sign was posted in front.

Sofia parked her car and walked inside. The lobby was decorated with vintage Italian Commedia dell'arte photos and colorful masks from the Venice Carnival. Once she had checked in, she headed upstairs.

Arriving at her room, she unlocked the door and entered the comfortable space. There was a four-poster bed, a small desk and chair, and a cozy seat nestled in the curve of the bay window overlooking the street. She placed her backpack on the desk and headed to the bathroom. After sleeping in her clothes on the overnight flight and meeting with Kieran, she was weary, grungy, and dying to take a bath. Fortunately, there was a white porcelain claw-foot tub and toiletries on the counter. In keeping with the Harlequin theme, the small hexagonal floor tiles were made of white marble with black marble rosettes. While the bathtub filled, she undressed, then stepped into the soothing warm water.

While soaking in the bubble bath, Sofia's mind drifted. Only a week ago, she was worried about pleasing her father and wondering what career path she should take, but the extreme changes in her life made those concerns seem trivial. The duplicity and treachery of his actions forced her to grow up almost overnight and now she was in Boston, attempting to find him. She tried to push down the bitterness welling up inside as uncontrollable tears streamed down her cheeks. The paintings of crying and laughing clowns on the bathroom walls stared back at her. It was all beyond belief and yet the clowns were emblematic of what her life had actually become—a surreal, tragic comedy.

After drying off and dressing in a black tank top and jeans, she sat in the bay window with a phone book she found on the desk. She flipped through the M's and to her dismay, there were hundreds of Malones in Boston, but since she didn't know her grandparents' first names, she couldn't identify them. All she knew was her aunt's maiden name, Margaret Grace Malone, and there was no listing for her. Kieran said she married an attorney in Boston, so she would need to check the city marriage records to learn her aunt's married name. She looked up the address of the county records office, jotted it down, and hurried out of the room.

Sofia parked downtown and walked through the brick

multi-level public plaza then entered the Boston City Hall building constructed of exposed concrete, steel and glass. She located the Registry Division and approached a lady sitting behind a desk at the entrance, her head buried in a book. The matronly administrator, wearing a lilac mohair sweater, had a nameplate that read Harriet Hildy.

"Hello, Harriet," Sofia said. "I'm looking for my aunt's marriage records."

She lowered her half-moon shaped reading glasses to the tip of her nose. "Do you have an appointment?"

"No. Do I need one?"

"Yes. Let me see when I can fit you in." Harriet consulted her appointment book. "An archivist is available next Monday at 1:00. Will that do?"

"Unfortunately, no. I'm from San Diego and won't be here on Monday. Is there any way I can see someone now?"

She frowned. "I'm afraid not. The archives are closed to the public on Friday."

"That's disappointing. We've been out of touch, and I was hoping to reconnect with her while I was in Boston. Can you help me?" she asked.

She shook her head. "Sorry, it's really not my job."

"I understand," Sofia said, then looked at Harriet, admiringly. "I love your mohair sweater. It's so beautiful, and you chose a gorgeous shade of lilac."

A smile lit Harriet's face. "Well, thank you, it's my favorite."

Sofia sighed. "It's such a shame I won't be able to see my aunt. My timing is terrible."

I'll tell you what," Harriet said, clearly sympathetic to her plight. "Since you're from out of town, I'll help you myself. Please, follow me."

Harriet escorted her down the hall to the archives where

the marriage records were stored. The instant she opened the door, the cold air hit them, and Sofia shivered and wrapped her arms around her chest.

"Sorry it's like the North Pole in here, but we need to keep the temperature low to protect the media. Thus, the mohair. I have a shawl you can borrow." Harriet took a white wool wrap off a shelf and handed it to her.

"Thank you," Sofia said and draped it over her shoulders.

"Have a seat." She gestured to two chairs in front of a machine with a large screen and flatbed scanner and they sat. Harriet picked up a piece of paper and a pencil. "What year was your aunt married?"

"I'm not sure, but it must have been in the 1930s or 40s."

"Oh dear. You'll have a lot to look through." She stood. "Wait here. I'll be right back."

In a few minutes, Harriet returned with a box of microfiche and gave Sofia a quick tutorial on how to use the reader. "We close at five. I'll check in on you before then," she said, then left.

The hours dragged on as Sofia slogged through hundreds of records and found nothing relevant. She glanced at the clock on the wall and noticed it was almost five. Her eyes were strained from staring at the black screen with small green letters, and she felt discouraged. If only she knew more about her aunt, the entire process would be easier. Shaking off her frustration, she resumed the tedious process.

After scanning several more sheets of microfiche, she hit gold. On the screen in front of her was the 1936 marriage record for Margaret Grace Malone and Declan Gallagher II, at the Church of the Holy Trinity in Boston. Sofia studied the document in astonishment. This must be her aunt! She wrote down their names and rushed out of the frigid room.

Waving the paper in triumph, she arrived at Harriet's desk and announced. "I found it!"

"Fantastic. I'm so happy for you."

"It was on the last sheet."

"Good work!" Harriet said. "Your perseverance paid off."

"I hate to trouble you, but could you look up a phone number for my aunt and uncle?"

"Sure."

"Here are their names." Sofia handed her the paper.

Harriet opened a phone book and quickly found the information. "Bingo! There's no home phone number but there is a business listing for Declan Gallagher II."

"That's great! I'll start there," Sofia said.

Harriet noted the address and phone number and handed it to her.

"Thank you so much. Only one more favor. Can I please use your phone?"

"All right, then." She turned the phone on her desk around, so the dial faced Sofia. "But make it quick. I need to get home and feed my toy poodles."

"I promise." Sofia said and dialed the number.

A woman with a high-pitched voice and a southern accent answered. "Faith and Family Federation and law offices of Declan Gallagher the second. This is Birdie Lee. How may I help you?"

"I'd like to speak with Mr. or Mrs. Gallagher, please," Sofia said.

"They're not available right now. If you give me your name and number, one of them will return your call next week."

Reluctant to reveal her name, Sofia said, "Unfortunately, I'm only in town for the day, so I'll need to call them back, but I have a quick question. Does Margaret Grace have a brother named Aidan Malone?"

"Why do you want to know?" asked Birdie Lee, suspiciously.

"It's a personal matter."

"Well, I don't know who you are, but I'm not allowed to share private information," she said, then hung up the phone.

Harriet looked at her sympathetically. "Maybe you should go to the office in person. Sometimes the gatekeeper is the biggest obstacle."

"You're right. I'll give it a try."

"Good luck," Harriet said.

"You've been so kind. Thanks for all your help." Sofia returned Harriet's shawl then hurried out of the building.

Chapter 19
Faith & Family

Sofia rushed out of the Boston City Hall complex and drove toward the affluent neighborhood of Beacon Hill. It was late afternoon when she arrived at historic Acorn Street, with its cobblestone sidewalks and perfectly preserved brick row houses. She parked at the address that Harriet gave her and got out of the car. A plaque on the office door read: *Faith & Family Federation, CEO Margaret Grace Gallagher and Law Offices of Declan Gallagher II.*

As she entered the spacious reception area, which was furnished with period antiques, a perky blonde secretary looked up. "Good afternoon. I'm Birdie Lee. May I help you?"

The instant she heard her voice, Sofia knew this was the woman she spoke to on the phone. "Nice to meet you, Birdie Lee. I'm here to see Mrs. Gallagher."

"We're about to close. Is she expecting you?"

"No. But I think she might be my aunt, and I'd like to speak with her."

"How peculiar. You don't know your own aunt?"

"No, we've never met. I was in town and hoped she'd have a moment to chat."

"Your voice sounds familiar. Did you call earlier?"

"Yes, I'm Sofia Ryan."

Birdie Lee eyed her skeptically. "Let me check with her. I'll be right back."

When she stepped away from her desk and disappeared down the hall, Sofia perused the framed pictures on the walls. Prominently displayed were newspaper and magazine stories extolling the legal successes of the Federation. The articles praised attorney Declan Gallagher II and his wife, Margaret Grace Gallagher, whose efforts helped block gun control, abortion rights, desegregation busing, and sex education classes in schools, among other social and political crusades.

Sofia scanned the various awards and articles and vehemently disagreed with everything the Federation stood for. How could this woman be Aidan's sister? Their values were diametrically opposed. Maybe that's why he never told her about Margaret Grace. Her father was a social and political progressive; or was he? In truth, she really didn't know who he was anymore.

Birdie Lee returned a moment later. "Mrs. Gallagher has agreed to see you, but she only has a few minutes."

Sofia followed her down a hall and into an office crowded with trophies, awards, and corkboards crammed with charts and schedules. It looked like a war room. At the epicenter of the controlled chaos sat Margaret Grace, a Brunhilda of a woman in her mid-sixties with frosted hair and an intense, pudgy pink face presiding over a desk littered with file folders. She took a final drag on a Camel cigarette and stubbed it out in an overflowing beanbag ashtray as she talked acerbically on the phone. "Absolutely not! If your school district allows filth like *The Catcher in the Rye* to pollute the minds of our children, I'll torch every copy myself. And I'll throw you and your degenerate flunkies on the bonfire! We're filing suit today!"

Margaret Grace slammed down the receiver, proud of herself, then flashed her piercing blue eyes at Sofia, who withered in the heat of her intense gaze. Everything about this loathsome lady made Sofia want to leave, but she steadied herself and tried to maintain her composure.

"Mrs. Gallagher, this is the young woman who wanted to see you," Birdie Lee announced.

"I know who she is. You may go now."

After her secretary left, Margaret Grace eyed her niece condescendingly. "Well, well, look what the cat dragged in. Sofia Ryan. I recognize you from the pictures my brother has sent me over the years. He's told me all about you."

"I can't say the same about you."

"He had his reasons. Why have you come here?"

"I'm looking for my father and when I found out he had a sister, well, I hoped you could help me find him."

"Aidan's missing? Good Lord!" Margaret Grace clutched her chest.

"I thought he might have confided in you. He retired and moved away without warning."

"There was warning all right. I've known for years how miserable he was."

"My dad wasn't miserable! We had a wonderful life together."

"He may have cared for you, but he was living a life that was way beneath him."

"Look, I just need to make sure he's safe," Sofia said.

"My brother's well-being is none of your concern."

Sofia marched up to her boldly. "Aunt Margaret, you obviously have no interest in me, and I don't really give a shit, but—"

Margaret Grace interrupted. "Watch your mouth, girl. If you don't leave now, I'll have you removed." She rose threateningly to her imposing six-foot height.

Sofia held her ground. "Why did my father never tell me about you?"

"There were things he wanted to keep private, and I respected his wishes."

"Can you at least introduce me to my grandparents?"

"They're no longer with us." She made the sign of the cross. "God rest their souls."

"What about Uncle Seamus?" Sofia asked.

"Quite the nosy little thing, aren't you?"

"I'm not nosy. I want to know what happened to my father and hoped someone in our family would help me!"

"We are not your family!" Unable to hold back her resentment, Margaret Grace's words spewed out. "Aidan had a promising future until he met your low-life Italian mother. She was a bloodsucking parasite who poisoned him against us."

Infuriated by her hateful words, Sofia lashed out. "You're insane. My mother may have her problems, but she would never do that!"

"She did, but you're too ignorant to see it." Margaret Grace hit the desk with her fist, sending her papers flying. "Marrying her was a dreadful mistake. The worst mistake of his life."

A tall, obese man in a beige suit, stinking of Brut cologne, burst into the room and glared at Sofia with disdain. He turned to his wife. "Who is this little street urchin?"

"Aidan's daughter. And I've told her to leave."

"I assume you're Declan Gallagher Jr?" Sofia asked.

"Declan Gallagher the *second*," he corrected her, then unbuttoned his tight coat with pudgy fingers encircled with ostentatious gold rings. "You're white trash, like your mother. Get the hell out of here or I'll call the police."

Sofia clenched her fists as the desire to strangle them became nearly overwhelming. "Meeting you was a revelation. I finally understand why my father was ashamed to tell me about you." She grabbed Margaret Grace's ashtray and hurled the cigarette butts at Declan, staining his clothes with a cloud of ash. His face turned red as he coughed and sputtered.

"Who's the white trash now?" Sofia asked, mockingly.

Her aunt charged up to her like a raging bull. "You spiteful little bitch!" As she raised her arm to slap her, Sofia shoved Margaret Grace with all her might. Losing her balance, she fell backward onto her desk with a crash.

"Thanks for the hospitality!" Sofia shouted and raced out of the office, slamming the door behind her.

Chapter 20
Confession

Adrenaline surged through Sofia's body as she rushed out of the Faith & Family offices and got into her rental car. On the drive back to The Harlequin Hotel, her thoughts were a torrent of rage, confusion, and disbelief. What had come over her? It seemed like a wildcat had been unleashed from the depths of her once timid soul. She'd assaulted her aunt and uncle, but they deserved it. Declan and Margaret Grace were the most repulsive human beings she'd ever met.

Why would her father stay in touch with such vile people merely because they were relatives? Aidan always said that blood was thicker than water, but consciousness was thicker than blood. What happened to his high ethical standards? She didn't understand it, and the situation made her even more depressed.

Sofia arrived at the hotel drained of energy, parked her car and slipped through the lively lobby like a ghost. After trudging up two flights of stairs, she entered her room and collapsed on the bed. It would be a relief to give up her search and go home, which sounded like the most sensible idea, as she craved a peaceful life without conflict. If only she were religious, she could become a nun and live in a quiet convent surrounded by sweet, supportive, soft-spoken women. But unlike her mother, who considered the Catholic Church infallible, she felt most religions did more harm than good. So, being a nun was definitely not an option. As much as she desired to give up her quest, she couldn't allow her father to get away with his treachery. She would find his sorry ass, come hell or high water, but how? Her mother was no help at all, and she had run out of leads.

Exasperated, she raided the minibar and devoured potato chips, Cheetos, corn nuts, pretzels, and a dozen Hershey's kisses. To wash down her junk food orgy, she polished off two cans of Budweiser. She felt better for a minute, then ran to the bathroom, kneeled over the toilet, and threw up.

After rinsing her mouth, she perched on her bed and flipped through Aidan's journal, desperately looking for clues. She decided to focus on his numerous sketches of mythical beasts, including griffins and gargoyles. A detailed drawing of a magnificent, winged angel killing a serpent with his sword caught her attention. What was her father thinking, and where was this bizarre imagery coming from? Worn out and barely able to keep her eyes open, she set his journal on the nightstand, turned off the light, and fell asleep.

In the morning, Sofia awoke gripped by a sense of dread, but she shook it off. While getting dressed for the day, she pondered what to do next and decided to go to the Church of the Holy Trinity, where Margaret Grace and Declan were married. Maybe someone there would know her family. Although it was almost a mile away, a brisk walk would help clear her troubled mind.

As she hurried down the street, an unbearable loneliness overcame Sofia. Her heart ached in a way she hadn't felt since she'd lost her twin. There was a hollowness in her chest, a void so deep she wondered if it would ever be filled again. She burst into tears and couldn't stop. Her life was in freefall, and there was no one to lean on. Ella's words echoed in her mind. *I'm warning you, don't search for him. You may not like what you find.* Her mother was right; she didn't like what she'd found so far. Aidan had deceived and rejected her, so why should she still care about him?

Before she knew it, Sofia found herself in front of the Church of the Holy Trinity. Although raised a Catholic, she had grown to distrust all religions. She revered Christians like Mother Teresa and Dr. Martin Luther King who embodied the precepts of Jesus and found wisdom in the teachings of Lao Tzu, Buddha, and Krishna, but many people seemed to blindly accept their religious texts as literal truth, even the laughable parts.

When she and Liam were ten, their mother took on the dutiful task of reading them the entire Bible in nightly installments to give them a strong moral foundation. The story of Noah's Ark horrified Sofia and her brother. They couldn't understand why a loving God would flood the Earth and drown millions of innocent people and animals. To them, he seemed like a mass murderer, as cruel as the Devil. Ella's explanation failed to convince them of God's righteousness, and after several nights of being unable to answer her children's probing questions, the Bible readings came to an end, much to their relief.

Sofia's final shred of religious faith died when she was eleven and had to listen to the priest spout platitudes at Liam's funeral. Aidan must have felt the same way as they both stopped attending church, leaving Ella to go alone. If a benevolent, omnipotent deity truly existed, there's no way he would have let her innocent brother die.

She hadn't entered a church since the funeral and was apprehensive, but she needed a quiet place to calm down and collect her thoughts, and the Church of the Holy Trinity was part of her family history. When she walked through the massive open doors of the old stone building and into the chapel, strains of Bach's *Jesu, Joy of Man's Desiring* played softly, and the sweet smell of frankincense wafted through the air.

Surprisingly, she found the music and environment peaceful and wiped the tears from her eyes. In the pews, several parishioners kneeled in silent prayer. Sofia took a seat and studied her surroundings. Alcoves with marble statues lined the left and right aisles.

A sculpture of Saint Michael with his wings spread and sword drawn as he killed an enormous snake coiled at his feet, caught her eye. It reminded her of one of the drawings in Aidan's journal. She pulled it out of her purse and compared the drawing to the sculpture. The images were identical, as if Aidan had based it on this very statue. The only difference was that beneath her father's drawing, there was an inscription that read:

Michael the Archangel . . . The Brotherhood serves your Holy Mission . . .

At the rear of the sanctuary, she saw several ornately carved wooden confessionals. A green light on one booth lit up, signaling that a confessor was available. Impulsively, she stood and approached the confessional. She paused in front of the door, then entered.

A small window slid open in the dark chamber, and the profile of a priest appeared through the lattice partition. He spoke in a soft, caring voice. "May God, who has enlightened every heart, help you atone for your sins and trust in His mercy."

"I haven't come to confess," Sofia said. "But I hope you can answer some questions for me."

"All right, my child, what's on your mind?"

"I'm doing genealogical research and learned that my father, Aidan Malone, and his family were parishioners at this church. And my aunt, Margaret Grace, was married here in 1936. Do you know them?"

"No. That was quite a long time ago, and I've only recently come to this parish."

"Is there another priest here that might remember my family?"

"Unfortunately, no one from the 1930s is still here," he said.

"Just one more question if you have the time."

"Of course. What is it?"

"I saw the statue of Saint Michael in the chapel, and there's a similar image in my father's journal. May I show it to you?"

"Certainly."

Sofia opened the journal and held it up to the lattice window.

"What a marvelous drawing. Is your father a professional artist?"

"No, he's a professor and a scholar. Do you know what the inscription under the drawing means?" she asked.

The priest looked at the intricate pen and ink sketch. "It may refer to The Brotherhood of Archangels, who were followers of Saint Michael."

"I've never heard of them."

"Most people haven't. The stories of their heroic deeds characterize them as a kind of Irish Knights Templar."

"That's fascinating. Can you tell me more?" Sofia lowered the book and set it on her lap.

"I can share what little I know about them."

"Great. I'd appreciate whatever you can tell me."

"Well, according to legend, they were zealous religious warriors who vanquished the enemies of the Catholic Church. There are many fanciful stories about their exploits, but it's merely folklore."

"I'm researching my family history and since there was a notation about them in my father's diary, I thought it might be significant."

"Perhaps he was writing about The Brotherhood for an academic paper."

"You're probably right. Can you recommend any books about them?"

"Not that I know of, but you might want to contact Trinity College in Dublin. They have the world's most extensive archive of Irish history and mythology."

"Thank you, Father. I appreciate your help."

"I pray God will bring you the peace and knowledge you seek."

On her walk back to the hotel, Sofia was exhausted and thought about going home. She desperately wanted to curl up on her own bed and forget about her father's lies and monstrous relatives, but although she tried to talk herself into giving up, not knowing the truth would torment her for the rest of her life. It might be a fool's errand, but she resolved to fly to Ireland. Hopefully, in the land of Aidan's birth, she might locate some of his relatives or find information that would lead her to him. *Good thing I brought my passport!*

Chapter 21
Irish Roots

Sofia exited the plane at Dublin Airport, and the early morning breeze was exhilarating. Amazingly, she actually enjoyed the flight. Something inside her had changed and the fear of flying, and fear in general, had loosened its grip on her.

Setting foot on the tarmac, she instantly felt at home, as if she'd been living in an alien land all her life and was finally back where she belonged, on Irish soil. Except for crossing the border into Tijuana, Mexico, with her parents and brother to watch the jai alai games, eat fish tacos, and pose for pictures on top of a burro, she'd never traveled internationally and looked forward to her new adventure.

Upon leaving the terminal, Sofia hailed a taxi. On the drive to Trinity College, she gazed out the open cab window. The sights and sounds of Dublin seemed to resonate in her ancestral bones. Soulful old book shops and lively pubs beckoned her to enter, but this was not a vacation, so she pressed on to her destination. When she heard a busker playing guitar and singing one of her favorite songs, "Moondance" by the Irish musician

Van Morrison, she knew the city had captured her heart and hoped to return someday.

Soon she arrived at Trinity College, which was founded in 1592. Sofia was starstruck; many of her favorite authors were educated here, including Oscar Wilde, Jonathan Swift, Bram Stoker, and Samuel Beckett. She felt more intelligent just breathing the rarified air as she strode across the campus teaming with a diverse group of students, faculty, and visitors.

Sofia made a beeline for the renowned Old Library's Long Room, home of the Genealogy Archives, to find information on Aidan's family. Since he was born in Ireland, maybe he was still in contact with some of his Irish relatives.

On her way, she noticed the *Book of Kells* which was on display. The beautiful, illuminated manuscript of the four Gospels from the New Testament, created in 800 CE, stopped her in her tracks. The stunning gilded pages combined Christian iconography with figures of animals, humans and mythical beasts, and Sofia marveled at the artistry of the book.

After leaving the display, she entered the main chamber of the two-story Long Room and looked up in awe at the wooden barrel-vaulted ceiling. Sofia inhaled the intoxicating musty scent of ancient tomes and relished being surrounded by such an inspiring repository of knowledge. Towering stalls on each side held over two hundred thousand of the oldest books in the library's collection, with innumerable documents from the 12th century to the present, representing all aspects of human endeavor and intellectual pursuits. Between each stall were marble busts of writers, philosophers, and scientists, including Socrates, Shakespeare, and Sir Isaac Newton.

Sofia began researching her ancestry in the archives to see if she had any living relatives in the country, but after a quick search, she realized it might take days to locate the information she was looking for using their unfamiliar and complex filing system.

To expedite the process, Sofia stopped at the information desk of the Genealogy Department. Caitlin, an elfin young woman with red hair in a pixie cut, informed Sofia she could hire a researcher by the hour and the fee would include a written report. After Sofia explained her situation, Caitlin estimated it would take a minimum of two hours to locate the information she was looking for, so she hired the service and filled out a form with what little she knew about her ancestors.

While waiting for the results, Sofia located and skimmed several books on The Brotherhood of Archangels which confirmed what the priest in Boston told her. If the group ever existed, which seemed unlikely, the history of the mysterious society was lost in the mists of time. One of the gilded manuscripts about the group reminded her of the *Book of Kells*. There were many elaborate drawings of the warriors' battles and an image of their crest, a majestic, golden-winged lion with a crown of silver stars. The discovery convinced her that Aidan had been researching The Brotherhood for a scholarly paper. While waiting, she wandered through the stalls, perusing the fascinating manuscripts until she heard her name called.

She walked up to the counter and met Ian, a handsome young archivist with thick shoulder length dark hair topped by a green Irish flat cap. He introduced himself and gestured to a desk. "Please, have a seat, Miss Ryan, and I'll explain the report." They sat across from each other, and he handed her a one-page typed document.

"This is incredible," Sofia said, her spirits buoyed.

As she reviewed the summary, Ian went over the details. "Your immediate ancestors were born and raised in Londonderry, Northern Ireland, which the Irish call Derry. Your father, grandparents, and aunt all emigrated to Boston on April

5, 1926, crossing the Atlantic on the *Celtic Queen*. And many of your relatives are buried in Derry, including your father's brother William and your great uncle Seamus Malone and his wife Nelda."

"Didn't my Uncle Seamus emigrate to America too?"

Ian shook his head. "There are no documents showing Seamus Malone or his wife ever left Ireland, and his son, Finn, your first cousin, was born in Derry and may still live there. That's all the information I could find on the initial search. Would you like me to look into previous generations?"

"This is good for now. How far away is Derry?"

"About five hours by train, but I wouldn't recommend going. Since Bloody Sunday, there's been a lot of political violence in Northern Ireland."

"Thanks for the warning, but if there's a chance my cousin lives there, I have to go."

"Well, be careful then."

"I will. Do you know what time the train leaves?" she asked.

"Let me check the schedule." Ian consulted a chart, then glanced at his watch. "The last train to Derry leaves in an hour and fifteen minutes."

"I'm in luck. How do I get to the station?"

"You can take the bus or it's about a twenty-minute stroll."

"I'd love to walk. Can you give me directions?"

Ian handed her a map and pointed out the route. "Dublin Connolly is north of the campus, across the River Liffey."

"Thanks so much for your help, Ian," she said and hurried out of the archives.

As Sofia walked along the river which flowed through the center of the vibrant city, Dublin Connolly with its beautiful and distinctive Italianate facade and tower came into view.

When she reached the station, she bought a ticket, located the platform, and boarded the train to Derry.

Sofia settled in a window seat, grateful to have no one sitting next to her. The whistle blew, and the sparsely filled train left the station. She was famished, as it had been hours since the light breakfast on the plane. Fortunately, an attendant rolling a food cart down the aisle was heading her way. She bought a cheese and chicken sandwich, potato crisps, and black tea.

While eating her lunch, she stared out the window as the bucolic countryside came into view, leaving the bustling city behind. The train sped past charming towns and villages and lush green meadows where hundreds of sheep splotched with pink, blue, and orange identifying colors, grazed happily. It was the most peaceful scenery imaginable and was in sharp contrast to the tumultuous thoughts and feelings churning inside her. *Why did my father claim his entire family died in Ireland?*

She took off the Irish friendship ring he gave her and read the faint inscription that years of wear had worn smooth: *May God be with you.* The pain of William's death at such a young age seemed very real to her now, and she understood why it was so difficult for Aidan to talk about his brother.

There was a long journey ahead, so she pulled out the journal and photographs from Aidan's satchel and laid them out on the fold-down table in front of her. She wanted to take a closer look at the picture of her father with William and Finn, but couldn't find it, so she carefully searched the empty bag and discovered the photo had slipped behind the dark blue silk lining. When she lifted the lining to retrieve it, she noticed a hidden compartment at the bottom of the case. Inside, she found a small, elegant envelope containing a picture of the glamorous Italian opera singer Gemma Ricci and a handwritten note on lavender-scented stationery embossed with flowers. Sofia read the message:

Dearest Aidan,
Our weekend in Capri was divine. You're the most
brilliant man I've ever met, and our connection is eter-
nal. I adore you and hope we share many more adven-
tures in the coming years. You are so special to me.
Your Dolce Diva, Gemma

Sofia was shocked and felt numb. She knew her father loved the diva's singing, but he never mentioned they had a personal relationship and there was no date on the note. *They must have had an affair. But when? And was it still going on?*

Every time she found an answer, more questions appeared. Frustrated and weary, she packed up Aidan's satchel and closed her eyes, hoping to get a little rest before arriving in Derry.

Chapter 22
Divided City

"Next stop, Londonderry Station," the conductor announced, waking Sofia from her nap. As the train slowed, she quickly gathered her belongings and exited the carriage. Although it was early evening, the sun was still bright in the sky as the city was so far north, and it didn't get dark until late at night. Inside the station, she located a rental car agency and selected a white Volkswagen Beetle for her stay.

Sofia planned to explore the town before finding a hotel, so she headed for central Derry while glancing down at a map on her lap for directions. It was unnerving, as everything about driving in Ireland was different. The steering wheel was on the right and the stick shift on the left. Even worse, she had to drive on the opposite side of the road.

Suddenly, the vehicles in front of her slowed, and she slammed on the brakes to avoid rear-ending an enormous beer truck with a cylindrical tank shaped and painted like a giant can of Guinness. The reason for the traffic jam soon became clear when she passed bright red signs on either side of the motorway declaring:

STOP! WAIT UNTIL CALLED FORWARD

The cars in both lanes inched toward the checkpoint. Startled, Sofia saw four Royal Ulster Constabulary police officers with body armor and machine guns flanking the road. She'd never experienced such a military presence, and it was alarming.

At the checkpoint barrier, a stern officer rapped his knuckles on the driver's side window. "Get out of the vehicle and open the boot."

She got out warily and opened the trunk. He scrutinized her and thrust out his open hand brusquely. "Identification, miss."

Sofia handed him her passport. As he examined it, a second officer searched inside the car, then walked around, scanning the undercarriage with a mirror.

"I see you're an American. What is your business here?"

"I'm on vacation," she said, trying to act calm.

"Very few tourists visit Northern Ireland these days," he said. "How long do you plan to stay?"

"Maybe a week. If you don't mind my asking, what are you looking for?"

"Weapons and explosives. We have a lot of troublemakers in Londonderry." He waved to the second officer, who gave him the all-clear sign, then returned her passport. "You're free to go, miss."

Sofia got in her car and, when the officer lifted the barrier arm for her to pass, she continued driving.

The River Foyle split Derry into two areas, the Cityside, which was predominantly Catholic, and the Waterside, which was mainly Protestant. It was as if the river was a symbol of their divided ideologies. As she crossed the waterway on the Craigavon Bridge, which connected the east bank to the west bank, she recalled her father's lecture on the history of Derry. He spoke about the centuries of violence between Protestants and Catholics over religion and independence, and it made her sad that people could so easily justify killing each other in the name of God and country.

Upon reaching the walled city, built in the 1600s, Sofia parked on Foyle Road. As she walked along the picturesque streets, she felt like she'd gone back in time. Ancient thirty-five-foot-high stone walls surrounded the old town which was accessible through seven gates. But the modern world came into sharp focus when she passed streets barricaded with barbed wire and looked up at the armed police officers patrolling on top of the ramparts.

Although it was a long shot, she decided to approach a few locals, because if her cousin still lived there, she might get lucky and meet someone who knew him or his family. She looked around and spotted the Greta Goose Pub, a busy establishment with music playing and people eating and drinking at wooden tables on an outdoor patio.

At the entrance was a six-foot tall bronze statue of a pink-footed Icelandic goose sipping beer from a mug. Sofia read the posted story, which claimed a migrating goose that the locals named Greta flew into the pub on September 1, 1899, landed on a table, and drank from an unattended pint of Guinness. The employees and patrons welcomed the gregarious goose, and to their delight, she returned on her annual migration every September 1 for twenty years. On the twenty-first year, when she was a no show, the pub hosted a memorial for the beloved bird and renamed the business Greta Goose Pub in her honor.

Charmed by the tale, Sofia entered the patio and a bubbly young hostess, her black hair swirled up in a beehive, greeted her. "Hello. Table for one?"

"I don't need a table right now," Sofia said. "I just arrived in town and I'm looking for my cousin, Finn Malone. Do you know anyone by that name?"

The hostess chuckled. "Not personally, but there's an infinity of Finns in Derry. And even more Malones. Throw a rock, and you'll hit two of them. What does the bloke look like?"

"I'm not sure. He's about sixty years old. I've never met him, but he might be a musician."

"Every Irishman worth his salt is a musician. As we say around here, you might be in for a wild Greta Goose chase."

"The story of my life. Thanks, anyway."

Sofia left the pub and strolled down a footpath lined with bars and restaurants. Noticing a British red telephone booth, she went inside and flipped through the white pages. Sure enough, there were scores of listings for Finn Malone, F. Malone, F.R. Malone, etc. She called the first three listings. Two rang with no response, and the third was out of service. It would take hours to call them all, so she planned to review the public records at the city administration office when they opened in the morning, to help narrow her search.

It was getting dark, and Sofia realized she needed a place to stay. As she continued down the street looking for lodging, she heard the sound of footsteps behind her and turned around. Two tattooed skinheads in wife-beater T-shirts and torn jeans were a few steps away, snickering and gawking. Excited by making eye contact, they hurried after her, their heavy steel-toed red boots clicking on the footpath.

Frightened, she ran away, looking for help. Most of the shops were closed but she noticed a man working inside O'Neill's Smoke Shop, a tiny business filled with pipes, tobacco, and cigars. She banged on the window to get his attention.

The owner, a gray-haired, broad-bellied man, stepped away

from the counter and opened the door. "Sorry, I'm about to leave."

"I hate to bother you, sir, but there are two men outside harassing me. Can you please help?"

"Of course. What do you need?"

"If you don't mind, I'd like to stay here for a few minutes until they leave."

He let her in, closed the door, then peered out the window. Spying the two punks loitering nearby, he shouted, "Get the hell out of here, or I'll call the police!"

The men guffawed, raised their middle fingers, and swaggered away like crazed coyotes.

O'Neill turned to Sofia. "They're gone now. Just a couple of worthless delinquents."

Sofia heaved a sigh of relief. "Thank you, sir."

"A young girl like you shouldn't be out alone at night."

"Sorry for the inconvenience. This is my first day in Derry and I'm a little out of my element."

"Well, you should get back to wherever you're staying."

"I don't have a hotel yet," Sofia said. "Is there one nearby?"

"There's a nice bed and breakfast down the road." He gestured for her to follow him; they walked outside, and he pointed to the right. "It's two blocks down, next to the Drunken Druid Pub. You can't miss it."

"Before I go, I have a quick question. I'm looking for my cousin, Finn Malone, who grew up in Derry. He's around sixty and might be a musician. Have you heard of him?"

He considered it for a second, then shook his head. "The only musician named Finn that I know of is Mighty Finn. The bloke has played around town for years, but his last name is Quinn."

"Thanks for everything. You've been very kind."

"Take care now." O'Neill locked the door and walked away.

As Sofia hurried down the footpath, a plan emerged. She'd spend the night at the bed and breakfast and see if she could find Finn Quinn. Since he was a local and an established performer in Derry, he might know her cousin.

Without warning, the two skinheads jumped out of an alley in front of Sofia. Her heart raced as they leered at her.

"Hello lass, what's your name?" the stocky one with a large black nose ring asked.

"We're going to a hooley. You should come with us," the other man said. He was pasty white with a crooked grin and uneven buck teeth.

"I don't know what a hooley is, but I'm not going anywhere with you two jerks. Get out of my way!" Sofia tried to walk around them.

"You're a feisty one," the stocky man said.

With every step she took, the punks jumped in front of her, laughing and blocking her way.

"Relax, Yank. We'll show you a hot time," the short punk sneered.

"You're revolting!" Sofia's adrenaline spiked and she elbowed him in the face with all her might and kicked the other man in the balls, leaving them yelping in pain. She felt empowered and was proud of herself for not taking shit from such sleazebags. Breaking away, she bolted down the street with the cursing men in hot pursuit.

When she reached the Drunken Druid Pub, they caught up to Sofia, grabbed her and tried to drag her away, but she fought back ferociously and screamed. During the struggle, she tripped one of them, and the disgusting duo fell over each other, tumbling into the road. A car blared its horn and screeched to a stop, almost running into them.

A tall man with long brown hair, wearing a green plaid jacket, stepped out of the pub. Assessing the situation, he rushed toward the commotion. "Hey, you gobshites, leave her alone, or I'll shove your bollocks down your throats!"

Intimidated by the commanding man, the punks scrambled to their feet and ran off.

He hurried to Sofia's side. "Are you all right?"

Although rattled, she brushed herself off. "Yes, I'm fine, now. I was on my way to the bed and breakfast to book a room."

"No worries, I'm the manager of the pub and we own the lodge next door. There are plenty of vacancies."

"Thanks for your help," she said.

"My name's Rory. Sorry for the rude introduction to our fair city. Trust me, not every lad in Derry is a reprobate."

"I'm sure that's true."

"Before you check-in, please come inside as our guest. We have the best fish and chips in town, and there's a great show tonight. The band is playing traditional Irish music."

"I'd love that. Thanks so much."

"My pleasure. Follow me, my lady."

Rory led her to the Drunken Druid's entrance. The historic two-story white stone building had a bronze plaque that read: *Established in 1686.*

Sofia was amazed. "Has the pub really been here for nearly three-hundred years?"

"Aye. We're the oldest in Derry." Rory held the door open.

"Thank you. You're a life saver." Sofia walked inside, grateful to have found a safe haven.

Chapter 23
The Drunken Druid

Rory led Sofia into the lively pub, crowded with blue-collar workers, young hipsters, seniors, and families eating, drinking, and playing darts while waiting for the show to begin. The walls were decorated with vintage Irish sports memorabilia and autographed photos of famous rugby and soccer players. As he led her toward the front of the stage, they passed a long, mirrored bar with a remarkable array of liquor bottles and a dozen beers on tap.

When they reached a small table in the front row, he gallantly pulled out her chair. "Enjoy your dinner. And please ask for me if you need anything at all."

"Thanks, Rory."

"Duty calls," he said and dashed off.

She sat and was instantly at ease in her new environment. A moment later, an outgoing young woman with curly black hair took her order and left. Sofia appreciated the enthusiastic energy of the audience and realized that Ireland couldn't be blamed because of a couple Homo Ignoramuses; it was a global affliction. Her father was right—nowhere was safe from them.

Soon the hot crispy fish and chips arrived, and she savored the meal along with Aidan's favorite beer cocktail, known as a Half and Half, which had pale Harp Lager on the bottom and black Guinness floating on top. Her dad told her never to order a Black and Tan with Bass Ale from England, which polluted the drink. It was an insult to the Irish because the Black and Tans were the British paramilitary force who suppressed the Irish independence movement, and the name referred to their khaki military pants and dark shirts. Sofia recalled an Irish folksong "Black and Tans" that he used to sing to her and Liam. She tried to stop thinking about her father, but it was impossible to entirely banish him from her thoughts.

Spotlights lit the stage as the band, three attractive lads and three lovely lasses in green and gold traditional outfits, appeared. The crowd whistled and cheered as they performed an exciting instrumental on tin whistle, concertina, bodhran drum, fiddle, mandolin, and guitar.

When the lead singer danced from the rear of the pub to the stage, the audience went wild. He wore a bright saffron Irish kilt and played the uilleann pipes as he basked in the adoration of his fans. An immensely charismatic performer with a lithe body and an expressive face crowned with a leonine blonde mane and a neatly groomed beard, he reminded her of a modern-day Viking in a kilt. He was sexy and graceful with a charming smile. Leaping onto the stage, he sang "The Rocky Road to Dublin" as the crowd clapped along to the rousing beat.

> *In the merry month of June, from my home, I started*
> *Left the girls of Tuam nearly broken-hearted*
> *Saluted father dear, kissed my darlin' mother*
> *Drank a pint of beer, my grief and tears to smother*
> *Then off to reap the corn and leave where I was born*

I cut a stout blackthorn to banish ghost and goblin
Brand new pair of brogues rattled o'er the bogs
And frightened all the dogs on the rocky road to Dublin

The song ended with a rhythmic stepdance by Finn and two of the girls. After the applause finally died down, the musicians performed a series of crowd-pleasing tunes that spanned Irish history, many of them riotous and tragic tales of the Irish Rebellion, The War of Independence, and the Northern Ireland conflict. Unforgettable songs of bombings and betrayals, heroism, and love.

At the conclusion of the medley, the bandleader said, "Welcome, friends! I'm Mighty Finn and these are The Marauders."

The audience applauded as he introduced each member of the ensemble. Sofia's cousin, Finn, would be around sixty years old, and this god of a man appeared to be closer to forty, so they couldn't be peers, but maybe they knew each other. Her search had just begun, and it felt good to relax for the night and watch the show.

Finn announced they had a repertoire of over three hundred Irish songs, and to end their set, he'd like to take a request from someone who hadn't seen the show before. When several people, including Sofia, shot their hands up, he pointed to her.

Sofia shouted, *"Black and Tans!"*

"Grand! We have an American in the house. What's your name, luv?"

"Sofia."

"Welcome, Sofia!" he boomed. "Please give our new friend a round of applause!" The audience clapped, and Sofia's spirits were lifted by the warm reception. Her father always said the Irish were the friendliest people in the world. At least he was right about a few things.

The Marauders played "Black and Tans" as Finn sang in a thrilling, rich baritone voice.

I grew up on the streets of Derry,
Where the folk were free and merry
Then the British came with their guns and chains,
Our hopes they planned to bury
But the Irish are brave, and the Irish are strong
And every night we would all sing along

Sofia and the audience enthusiastically joined in on the chorus.

To hell with ye, Black and Tans!
Cockwombles won't rule our sweet lands
We'll never bow down to your King or your Crown
We'll chase your invaders from our sacred ground
Independence is ours if we all take a stand
To hell with ye, Black and Tans!

The song deeply moved Sofia and reminded her of the first time her father sang it to her and Liam on Saint Patrick's Day, when they were little. Aidan was usually very formal, but while singing, he awkwardly danced an Irish jig, which made them laugh so hard it was permanently etched in her memory. At the thought of never hearing his voice again, tears filled her eyes; the prospect of losing him forever was shattering. The more she reflected on his disappearance, the more she was convinced he must be in trouble. Nothing else made any sense.

As Sofia was getting ready to leave, Rory approached her table with Finn. "I'd like you to meet the one and only Mighty Finn Quinn," he said.

Finn smiled warmly. "Welcome to Derry, Sofia."

"Thanks. I really love your music. Do you have a minute to chat?" she asked.

"Sure. I have a bit of time before our next set." He sat beside her.

"I'd love to stay and chat too, but my work is never done," Rory said and hurried away.

"How do you happen to know 'Black and Tans'?" Finn asked.

"My dad was born in Ireland, and he taught it to me."

"That's grand. What brings you to Derry?"

"I found out I have an Irish cousin named Finn Malone who used to live here, so I'm trying to find him."

"Boys, a dear!" he said in astonishment. "That's my name."

"But I thought your last name was Quinn," Sofia said.

"My birth name was Malone, but my father changed our surname when I was a child. It's complicated. Who's your father?"

"Aidan Malone."

"Aidan?" he asked, surprised.

"Yes. His older sister is Margaret Grace, and he had a brother named William and an Uncle Seamus. Do you know any of them?"

"Know them? Seamus is my father, and Aidan is my first cousin. We were inseparable until he moved with his family to America after William's death."

Thrilled, Sofia threw her arms around him. "It's a miracle that I found you!"

Finn beamed. "I'm glad you found me too. I haven't heard from your father in years. How's he doing?"

"It's a long story. Can we get together in the morning and catch up?"

"Absolutely. I'd love to."

"Sorry, I'm going to miss your next set, but I need to check into the bed and breakfast next door."

"No need. You can stay with me. I have a comfortable guest room, and I make a much better breakfast."

"Thank you, but I wouldn't want to impose."

"Don't be ridiculous, we're family. I insist."

"That would be fantastic, and it would give us more time to visit," she said.

"I have another set to play, then we'll go. May I buy you dinner?"

"I've already eaten. Rory treated me to the awesome fish and chips here."

"Excellent. He's a good lad."

"Please forgive me if I doze off. I arrived from Boston this morning and can hardly keep my eyes open."

"It wouldn't be the first time someone nodded off during my show," he teased. "I'll be back soon."

Finn gave her a fatherly hug and headed backstage. Sofia felt fortunate to have found her cousin. Maybe it was true about the luck of the Irish. Or maybe it was fate. It had been a long and harrowing first day in Ireland, but she was happy she came. Exhilarated but weary, she rested her head on the table and instantly fell asleep.

Chapter 24
Beneath the Surface

Heavy rain pelted the second-story window of an 18th century flat, awakening Sofia from a deep sleep. When she opened her eyes, she was lying under a soft feather comforter in a wooden bed shaped like a sleigh. She sat up and remembered coming home late with Finn and falling asleep in his guest room. Shadow boxes displaying handwritten musical scores hung on the walls. She noticed the antique grandfather clock standing prominently in the corner. It was almost eight in the morning, and since her cousin performed until midnight, she assumed he was still in bed.

Sofia got up and took a relaxing shower, savoring the lemon scented soap as the warm water poured over her body. After drying off, she dug through her backpack, put on a green cashmere sweater and black jeans, then headed downstairs.

The apartment was neat, clean, and overflowing with Celtic art, books, and exotic musical instruments. Drawn by the aroma of coffee mingling with the strains of a haunting melody, she entered the kitchen and saw Finn playing a four-foot-tall flame maple Irish harp. With a final strum, he muted the strings. "Good morning."

"That song is gorgeous. Did you write it?" Sofia asked.

"No, I wish I had. It's called 'O'Carolan's Dream' and was composed by a blind Irish musician in the 1700s."

"Well, it's a great way to start the day."

Finn carried the treasured instrument to its special niche. "Did you sleep well?"

"Yes, your guest room is very comfortable," she said. "Thanks for inviting me to stay."

"It's brilliant having you here. Would you like a wee cup of coffee?"

"I'd prefer a large cup."

Finn smiled. "Don't worry, luv, everything in Ireland is called wee, regardless of size."

"That sounds wonderful."

"Please, make yourself at home." He gestured to a small wooden table with two chairs, then prepared her drink in his French Press.

"Do you have cream?" she asked.

"Aye. Irish cream is the best."

Sofia sat and took in the charming surroundings. The galley kitchen had copper pots dangling from hooks on the wall and butcher block countertops with fresh fruit in woven baskets. Through the picture window above the sink, there was an exquisite view of Bishop's Gate, with its stone arch topped by the sculpted head of a bearded river god.

Finn brought her a cup of coffee and placed a small pitcher of cream on the table.

"Your home is delightful, and the coffee smells amazing!"

"Only the best for my long-lost cousin." He carried a basket of freshly baked scones and raspberry jam to the table and joined her. "Any plans for the day?"

"Not yet, but I came to Ireland to find out if my dad had any relatives, and I found you. So, my trip is off to a perfect start." Sofia took a bite of the scone. "Oh my god, you make the best scones I've ever tasted!"

"Told you I make a good breakfast." He took a sip of coffee and studied her face. "You look so much like your da. I'm glad Aidan finally came to his senses and left the Church to start a family."

"What do you mean?" she asked, puzzled.

"Well, the last time I saw him, he was a priest."

Sofia stared at him, dumbstruck. "Really? He never told me."

"Maybe being conned by the Church embarrassed him."

"I thought I knew my father." Sofia struggled to process the revelation. "Turns out, his entire life is a mystery."

"Where's your mother?" Finn asked.

"In California. They divorced years ago."

"That's a shame. You mentioned last night that Aidan is missing?"

"Yes, he left a note telling me not to look for him and vanished. Until then, I thought everything was fine."

Finn reached over and patted her hand reassuringly. "This must be so hard on you, luv. Aidan can be a hothead. Maybe something ticked him off and he needed to get away for a while."

"I really need to find out why he deserted me," she said.

"Of course you do. And I made a call this morning to my fiddle player to see if his wife can help. She works at the church our families attended when we were lads and is going to ask if anyone is still in contact with Aidan."

"I appreciate you reaching out."

"Hopefully, she'll find someone," Finn said.

"I can't understand why my dad told me he lived with your father after he arrived in Boston."

"It's odd that he would lie about my parents. They never went to America and sadly, they passed away a few years ago."

"I'm so sorry. I wish I could have met them."

"None of us get out of here alive, so we should enjoy every day to the fullest," Finn said.

As they sipped their coffee, Sofia remembered the old photo of her father with two other boys. "I want to show you something. I'll be right back."

She rushed upstairs, returned with the picture, and showed it to Finn. "Is this you with Aidan and William?"

Finn nodded, recalling the afternoon. "We were playing in our garden when my da took that photo."

"My father told me that William died, but he wouldn't explain what happened."

"There was a political demonstration outside the church on Easter Sunday. Aidan and I were only eight, and we were leaving after our first communion when the protest turned into a riot. Several people died. Poor William was in the wrong place at the wrong time."

"That's tragic," Sofia said. "No wonder he never wanted to talk about it."

"Many of our friends were involved in the free Ireland movement, so our families were afraid of British retaliation. After that, my da changed our last name, and Aidan's family moved to America."

"Did you stay in touch with my dad after he left?" she asked.

"I tried. We corresponded for years, but he stopped replying. According to my ma, his parents thought I was a bad influence. They threw away my letters and told Aidan not to contact me again."

"When I was in Boston, I met his best friend from high school, and he said the same thing. My dad's parents sound horrible."

"Gareth and Clare were extremely religious and didn't approve of my lifestyle. Then when I stopped going to church, they branded me a sinner."

"I don't go to church either, so I'm sure they'd hate me if they were still alive," Sofia said.

"I wasn't aware that they died."

"Well, I never met them, but Margaret Grace said they passed away."

"His sister was a religious nut too. Aidan's family and his godfather pressured him to join the priesthood. They were afraid I might try to talk him out of it, and they were right."

"Who was his godfather?" she asked.

"Our priest, Brendan O'Connor. Aidan's parents worshipped him, but he was a pompous arsehole and very ambitious. He rose through the Church hierarchy and became a bishop in Rome, where he took Aidan under his wing."

"I feel like you're talking about a stranger, not my father."

"Sounds like he kept a lot from you."

"More than I ever imagined," Sofia said. "When did you last see him?"

"After Aidan became a priest, he came to Derry occasionally and would drop by for a visit. I think he wanted to save my soul." Finn laughed. "We had fond memories from our childhood, but our interests were so different we drifted apart. On his last visit, it was clear he'd gone away with the fairies."

Sofia was stumped. "Fairies?"

He chuckled. "It just means his head was in the clouds. He was obsessed with a strange organization called The Brotherhood of Archangels."

"I recently learned about that group, but I thought they were apocryphal. What did he tell you?"

"Aidan claimed they were divinely inspired to rid the world of evil. A lofty goal, but it sounded like balderdash to me. Apparently, they'd meet at the Church of Saint Sulpice in Carndonagh."

"Where is Carndonagh?" she asked.

"About twenty miles north of Derry on the Inishowen Peninsula."

"I should go. Maybe somebody will remember my father."

"I have a recording session today, but I'll be happy to drive you there tomorrow," Finn said.

"Thanks, but I'd rather not wait."

"Are you sure?" he asked. "The roads can be pretty rough in the rain."

"Don't worry. After almost rearending a Guinness truck, I think I have the hang of driving in Ireland now."

"Glad to hear it. The drive takes about an hour. And fortunately, there's no military checkpoint to slow you down when you cross the border into the Republic of Ireland. But be careful; there are a lot of political agitators in the area."

"I'll be careful. How do I get there?" she asked.

"Drive north out of Derry along Loch Foyle. At Quigley's Point, you'll go inland. Follow the signs to Carndonagh. You can't miss the church. It's the tallest building in town."

"Thanks, Finn. You're the best cousin I've ever had!"

"Or ever will have," he smiled. "I'll see you when you get back. There's an umbrella by the door. You'll need it. It's Baltic out there."

"Thanks. Wish me luck." Sofia finished her scone and headed for the door, eager to see what she might discover at the Church of St. Sulpice.

Chapter 25
Into the Storm

Sofia slogged through the wet windy streets toward her car, holding on tight to the umbrella, which shielded her from the pouring rain. Huge cannons, which once repelled the forces loyal to the British King during the Siege of Derry in the late 1600s, towered above her on the ramparts of the city walls. Although the cannons were from ancient history, it was clear the intransigent conflict still smoldered in the daily lives of the citizens and could flare up at any moment.

Relieved to get out of the rain, she hopped into her rental car and drove through Derry on her way to Carndonagh in County Donegal. As she left the city behind, she drove along the scenic road overlooking the loch. The storm blew gales of wind across the wide estuary of the River Foyle, pushing waves that crashed on the rocky shore below. Torrents of rain battered her windshield and even with the wipers flapping wildly, she could barely see well enough to drive. Peals of thunder shook her small VW Beetle and lightning streaked across the morning sky, but Sofia was resolute. Her foray would probably lead to nothing, but since her father mentioned the Church of Saint Sulpice to Finn, she had to go there.

After passing the ruins of castles and through small villages tucked along the shores of Loch Foyle, she crossed an old stone bridge and arrived at Quigley's Point on the Eastern shore of the Inishowen peninsula. There was a sign pointing the way to Carndonagh, so she followed the winding road inland through the rural countryside for a few miles until she entered the town with its traditional shops and pubs. As Finn said, it was impossible to miss the church, which dominated the skyline and had a park on one side and a cemetery on the other.

Sofia parked her car and crossed the street to the black wrought-iron entry gates that surrounded the stately red brick Gothic building, topped by a gold spire. The front of the structure had four stained-glass lancet windows with a large rose window in the center. While walking up the steps, a gust of wind nearly blew the umbrella out of her hand. She tried to open the massive door, but it was locked. Refusing to give up, she looked around and saw the adjacent priests' quarters with a light on inside.

Hoping to speak with someone, she hurried over to the elegant two-story building with a covered porch and rang the bell at the rectory entrance. When there was no response, she pounded on the door repeatedly with her umbrella. As Sofia was about to leave in disappointment, the door opened. A stout priest with brooding dark eyes studied her suspiciously. He had short white hair and wore a black satin cassock with gold buttons.

"Sorry to disturb you," Sofia said. "Do you have time to talk?"

"The church is closed until noon. Come back later," he replied.

As he closed the door, Sofia grabbed the handle, holding it

open. "Please, it's urgent. I need to speak with a priest right away."

The man frowned at her, then relented and opened the door. "All right. Come in if you must. I'm Father Dolan."

Leaving her wet umbrella on the porch, she walked inside the luxurious foyer with tapestries on the walls and black marble floors.

He closed the door behind her and gestured to two plush leather chairs. "I only have a minute."

"Thank you. I appreciate your time."

They sat across from each other as the priest, who appeared to be in his late sixties, scrutinized her. "What is so urgent that it can't wait?"

"I thought someone here might have information about my father, Aidan Malone."

The man grimaced as if she'd said something stupid. "You're an American. Why on earth would anyone here know your father?"

"Because he was a priest who grew up in Derry and—"

"Excuse me, young lady," he interrupted. "Perhaps you're unaware that priests don't have children."

"Of course, I know that. But he left the Church when he married my mother."

"Well, he has nothing to do with this parish," he said dismissively.

Sofia pressed on. "Also, his godfather, Bishop Brendan O'Connor, was from Derry. Do you know him?"

"I've never heard of either of these men. And if you know so much about your father, why are you wasting my time?"

"Because he was involved with a group called The Brotherhood of Archangels who used to meet here."

"Nonsense. No such organization was ever here. I don't

know who's been feeding you this malarkey, but since you have so many questions, why don't you ask your father?"

"I can't. He's missing."

Dolan gave her a skeptical look. "That's quite a tall tale. I've never met Aidan Malone or Bishop O'Connor, and I was born in Derry and have been a priest here for forty years."

Infuriated by his arrogance, Sofia walked up to him, and said, "I thought priests were supposed to help people."

"Some people are beyond help." He stood and faced her. "You should leave now."

She held her ground. "No. I'd like to talk to someone with more authority."

"I'm in charge here, and I have duties to attend to." He strutted to the door and opened it.

Sofia followed and locked eyes with him. "You don't fool me with your holy man act. You're a lousy liar and a pathetic priest. Here's a ten penny for your time." She pulled a coin out of her pocket, then tossed it skittering on the marble floor. Incensed, his face reddened as she stomped out of the rectory and into the storm.

Chapter 26
Secrets and Lies

As the rectory door slammed behind her, Sofia opened her umbrella against the deluge of rain. She didn't trust Father Dolan and suspected him of hiding something, so before she left the Church of Saint Sulpice, she might as well snoop around a little.

While exploring the grounds, she searched every entrance for a way in, to no avail. At the back of the building, faint light from a basement window caught her eye. She peered through the panes of circular crown glass and saw the distorted image of a mason chiseling a gravestone in a large workshop. He finished his task and wheeled the heavy stone away on a dolly.

Sofia tried the window, and to her surprise, it was unlocked. Although apprehensive, she worked up the courage to push the heavy leaded window open. Setting down her umbrella, she climbed inside, stepped on a wooden crate, then lowered herself to the floor.

She silently followed the mason down a long passageway and into a claustrophobic crypt. Light from the man's lamp cast wavering shadows on the walls of the cold, humid space. When he reached his workbench, she slipped past him, hiding behind the tombs and monuments. On one side of the room, there was a stairway leading upwards, and she began her ascent into the darkness.

At the top of the stairs, she opened a door and discovered a hallway with offices on either side. She crept down the corridor past the darkened suites, her footsteps muffled by the thick red carpet. At the end of the hall was a room with a sign above its double doors:

SANCTUM SANCTORUM

Sofia knew the Latin phase meant Holy of Holies, a sacred chamber of utmost secrecy. She opened the door, looked inside to ensure no one was there, then entered. The majestic stained-glass rose window was at one end of the room, allowing dim light to permeate the richly appointed chamber. In the center was a large cherry wood conference table with dozens of high-back chairs upholstered in red velvet.

On a pedestal in front of the window rested a towering marble sculpture of a golden-winged lion with a crown of silver stars. It looked exactly like The Brotherhood's crest she'd seen at the Trinity College Archives. Far from being a legend, the society was real.

Framed paintings of priests lined the walls. Sofia scanned the gallery, and what she saw took her breath away. One portrait was of her father looking solemn, dressed as a Catholic Monsignor in a purple cassock. The inscription below his image read:

Aidan Matthew Malone,
Servant of Michael the Archangel, 1944

A canvas with the image of Father Dolan hung next to Aidan's. He was younger, but she recognized him. Now she knew for sure that her dad had belonged to the secretive order and understood why the priest lied about knowing him.

The sound of approaching voices coming from the hallway startled her, and Sofia hid behind the lion sculpture seconds before two men entered. When they turned on the lights, Father Dolan walked in, accompanied by a weathered, rough-hewn man with slick red hair who looked strangely familiar.

Jolted by the vivid memory of his menacing face in Yosemite, she realized this was the creepy man who frightened her when she was a child. As she eavesdropped on their conversation, her heart pounded so loudly she feared they might hear it.

"The young woman claimed to be Aidan's daughter, but we can't be sure," Father Dolan said.

"Don't you worry—I'll get to the bottom of it. She's been on my radar for a long time."

"Very well. Keep me apprised of what you learn."

"You can count on it," Jack said.

The priest reached into a cabinet, pulled out a briefcase, and placed it on the conference table. "I have something for you." Dolan opened the case, which was filled with British pounds. "Are the plans for the special military operation confirmed?"

Jack nodded. "Yes, they are all in place."

"Good." Father Dolan closed the case and handed it to him. "Make sure the patriots' families are well taken care of."

"Of course, boss."

"All glories to Archangel Michael," the priest said.

"All glories to The Brotherhood."

The men turned off the lights and left the room.

Sofia came out from her hiding place, peered out the door,

and quietly observed them heading down the hall toward an exit.

She followed at a distance and waited on the landing at the top of the stairs as they descended into the church. The priest entered the sanctuary, and Jack left through a side door. Despite the risk, Sofia was determined to confront Jack. This mysterious man had lurked in the shadows of her life since she was a child, and she had to know why or die trying.

Chapter 27
Old Jack

Sofia stealthily left the church and was grateful the rain had stopped. She shadowed Jack down the street and watched him enter a rustic pub named The Black Rose. When she stepped inside the noisy neighborhood hangout, filled with working-class men and gnarled old geezers engaged in rowdy conversation, the room became silent, and all heads turned to gawk at her. Clearly, she was an outsider. Except for the buxom barmaid with waist-length dark hair, there wasn't a woman in sight.

A husky voice called out, "You don't belong in here." Sofia turned and saw Jack standing behind her, scowling. "Best be on your way, little lady."

She shook her head. "Not a chance, asshole. I need to talk with you. Unless you want me to make a scene."

He shot a fiery glance around the room and bellowed, "Get back to your drinking! You never seen a lady before?"

The barmaid held up her fist. "Shut that hole in your face, Jack, or I'll show you a lady!"

The patrons laughed raucously, then returned to their beers and bullshit.

Jack studied Sofia. "I didn't catch your name."

"I didn't give it to you."

"Loosen up," he said. "Would you care for a pint?"

"This is not a social call," she snapped.

"I'll order it, anyway. It looks like you could use a drink." Jack held up two fingers to the barmaid.

Sofia pointed to a quiet area across the room. "Let's talk over there."

"As you wish." He followed her to a table near a dartboard. "While we're waiting for our beer, would you fancy a wee toss?"

"Why don't you show me how?" she asked mockingly.

"It's easy. Watch a master and learn." Jack set his briefcase on the table, selected two darts, and handed one to her. He smiled confidently and threw the dart, hitting the outer bull.

Sofia threw her dart, nailing a perfect bullseye. "I guess I'm a quick learner."

"A lucky throw," he said.

"Not really. I love beating men at their own games."

The barmaid arrived with two frothy pints of Guinness Stout. Jack sat, took a long drink, then fixed his pale blue eyes on Sofia. "Quite the little troublemaker, aren't you?"

"It's my new favorite pastime."

"Well, we don't like troublemakers around here. The good father at Saint Sulpice said you were very rude to him this morning."

"I'm not so sure how good he is. He lied to me."

"That's a dangerous accusation, and we don't take slander lightly. Why were you following me?" he asked.

She stared him down. "I'm looking for my father, Aidan Malone."

"Don't recall anyone by that name."

Sofia's gaze was unwavering. "That's rubbish. When I was a kid, you were spying on my family in Yosemite."

He scoffed and took a swig of beer. "You have quite a lively imagination."

"Stop lying! I heard you talking about him with Father Dolan in the church."

Jack's cold eyes narrowed. "Trespassing, eh? I could have you arrested."

"And I could expose your secret society."

"Don't get your knickers in a twist. If you can't find your own father, that's your problem, not mine."

"I can make it your problem." She leaned in aggressively. "Start answering my questions truthfully, or I'll go to the press."

"Settle down. I vaguely remember Aidan from years ago, but he's no longer involved with us."

"Then why did you say you didn't know him?"

He glanced around the room to confirm no one was listening. "I wasn't sure if you were trustworthy. Hopefully, no one has harmed him."

"Why would someone harm him?" she asked.

"It's impossible to say, but over the years he ruffled quite a few feathers."

"Who are you talking about?"

"Could be anyone. Your father alienated a lot of powerful people, so you should go home before you get into serious trouble. Not everyone's as understanding as old Jack."

"I'll go when I'm good and ready. I don't respect dishonest priests, like Father Dolan, or petty criminals like you who carry around a case of blood money." She shoved the briefcase toward him.

"Listen to me." He grabbed her arm roughly. "It's not wise to pry into matters that are none of your goddamn business."

Sofia jerked her arm away. "I don't care about your business, but I'll never quit searching for my dad."

Jack softened and tried a new tact. "Of course. I understand and admire your loyalty to him, so if you promise to keep it confidential, there's something I can share that might help you."

"Agreed. What is it?"

"Your father's not in Ireland or I'd know about it. After leaving The Brotherhood, he tried to get back in our good graces and begged to be reinstated. We had a plan to meet, but he was a no show."

Sofia's eyes narrowed. "I don't believe you."

"It's true, but where he is now is anyone's guess. If you want my advice, since he abandoned you and your mother, you should let him go."

Sofia was thrown by what he revealed. "I never said he abandoned us."

"I assumed that's what happened. Even before he took up with Ella, he was a ladies' man. He couldn't control his lust. It was his fatal flaw. Perhaps he has a new family now."

Outraged, Sofia stood up. "You're despicable, and I'm sick of all your lies."

"One last bit of advice, Sofia Ryan, if you don't leave Ireland immediately and return to San Diego, I can't guarantee your safety."

Sofia was rattled. How did he know her name and where she lived? He even knew her mother's name. Feeling cornered, she furiously lashed out, hurling her mug of Guinness at him. The glass bounced off Jack's chest, spraying him with black beer and foam, then rolled across the floor. "If anything happens to my father, I'll hold you personally responsible!" As she stormed out of the pub, silence enveloped the room, and all eyes watched her leave.

On her drive back to Derry, Sofia tried to make sense of what happened. She was deeply concerned about her father's well-being and couldn't stop thinking about how Jack threatened her. Who was this treacherous man and were his claims about Aidan's womanizing true? The thought made her feel sick. Although she didn't want to believe it, over the years she'd seen him flirt with some of his female students, but always thought he was being playful. Maybe he left to be with the opera singer. She recalled Gemma Ricci's romantic note.

Our weekend in Capri was divine. You're the most brilliant man I've ever met, and our connection is eternal. I adore you and hope we share many more adventures in the coming years. You are so special to me.

There was clearly more to the mystery of Aidan's disappearance than could be discovered in Ireland and she considered what to do next. By the time Sofia arrived at Finn's flat in Derry, she had a plan.

When she entered her cousin's apartment, the sound of harp music floated from the living room. Finn looked up at her with concern and stopped the vibrating strings with his hand.

"Hi, Finn. I'm sorry, I lost your umbrella."

"No problem, luv, I have a lifetime supply. It looks like you've had a tough day."

"That's an understatement," she said.

"Seems we both struck out. My friend at the church called around and couldn't find anyone who's still in touch with Aidan or his family."

"Thanks for trying. I need to call my mom. Can I use your phone?"

"Sure, it's right there." He gestured to the black rotary dial phone sitting on a side table next to the leather sofa. "I'll give you some privacy."

"Thank you," she said, and he left the room.

Sofia dialed her mother's number. It rang five times before Ella answered in a groggy voice. "Pronto."

"Mom, it's me. I hope I didn't wake you up."

"That's okay, Sofia. You sound upset. Are you all right?"

"Yes, but I've discovered some terrible things about Dad. We have a lot to talk about. I can't explain everything now, but I'm going to Rome, and I want you to meet me there."

"Roma?" she asked, confused. "When are you going?"

"Right away," Sofia said.

"Just come over, and we'll talk about it."

"That's not possible. I'm in Ireland."

"Ireland! Why did you go there?" Ella asked.

"I'll tell you later. I think Dad might be in Rome. Will you please come with me?"

"No. I never want to see him again."

"Please, I'll pay for your trip," Sofia said.

"How could you possibly afford that?"

"Dad left me quite a bit of money."

"Darling, I really want to help you, but that part of my life is over," Ella said. "I want nothing to do with your father."

Sofia steadied her voice, trying to hide her exasperation. "Okay, but if you change your mind, call me. I'm staying with my cousin, Finn, in Derry. Please write down his number."

"Hold on. Let me get a pen," she said. "Okay, I'm ready."

"It's 011.44.28.555.6488. Did you get that?"

"Yes, I wrote it down."

"I'm leaving for Rome tomorrow with or without you, and I could really use your help."

"Sorry, I can't go, and I don't think you should go either," she said. "It's a bad idea and no good will come from it."

When the line went dead, Sofia hung up the phone in despair. *Mom, why do you always let me down?*

Chapter 28
Behind the Mask

Shaken by the phone call with Sofia, Ella got back in bed and turned off the light on her nightstand. Although she wanted to help her daughter, she felt deeply conflicted. As she tossed and turned, unable to sleep, her calico cat jumped on her chest, stretched out, and purred softly. "Thanks, Luna. But I don't think purring is going to fix this," she said, petting the feline's silky fur.

Ella's life had been a series of disappointments and tragedies she learned to cope with by hiding behind a mask of lies, ashamed and paralyzed by her choices. Ever since Liam died in the car accident, fear and guilt had been her compass. And after her marriage fell apart, she neglected Sofia, unable to escape the depression and hopelessness that engulfed her. Weighed down by years of secrets, she dreaded what might happen if she revealed the truth, but now that the fiction about Aidan was unraveling, she wondered if she could finally be honest with her daughter and even heal their shattered relationship.

It had been decades since she'd been to her homeland, as

America never really seemed like home. Italy was the land of her birth, and she missed it. However, if going to Rome meant confronting Aidan, she wasn't sure she could do it. He'd broken her heart, and the pain of facing him would be intolerable. She always believed God was punishing her for the sin of marrying a priest, but now she wondered if it was Aidan, not God, who stole all the happiness from her life. *Why did I ignore all the signs of his dishonesty?*

ROME, ITALY—1956

The sleek Pan Am Clipper took off in the early morning from Rome International Airport and ascended into the sky as Ella, twenty-four and filled with hope for her future, gazed wistfully out the airplane window. How quickly her world had changed. It had only been a few weeks since she met Aidan, but it seemed like they'd known each other forever. She'd found her soul mate and was sure nothing would ever keep them apart. Feeling a mix of gratitude and apprehension, she could hardly believe she was bound for America.

She touched the strand of pearls around her neck, which were a gift from Francesca, who saved her life and had been like a second mother. After Ella's family died, and she became an orphan, the kind woman took her in and cared for her like a daughter. Everything she knew about Rome and all its cultural riches, she learned from Francesca. Although she'd passed away, Ella still felt her presence and knew she would be pleased by her good fortune.

Dressed in a white silk blouse with embroidered red roses and a red velvet skirt that Aidan had bought her for the occasion, Ella was excited to meet her new family, but as she saw

Rome recede in the distance, a tinge of sadness filled her heart. She turned to Aidan, who sat next to her, eyes downcast, his mood as gray as the suit he wore, and gently caressed his arm. "Do you miss Roma too?"

"Not at all. I'm glad to put it behind me."

"But I thought you loved living in Italy."

"For me, it's been a blessing and a curse," he said despondently.

"I don't understand."

"Of course. How could you?" Aidan took her hand. "There's something I need to confess before we get married."

His somber face alarmed Ella. "Are you having second thoughts about us?"

"No. However, if you can't accept my past, it wouldn't be fair to you."

"What are you trying to say?" she asked.

"I'm sorry for not telling you sooner, but . . . I used to be a Catholic priest."

Ella was bewildered. "I've never seen you in a clerical collar."

"The order I belonged to doesn't wear vestments."

"When were you a priest?"

"Until I met you. After we fell in love, I left the Church."

Her heart sank and she pulled her hand away. "Oh, Aiden... You shouldn't have left for me."

"I didn't. I left for love. Surely God approves even if the Church can't."

"Breaking your vows is a sin. And I don't want to be responsible."

"You're not responsible. I've known for years it was a mistake to join the priesthood, and the moment I saw you, I knew we were meant to be together."

"But I changed my entire life for you," she said. "Why didn't you tell me before we left Italy?"

"I was afraid of losing you."

She fidgeted in her seat. "This is a very serious decision. Are you sure?"

"I'm positive," he said fervently. "Meeting you changed everything. You're my heart and soul."

Ella silently stared out the window, wrestling with her thoughts.

Aidan tenderly turned her head toward him. "Please forgive me."

She looked into his pleading eyes and was convinced he was sincere. "I forgive you, but from now on, there must be no secrets between us."

"You have my word."

Ella took a deep breath. The revelation had unnerved her, but she desperately wanted to find a silver lining. "I've always believed God works in mysterious ways. Maybe he saved you for me until we met."

"Divine intervention indeed," he said.

There was a mysterious quality about Aidan that Ella cherished, and although troubled by his deception, she believed their love would be stronger than any challenges they might face. She squeezed his hand. "I've never been on an airplane before. I'm flying like a bird!"

Relieved that she'd forgiven him, Aidan kissed her. "And I'm free as a bird for the first time, all because of you!"

Chapter 29
Black Sheep

Boston, Massachusetts—1956

It was a warm afternoon as Aidan drove in a 1950 Chevrolet Deluxe Convertible with Ella beside him in the passenger seat. He had a sentimental attachment to the classic car, and for years, he paid a mechanic to keep it in pristine condition at a storage unit near the airport so it would be ready for him when he visited. Aidan reached his arm out the window and patted the metallic maroon car, its shiny chrome glinting in the sun. "She's a beauty, isn't she?"

"Yes, she's lovely . . . It must be nice to be home."

"It is. I couldn't be happier." He smiled at her.

Ella watched pensively as they drove through his old South Boston neighborhood. Everything seemed strange, and she got a sinking feeling. "I hope I'll be happy here, too. If I don't like it, can we go back to Roma?"

"Of course. I was apprehensive when I first arrived, but I learned to love America."

"How old were you when you came to Boston?"

"Eight. And I lived here until I left for the seminary in Rome right after high school."

When he mentioned the seminary, Ella panicked. "Wait. Does your family know about us?"

"Not yet. I wanted to share the good news in person."

"Maybe you should have told them we were coming."

"Don't worry. They love surprises."

"I hope they like me," she said.

"They'll love you like I do."

"I can't wait to meet your parents." Reassured, Ella placed her hand on his leg. "Tell me all about them."

"He smiled. Da was a stevedore, but he retired after injuring his back. Ma is a homemaker, and my sister is married to a lawyer. They have four sons."

"Family is such a blessing. When did you last visit them?"

"A few years ago."

"Why did you wait so long?"

"My work was extremely demanding," he said.

A glimmer of sadness crossed her face. "If my family was still alive, nothing could keep me away from them. We were very close."

"I'm so sorry, love. I know they are irreplaceable, but you have a new family now."

Aidan pulled the car over and parked in front of a row of three-story Victorian brownstones. "Here we are. Welcome to Malone Manor."

His parents' home had four steps leading up to the porch, where American and Irish flags fluttered in the breeze. Box shaped hedges, their lines trimmed so straight that not a leaf was out of place, surrounded the front yard.

He opened the door for Ella, who stepped out and nervously straightened the black patent leather belt around her slim waist. "How do I look?"

"Ravishing, as always." They walked arm in arm up the steps to the front door and Aidan rang the bell.

Moments later, a woman's voice called out. "Who is it?"

Aidan playfully disguised his voice. "Fuller Brush Man."

The door flew open, and his sister, Margaret Grace, in a bright pink pantsuit, greeted him, her round doughy face surrounded by a blonde bouffant hairdo. "Brother! We didn't know you were coming home." She hugged him, then glanced at Ella warily. "And who is this?"

Aidan beamed. "I'm so glad you're here. I'll have the pleasure of introducing my fiancée to my sister and my parents."

Ella held out her hand politely. "Hello, nice to meet you."

Margaret Grace ignored her and turned to Aidan. "What did you say?" She grasped the silver cross hanging above her copious cleavage.

"This is Ella Bellini, soon to be my bride." Aidan put his arm around Ella.

"Bride?" Margaret Grace pondered the bombshell.

Aidan nodded. "Yes. I've become laicized."

"Did you get permission?" she asked.

"I don't need their permission."

Ella tried to diffuse the tension. "Aidan has told me wonderful things about his family."

"Has he?" She furrowed her brow. "Well, come in then. Ma and Da will want to hear this."

Ella looked uneasily at Aidan, who smiled reassuringly as they followed Margaret Grace inside.

The Malone home was stodgy, filled with rococo dark wood furniture. On the wall above the fireplace was a gallery of photos spanning Aidan's illustrious career with the Church and Margaret Grace with her husband and their four rotund sons. The boys, a year apart in age, posed in identical black suits, with flat top haircuts, and goofy grins.

Gareth and Clare, a lanky, gray-haired couple in their late sixties, sat stiffly on the sofa, having their traditional afternoon tea and biscuits. Gareth wore a dark suit with an orange and green County Derry tartan vest, and Clare's black dress was embellished with a matching tartan scarf. They looked up in astonishment as Margaret Grace entered with Aidan and Ella.

"Aidan!" Clare said. "I can hardly believe my eyes."

"Why didn't you tell us you were coming, son?" Gareth asked.

"I wanted to surprise you."

"Well, you succeeded. Good thing you didn't give your father a heart attack," Clare said.

Gareth eyed Ella. "And who is this young woman?"

"Ella Bellini." Aidan nudged her forward to meet his parents. "She's the love of my life, and we're going to be married."

"Married?" Clare stood, jolted by the scandalous news.

"You'll do no such thing!" Gareth rose to his feet unsteadily.

Their hostility startled Ella, and she took a step back.

"Yes, I will, with or without your approval." Aidan pulled Ella to him.

Gareth's face turned red, and he rushed out of the room.

"After all your father has sacrificed for you, this is how you treat him? Go ahead, throw your life away on this . . . this . . . " Too distraught to continue, Clare flashed Ella a spiteful look, broke into tears, and hurried after her husband.

"What did you expect, Monsignor Malone? The family's blessings?" Margaret Grace asked scornfully, then followed her mother down the hall.

Ella thought she'd found a loving family with Aidan, but they had nothing but animosity toward her. "They hate me."

"No, they just want to control me, as usual."

When Ella saw a photograph on the mantle of Aidan in his priestly vestments, posing with his proud parents, she lost hope. "They think I took their son away from God. They'll never accept me."

"You've done nothing wrong. It was my decision," Aidan assured her. "Wait here. I need to talk to them."

He walked away, leaving Ella alone and despondent. Aidan and his family were speaking so loudly that she could hear them arguing behind the partially closed bedroom door. She crept quietly down the hallway and peeked in. Aidan, Clare, and Margaret Grace huddled outside the en suite bathroom, listening as Gareth splashed water on his face.

Clare called out to him. "Are you all right, dear?"

"I've never felt worse."

"You've broken his heart." Clare glowered at her son. "That's what you've done."

"Ma, please try to understand," Aidan pleaded. "I don't want to be a priest anymore."

"In the eyes of The Lord, you are a priest forever."

"It's my life, and I want a family."

She slapped him in the face. "Wake up! We are your family, and we've devoted our lives to your calling."

Aidan rubbed his stinging cheek. "That's what you wanted, not me."

Gareth emerged from the bathroom and glared at Aidan. "She's half your age. How could you throw your career away on that Italian floozy?"

Aidan's jaw tightened. "Spoken like an ignorant dock worker."

Stupefied, Gareth clutched Clare's arm to steady himself.

"How did you get entangled with her?" Margaret Grace asked as Aidan's family surrounded him like vultures. "You were supposed to be at the Vatican."

"We met in Rome at Trevi Fountain. She sells flowers."

"I'll bet that's not all she sells," Gareth said.

Aidan stepped up to his father, shaking with rage. "You have no right to pass judgment on her. She's your moral superior."

Margaret Grace grabbed his arm and held him back. "Hold your tongue, Aidan Malone. Show some respect for your father."

He pulled away. "I will when he deserves it."

"I'll forgive you, son, because you're in the grips of lust, but you must return to your rightful position immediately," Gareth said.

"It's not lust. It's love."

"This is shameful. You've worked for over twenty years and risen in the Church to become a monsignor," Clare said.

"Yes, and I've supported both of you and done everything you wanted until now."

"What about me?" Margaret Grace asked petulantly. "I've done more for Ma and Da than you have!"

"It's not a competition. We've both helped them."

"This isn't about money," Gareth said. "Can't you see that your immoral behavior disrespects your family and the Church? William would be ashamed of you."

"My brother is dead!" Aidan shouted. "And although you want me to be him, I can't play that role any longer. You've always told me what to do, but this is my choice. Accept me for who I am, or we have no relationship."

"So be it. Leave my house. You're not welcome here." Gareth turned away from his son.

"Now I see I never was." Realizing that reconciliation was impossible, Aidan left the room and found Ella waiting anxiously in the hallway. "Let's go." He took her hand and led her away.

As they reached the front door, Margaret Grace rushed up to her brother. "When you come to your senses, call me."

He cast a contemptuous look at her. "When hell freezes over."

"Don't become the black sheep of the family, Aidan. They always get slaughtered."

"I'm honored to be the black sheep. And I want nothing to do with this toxic family ever again."

Aidan and Ella left the house emotionally battered and headed to the car in silence.

Chapter 30
For Better or Worse

Aidan and Ella drove through Boston's financial district in glacial silence. The encounter with his family haunted her; it was the nightmarish opposite of all her hopes and dreams, and she couldn't keep her resentment bottled up any longer. "They think I'm trash! How could you let them treat me that way?"

"Please forgive me," he said.

Ella turned away from him and looked out the window. "They were so cruel."

Aidan touched her shoulder, gently. "I'm sorry. I was a fool to assume they'd be happy for us. Nothing ever changes with my family. They only care about themselves."

He pulled the car over and parked in front of the Art Deco Courthouse and Federal Building, clad in New England granite. "Since the Malones are no longer my family, I don't want their name. They're detestable and don't exist for me anymore."

Aidan reached into his coat pocket and took out two passports. He glanced at one, put it away, then handed the other one to Ella, who opened it. The official document featured his picture with the name Aidan Ryan. She stared at him, baffled. "Aidan Ryan? Why do you have two names?"

He made light of it. "Occasionally, my work required me to use different identities."

"Why would a priest need that?" she asked.

"Because my research for the Vatican was confidential."

She wanted to believe him but was skeptical. "That makes no sense."

"Of course it does. It's authorized and perfectly legal. No need to worry, love. Besides, that's all in the past," he said calmly, with total conviction. "What matters now is our future."

He was so sincere and self-assured that Ella's doubts began to dissolve. "I understand, I think . . . I just want us to have a good life together."

Aidan tenderly ran his fingers through her hair. "Trust me, I know what I'm doing and everything will be fine."

With a leap of faith, Ella willingly suspended her disbelief. "I shouldn't let you off so easily, but I like a little mystery in a man."

"And I like a lot of mystery in a woman." Relieved, he leaned over and kissed her. "Let's make it official. My love for you is immeasurable, and I can't bear to live another day without being your husband, if you'll still have me."

"Do I have a choice?"

"Absolutely not!"

She wagged a finger at him. "From now on, you better behave yourself."

"You can count on me."

They got out of the car and hurried up the steps to the courthouse.

A short time later, Aidan and Ella stood before Justice Marley, a marmoset of a man with unruly tufts of white hair on either side of his bald pate. He turned to Ella. "And do you, Ella Bellini, take Aidan Ryan, to be your lawfully wedded husband?"

"I do."

"I now pronounce you, man and wife." He turned to Aidan. "You may kiss the bride."

"I already have, your honor, but the experience bears repeating."

Ella wrapped her arms around Aidan, and he kissed her once, twice, three times.

The newlyweds left the courthouse, giddy with excitement. As they made their way down the steps toward the parked car, Aidan said, "I love being married. At last, my life has meaning." He wrapped his arm affectionately around Ella's waist. "And please, you must promise not to tell anyone I was a priest. My past is private and for your ears only."

"I promise, but I have one question. Where will we live?"

"Nowhere . . . and everywhere. Everywhere is our home!" Aidan said rhapsodically.

"Only God and fools can live everywhere."

"Then we're in good company."

She flashed him a get-serious look.

"You're right," he said. "I should have at least one foot on solid ground. We'll need little things like money and food. I guess I'll find a job."

"What will you do?" she asked.

"I can do anything! After all, our fates lie not in our stars, but in ourselves."

"Don't be silly."

"That's not merely a poetic utterance, Ella. I'll put my PhDs to work for us."

"Can degrees in history and philosophy really pay the bills?"

"Of course they can. Rest assured, I'll take good care of our family."

"Maybe I'm crazy, but I believe in you," Ella said.

When they arrived at the car, Aidan opened the passenger door with a flourish. "After you, Mrs. Ryan. A mellifluous name, isn't it?"

She got in and smiled to herself, enjoying his flowery language, even though sometimes she couldn't understand it. Aidan hopped into the driver's seat, and they sped away.

Chapter 31
Casting Caution to the Wind

When Ella and Aidan arrived at the elegant Parker House Hotel along the historic Freedom Trail, the valet and bellman took their car and luggage, and the newlyweds strolled arm in arm beneath the grand golden entryway through the bronze doors.

The luxurious lobby, with its burnished wooden columns and opulent furnishings, dazzled Ella. "Are you sure we can afford this?"

"Of course, or we wouldn't be here," Aidan said, and led her to the reception counter. After they checked in, he escorted her to the renowned Parker's Restaurant while rhapsodizing about the hotel's fascinating history and the many illustrious guests who had stayed there, including two of his literary heroes, Mark Twain and Charles Dickens.

The hostess seated them at an intimate booth by a window with a view of the twinkling city lights. Candles on their table cast a romantic glow.

"I feel like royalty," Ella said.

"You'll always be my queen." Aidan kissed her on the

cheek then handed her the menu. "Order whatever your heart desires."

Ella's eyes widened when she saw the prices. "Everything is so expensive."

"Don't worry about that. I'll get a job and start pinching pennies soon enough."

"All right, but after tonight we need to be more sensible."

"Agreed."

They dined on Waldorf salad, Lobster Thermidor, and scalloped potatoes garnished with cheddar cheese and chives. Although the lavish meal temporarily distracted Ella from the troubling encounter with Aidan's family, the sting of their rejection continued to haunt her. The day had been a tumultuous mix of extreme highs and lows, and she fretted about what the future might bring.

While sharing a slice of the restaurant's famous Boston cream pie, she hesitantly broached the taboo subject. "Aidan, I know you'd rather not talk about it, but do you think your parents and sister will ever forgive you for marrying me?"

His mood darkened, and he pushed the pie away. "I couldn't care less. I've unthought them and I don't want or need their forgiveness."

"But when we have children, I'd like them to meet their grandparents."

Frustrated, he slapped the table. "They don't deserve to meet our children. Please, never speak about them again. They're dead to me."

"I just hoped that someday they would accept us," she said.

"That will never happen; they're incapable of change. Forget about them."

Ella regretted bringing it up. "I'm sorry, sweetheart."

"We'll have our own family," he said.

Ella kissed him tenderly. "Maybe we should get started tonight."

"Absolutely." He refilled their champagne flutes. "I have a special treat for you in our room."

"What is it?" she asked.

"Patience. We're going dancing first." Aidan put his arm around her, and she nestled her head against his chest.

"You make me feel so safe," Ella said.

"I'll always take care of you."

She looked into his eyes. "Did you mean it when you said we could go back to Italy if I wasn't happy here?"

"Whatever you wish, love, but let's talk about it later. The Rooftop Ballroom awaits."

He led her to the sophisticated space, sparkling with crystal chandeliers and a panoramic view of Boston. After dancing to a big band playing classics from the Great American Songbook, Ella and Aidan went to their room.

Aidan had arranged for the hotel staff to have everything ready in their spacious honeymoon suite when they returned for the night. There was a fire burning in the antique fireplace and vases filled with red roses scented the air. In the marble bathroom, candles lined the rim of a large soaking tub, with rose petals floating on the water. Feeling blissfully free, they threw off their clothes and slipped into the tub. As Ella snuggled with Aidan in the soothing warm bath, the bleak events of the day melted away.

When the water cooled, they dried off, put on the fluffy hotel robes, and headed to the bedroom. Ella reached to turn off the lights, but Aidan stopped her. "No, please, I want to see your gorgeous body." He slipped off her robe and caressed her soft olive skin. As they kissed, he picked her up and gently placed her on the bed.

The fire of Ella's passion ignited when he kissed her breasts and sucked her erect nipples. She pulled him on top of her, and their bodies entwined, becoming one as they made love with wild abandon. They had always been ardent lovers, but tonight was transcendent, with several simultaneous orgasms. After making love for hours, they collapsed beside each other, suffused with the intoxicating joy of merging as one.

The next morning when Ella awoke, wrapped in Aidan's arms, she watched him sleeping peacefully and admired his full lips, regal nose, and angular features. She gently ran her fingers through the soft blond hair that framed his handsome face. Although filled with love for him, she couldn't stop questioning her good fortune. It shouldn't matter that his family rejected them or that he used to be a priest. God had brought this extraordinary man into her life. She should be grateful and embrace their journey together.

Ella quietly got up, put on the robe that was draped over the upholstered bench at the foot of the bed, and went into the bathroom. After freshening up, she opened the royal blue velvet curtains and looked out at the sun rising between the tall buildings of the city.

Aidan stirred when the morning light filled the room. He slipped out of bed, naked, then walked over to his bride. Enveloping her in his arms, he kissed the back of her neck. "Good morning, Mrs. Ryan."

She turned to face him. "*Buongiorno, amore mio.*"

"Shall we have an encore of our amorous evening?" he asked.

"Would you like some coffee first?"

"You're all the stimulation I need."

Ella blushed at the sight of his penis, standing at attention. "I can see that. Brush your teeth and we'll have a repeat performance."

"Agreed." He threw on his robe and rushed to the bathroom, emerging moments later smelling of spearmint. As he approached her, brimming with passion, the phone rang, interrupting their plan, and Aidan reluctantly answered it. After listening for a moment, he chuckled. "That's splendid. Of course, we'll join you for breakfast. See you soon!"

He put down the receiver and looked at Ella with a gleam in his eye. "We're in luck."

"Who was that?" she asked.

"Kieran Kelly, an old friend of mine. I called him before we left Rome, and he's got a lead on a teaching job for me in California. We're going to visit him this morning. It seems like our dreams are coming true, so we won't have to go back to Italy after all."

Ella sighed in resignation. "If that's what you want."

Chapter 32
Awakening

Sᴀɴ Dɪᴇɢᴏ, Cᴀʟɪғᴏʀɴɪᴀ—1978

Ella was in her apartment, still lying in bed with her calico cat sprawled on her chest. For years, she hadn't allowed herself to think about her life with Aidan, as it was too heartbreaking. But after her daughter's visit and phone call from Ireland, she couldn't hold back the flood of memories any longer. She was aware of how neglectful she'd been to Sofia, and it filled her with shame and guilt, but now she had an opportunity to make amends.

When she lifted Luna off her chest and sat up in bed, the intuitive feline perched on her lap and gazed at her with inquisitive green eyes. Ella patted her best friend on the head. "I have to go, baby. But don't worry, I'll find someone to take good care of you."

She picked up the phone and dialed the number Sofia had given her. After a few rings, she heard the Irish lilt of Finn's voice.

"Hello. Finn here."

"This is Ella, Sofia's mother. Is she there?"

"Aye, one moment. I'll fetch her."

Ella waited anxiously until her daughter answered.

"Hi, Mom. I was hoping you'd call back."

"Hello, darling. I've decided to join you in Roma."

Sofia was stunned. "That's fantastic! I'm so glad you're coming."

"When do you want me there?" Ella asked.

"As soon as possible. I'll set up a prepaid ticket today with TWA and you can pick it up at the airport anytime."

"Okay, I will." Ella petted her cat. "Do you need me to bring you anything?"

"No. Just yourself."

"All right, since you've never been to Roma and don't speak Italian, for once in your life you need me."

"I've always needed you, Mom," Sofia said, her voice quavering.

Ella was speechless and couldn't remember a time when her daughter sounded so vulnerable.

"Are you still there?" Sofia asked.

"Yes, sorry. Where will we meet?"

"I'll be staying at Hotel Tito Di Trevi near the Trevi Fountain."

Ella jotted it down. "Okay, I know the area. I'll meet you there."

"Thanks, Mom. I really appreciate what you're doing for me."

"I love you, Sofia. Bye for now." Ella hung up the phone and, for the first time in ages, had something to look forward to. She hopped out of bed, pulled a suitcase out of the closet, set it on the dresser, and opened it. "Roma!"

Chapter 33
Reunited

Rome bustled with morning energy as vendors opened their shops, and people hurried along the sidewalks, headed for work. A cab pulled up in front of a four-story, coral-colored Renaissance style building. Above the entrance, a blue neon sign read *Hotel Tito Di Trevi*. Ella stepped out of the taxi, carrying a small suitcase, and entered.

The charming lobby, with its smooth white marble floors and floral tapestries on the walls, was welcoming. Vases of fragrant pink peonies adorned the carved wooden front desk where a young receptionist, wearing a green, white, and red scarf—the colors of the Italian flag—looked up from her work and greeted Ella. "*Buongiorno*. May I help you?"

"I'm staying with my daughter, Sofia Ryan. I think she's already checked in."

The lady opened the guest roster and perused the names. "Yes, she mentioned you'd be joining her. She's in room 208, on the second floor. Shall I have someone help with your luggage?"

"No need. I only have one bag."

The receptionist gestured to the stairs. "It's one flight up and to the left."

"*Mille grazie.*" Ella headed toward the staircase.

When she arrived at the room and knocked, Sofia opened the door and embraced her. "Thanks so much for coming, Mom. It means the world to me."

"Sorry I'm late, but my plane was delayed," Ella said.

"When you didn't arrive last night, I was worried you changed your mind."

"No, I really want to be here for you."

Sofia took her suitcase. "Let me help with that."

Ella entered the clean, attractive space with two beds and a small sofa and looked around. Vintage photos of Rome from the early 1800s, including the Spanish Steps, Trevi Fountain and the Colosseum, decorated the walls. Sofia placed her mother's bag on a bench.

"What a pleasant hotel," Ella said.

"It's nothing fancy, but the beds are comfortable."

"How did you find it?"

"Finn suggested it," Sofia said. "He stays here when he's in Rome."

"It was very kind of him to look after you. I hope to meet him someday."

"He's a talented musician who looks like a Viking and is about as different from Dad as you can imagine."

"I was surprised when you called from Ireland. Why did you go there?"

"It's a long story and we have a lot to talk about. Let's sit on the balcony."

Sofia led her outside through French doors that opened onto a shaded veranda overlooking the city. Red geraniums spilled from flower boxes attached to the wrought-iron railing. On a table, there was a carafe of coffee and a basket of pastries.

She pulled out a chair for her mother. "The breakfast comes with the room."

Ella smiled. "I can hardly believe we're together in Roma."

They sat, and Sofia poured the coffee. "Sorry for what I said the last time we met. I was still in shock over Dad's disappearance and took it out on you."

"I understand," Ella said. "You've only heard one side of the story for most of your life."

The women took croissants out of the basket and ate in silence as Sofia tried to think of a graceful way to ask the hard questions about her father. Unable to come up with a subtle approach, she plunged in headfirst. "Mom, did you know Dad had another last name and that he used to be a priest?"

"Yes. We kept many secrets from you. I should have been honest about your father and his family years ago."

"Why didn't you tell me the truth? Things would have been so much better between us if I'd known."

"I couldn't. I felt trapped and was afraid of what might happen if I didn't go along with his lies."

Sofia sipped her coffee and held Ella's gaze. "I wasn't aware that you and Dad had any problems until Liam died."

"Far from it," she said. "Our relationship was falling apart for years."

Sofia wondered how she could have been so clueless. "Well, you hid it flawlessly."

"We held it together for you kids, but after Liam's funeral, nothing I did could make Aidan happy. He flew to Boston to visit his family and when he returned, he was very hostile."

"I remember that trip. I got mad at him for leaving us alone. He obviously lied about going to a conference, but I had no idea he was visiting his family. I thought they were all dead."

"He didn't want you to know anything about them."

"Maybe that was a good thing. Last week, I met his sister,

Margaret Grace, and her husband in Boston, and they were awful."

"I never met her husband, but Aidan's sister and parents were hateful to me."

"Did you ever meet his godfather?" Sofia asked.

"Yes. He was horrible too."

"Finn told me he had a lot of influence over Dad."

"True," Ella said. "Bishop O'Connor told him Liam's death was God's punishment for breaking his vows."

"God had nothing to do with it. It was a drunk driver," Sofia said.

"He was convinced the bishop was right and wanted to end our marriage. I refused, but he was so relentless he finally got his way."

Sofia shook her head. "I was unaware of all this."

"It broke my heart. The bishop and your father pressured me to accept the divorce and said if I didn't, they'd send me back to Italy, and I'd never see you again."

"Unbelievable. That was so cruel."

"When I finally agreed to the divorce, I had to swear not to tell anyone about Aidan's past, or he'd cut off my support."

"That's blackmail!" Sofia's face flushed with anger.

"Then, when I moved out of the ranch to find a place for you and me, Aidan went back on his word. He refused to let you go and took me to court to gain sole custody."

As the revelations sank in, Sofia felt the sting of remorse. "I feel terrible for blaming you all these years. He manipulated me into speaking against you at the hearing."

Ella gave her a hug. "It's not your fault; you were just a child. After he betrayed me, I was so afraid and confused, I gave up."

"The depth of his deception is mind-boggling."

"I should've fought harder to keep you, but by then, I was

so depressed I could barely take care of myself and believed I was a failure as a mother." Ella looked away, in shame.

Sofia touched her hand. "That's not true. Like you said, he deceived both of us. The only positive thing about Dad abandoning me is that we can finally get to know each other."

Ella met her gaze. "That's all I've ever wanted."

"You probably think I'm crazy for wanting to find him."

"It's not crazy. You have a right to know what's happened to your father."

Sofia looked out at the captivating Roman skyline. "How does it feel to be back in Italy?"

"Wonderful, but it stirs up many memories, and not all of them are good."

"Would you like to talk about it?" Sofia asked.

Ella lowered her eyes. "Aidan never wanted me to tell you about my life, but now that he's gone, I suppose I have nothing to hide anymore." She silently contemplated her past for a moment, then turned to her daughter. "I've been through so much; I wouldn't know where to begin."

"Please tell me everything. Start with your childhood."

"All right, I'll try."

Sofia waited, spellbound, as her mother gathered her thoughts.

Ella took a deep breath and closed her eyes. "I was born in a village on the south coast of Sicily near Gela. My family lived in an old farmhouse on a hill overlooking the Mediterranean Sea. It was a beautiful place to grow up. Then, when I was twelve, everything changed . . ."

Chapter 34
Shock Wave

Sicily, Italy—1943

Ella strolled through the garden, snipping red roses to create a bouquet for her father's birthday party. At twelve, she had a flawless olive complexion and the blush of youth on her cheeks. She inhaled the flowers' sweet scent and then carried them toward her home. The two-story house, which had been passed down for generations, had a terracotta tile roof and whitewashed walls that glowed golden in the setting sun. Ella ran in, placed the roses in the family's prized antique crystal vase on the large oak table, and hurried upstairs to get ready.

Later that night, the merrymaking was in full swing. Ella's relatives never needed an excuse to get together, but tonight was special; it was the eighth of July, and they were celebrating her father's thirtieth birthday. It had been a sumptuous meal and platters with remnants of Sicilian arancini, eggplant pasta, and salad lined the buffet. Along with her gregarious relatives, Ella sat at the table, enjoying a bowl of creamy chocolate gelato.

"*Buona fortuna*, Paulo," Ella's mother, Isabella, said and kissed her husband. She was in her late twenties, with a vibrant personality and rich brown eyes. Long chestnut hair framed her lovely, smiling face.

Ella's father, Paulo, a ruggedly handsome man with lively green eyes and a weathered complexion from years of fishing, held up his glass of red wine. "Thank you so much. I am blessed to have such a loving family."

"*Buona fortuna*," they all responded and drained their glasses of Paulo's homemade ruby marsala wine. Isabella opened another bottle for the family to share and walked around the table, refilling the empty glasses.

Except for Papa's parents who had passed away, the entire family had come to the party. Isabella's mother, Caterina, and her father, Franco, had traveled to Gela for the festivities. Her grandparents had a florist shop in Messina, on the east coast of the island, where they sold the flowers from their greenhouse. Despite the challenges of living under a ruthless dictator, they believed Sicily was the best place on earth and vowed to stay and fight for its freedom.

Isabella's older brothers, Rocco and Luca, lived nearby. Rocco worked with Ella's father on the fishing boat. He was a perennial bachelor who usually had a beautiful lady fawning on him and was tall and handsome, with a mischievous twinkle in his amber eyes. Luca and his wife, Valentina, married when they were teenagers and were still madly in love. They had an orange and lemon orchard near the Gela River and sold fruit for a living. Their daughter Bianca was the same age as Ella, and they were as close as sisters.

The girls sat next to each other, relishing the gelato. When they finished eating, they jumped up from the table and snuggled together on the couch to engage in one of their favorite pastimes, braiding each other's hair.

"Me first," Bianca said and handed her a brush.

"It's my turn," Ella teased, then began braiding her cousin's long, sun-kissed hair.

Luca raised his wineglass. "To Paulo, many happy returns!"

Valentina joined in. "To the women in this family . . . you men would be lost without us!"

Suddenly, the door burst open with a crash, and two Blackshirts stormed into the house. Sergio, a wiry and intense man, stood next to his aggressive boss, Vito. Both wore Fascist uniforms with black berets studded with a silver skull and crossbones. The thugs aimed their rifles at the family, whose jovial mood vanished in an instant.

Vito scowled. "Another Socialist gathering with the Bellini family, I see."

"It's my birthday, nothing more," Paulo said. "Now please leave. There are children here."

Ella and Bianca cowered, hugging each other in fear.

"You have no business barging into our home," Isabella protested. "This is a family party."

Vito surveyed the room and considered his next move. "I'll let you go this time . . . for a price." He grabbed the crystal vase filled with roses. "This will make a nice present for my wife."

"And from now on, without our permission, all gatherings are forbidden," Sergio commanded.

"We will not tolerate traitors!" Vito warned, and the Blackshirts left, slamming the door behind them.

The family was speechless for a moment, painfully aware they were no longer safe in their own home.

Rocco was furious. "Vito, that son of a bitch. He's always been a thief, but Mussolini gave him permission to be a gangster for the Fascists."

"Along with all the other scum in Italy!" Luca pushed away from the table.

"Sicily will not tolerate these criminals for long," Franco said. "In the end, we will prevail."

"If only Mussolini would drop dead, our lives would be perfect," Rocco said.

Paulo got up and paced. "He's a maniac, just like Hitler."

"Give them a slogan, a uniform, and a gun and there's no atrocity they won't commit in the name of Il Duce," Luca said.

Valentina couldn't take it anymore. "Enough about Mussolini! He's ruined Italy and now he's ruined our celebration."

"Don't worry, Valentina. We won't allow those monsters to rule our lives." Isabella stood and began clearing the table.

"And this family will get together whenever we want!" Paulo carried a load of plates to the sink. "But I'm sure we could all use some sleep now."

"You're right," Rocco said. "To hell with those Blackshirts and their oppressive rules. Let's meet for breakfast tomorrow morning. I'll make the best frittata you've ever tasted."

Everyone agreed, and the party broke up as Luca, Valentina, Bianca, and Rocco said their goodbyes to the rest of the family with hugs and kisses.

Paulo and Isabella continued cleaning up as Ella and her grandparents walked upstairs to their bedrooms.

Ella was sound asleep when an ear-piercing siren howled at four a.m. Although she didn't know it at the time, the first assault wave of American and British troops had already landed on the beaches of Gela. She jumped out of bed and ran to her parents' room. They were already up and getting dressed.

"Quick, go to the top of the hill," Paulo said. "We'll help Franco and Caterina and meet you there."

She ran back to her room, grabbed a jacket, and hurried outside. An ominous wind blew forcefully, and dark clouds obscured the moon and stars as Ella ran to the top of the hill. Shaking with fear, she stopped under the large olive tree, which was the meeting place the family had planned to use in case of an emergency.

As she waited with an increasing sense of foreboding, Ella could hear artillery fire and smell the acrid gunpowder from battleships shelling the beaches. Flares and tracers crisscrossing in wild patterns illuminated the night sky and distant shoreline, punctuated by blinding flashes and ear-shattering explosions.

Ella heard the roar of an airplane and looked up as it passed overhead. She could see the terrifying Nazi black crosses on the underside of its wings. Without warning, doors in the plane's belly opened and bombs plummeted toward the ground, whistling as they fell. The shock wave knocked her down and uprooted trees, snapping them in half like matchsticks. She struggled to her knees and watched horrified as a bomb shattered her home, reducing it to a flaming pile of rubble.

Chapter 35
Death of Innocence

Ella lay on the hard dirt, curled up in a ball for what seemed like forever. Her ears were still ringing from the blast when her uncle ran up to her. "Thank God, I found you!" Rocco said.

Her head ached, and his voice sounded as if he was underwater, but seeing him gave her a glimmer of hope. "Where is everyone?"

"I searched the house, but there's nothing left." Breathless and pale, Rocco sat on the ground next to her.

"Did they get out before the bomb?" Ella asked. The alternative was too awful for her to imagine.

Speechless, they huddled in silence for several minutes until Rocco reluctantly admitted what he'd seen. "I'm so sorry, Ella. They didn't make it."

"How do you know? It's possible they're safe."

"No. I saw it with my own eyes."

Hearing the words made the horrific loss all too real. Ella threw her arms around her uncle, and they held each other, sobbing uncontrollably. The family was together only hours earlier and, in an instant, her parents and grandparents had perished.

Finally, Rocco caught his breath long enough to speak. "We can't stay here."

"Shouldn't we wait for Luca, Valentina, and Bianca?" she asked.

"Luca and I had a plan to meet at the church of Saint Francis if something happened. We must go."

It was still dark as Rocco and Ella furtively headed toward the town, avoiding the main roads. The demolished streets filled with craters and rubble made the trek difficult for them. They passed dozens of dead bodies, many with severed arms and legs. The horrific sight and sickening smell of death made Ella nauseous, and she threw up. "I can't go on," she cried and fell to her knees.

Rocco took her around the waist and helped her stand. "Lean on me, I'll help you. We'll be safe in the church."

Ella pulled herself together and pressed on as high columns of black smoke filled the sky. In the distance, fires burned where bombs had destroyed many of the buildings in Gela, and she feared it would never be the same.

By the first light of dawn, Ella and Rocco arrived in town. The fighting was fierce on both sides, and they could see the Allies searching house to house for Fascist soldiers and snipers. They realized they couldn't trust anyone, as some locals supported the Fascists, and their family had long ago been accused of being Socialists. But the Americans and British might also consider them the enemy. Hopefully, they would find refuge in the church. There were many close calls, but they avoided detection and finally made it to Saint Francis of Assisi, a small 15th century sanctuary.

When Rocco and Ella entered, they discovered other villagers had also taken shelter there. Unfortunately, so had several Fascists, including the two Blackshirts who barged into their home, and they were all armed and ready to fight. The situation was chaotic as civilians and soldiers jostled for space and shared stories of the attack.

"Forgive me, sweetheart. I thought we'd be safe here." Rocco hugged her. "I'll try to talk some sense into these people."

Taking her hand, he led her up to the altar and hollered above the din of voices. "Friends and neighbors, please listen. The Nazis bombed our home and both sides are killing Italians. We must stand together!"

Sergio and Vito fired their guns into the ceiling, and plaster rained down. "You're a liar and a traitor!" Vito yelled. "We'll fight to the death for Il Duce!"

Rocco shielded Ella. "Please, there are women and children here. This is a house of God. It should be a sanctuary, not a war zone."

The Blackshirts aimed their rifles at them. "Follow our orders or die!" Sergio commanded.

Vito shouted the Fascist slogan, "Believe, obey, fight!"

The other soldiers joined in, stomping their feet with each word. "Believe, obey, fight! Believe, obey, fight!"

As the zealous chant intensified, Rocco and Ella desperately looked for a way out, but the fighters had blocked all the exits.

There was a deafening boom as the front doors were blown off their hinges and the U.S. Army Rangers rushed in. Rocco grabbed Ella's arm and pulled her behind the altar. He covered her small body as best he could, and they lay flat on the floor. Bullets flew in all directions, as a vicious firefight broke out among the pews. Some shots tore through the pulpit, hurling shards of wood like shrapnel. When the Americans had killed the last of the Fascists, the shooting finally stopped.

Ella and Rocco emerged from behind the altar with their hands raised in surrender, and the American soldiers led them outside along with the other captives.

ROME, ITALY—1978

Sitting on the balcony of their hotel, Sofia was stunned to learn what her mother had endured. "No child should have to live through such brutality."

Tears filled Ella's eyes. "My family was my entire world and losing them was unbearable."

"How did you survive?" Sofia asked.

"Rocco and I hoped the worst was behind us, but nothing prepared us for what we were about to face."

Chapter 36
Prisoners of War

Sicily, Italy—1943

Ella and Rocco sat on the parched earth, huddled together under a tarp, trying to find relief from the scorching August sun beating down on them. After five weeks in the makeshift prisoner of war camp, they were weary, filthy, and hungry. Although provided food and water, the conditions were dreadful.

The U.S. Army Rangers had herded hundreds of detainees, including Axis soldiers, and Italian civilians, into the crowded compound. The enclosure, created with wooden posts wrapped with rows of barbed wire, had a few highly sought after tarps hung to provide shade, but most of the detention area was open to the elements.

It was late afternoon, and the prisoners began pushing to find a place near the perimeter where their captors handed out water and C-Rations. Ella and Rocco reached through the wire, eager to receive the scant sustenance.

With the coveted rations in hand, they sat on the dirt, opened the cans, and devoured the bland meat and vegetable stew. They had just finished eating when a gruff U.S. Army Ranger pointed at them and shouted, "Hey, you two, get over here!"

Ella had seen many prisoners loaded onto boats and shipped to unknown places and hoped that would not be their fate. "What does he want from us?" she asked her uncle.

"Stay calm. I'll speak with him." Rocco and Ella walked up to the ranger. "How can I be of service, sir?"

"Mussolini is no longer in power," the soldier said. "What do you think about that?"

"Thank God," Rocco said. "He's a monster. Italy will be better off when he's dead."

"Good answer." He opened the gate. "Now get out of here. We need to thin the herd. But if I catch you fighting, I'll kill you myself."

"Yes, sir. Thank you, sir." Rocco took Ella's hand, and they stepped quickly through the open gate, glancing over their shoulders repeatedly, afraid the ranger had made a mistake. Much to their relief, no one came after them. Their nerves were raw from the stress of being imprisoned and the future was uncertain, but at least they were free, and would do everything in their power to make sure they were never captured again.

After an arduous trek in the heat, while avoiding the soldiers that patrolled the smoking ruins of their town, they arrived at Rocco's home and discovered it was demolished.

"Oh my God, *Zio*, what will we do now?"

Rocco reached out for her hand. "Come, we'll go to Luca's house. Hopefully, they made it back and are safe."

The fighting was everywhere, and the sound of gunfire

frequently shattered the silence. They walked along the once beautiful Gela River, now polluted with the debris of war, hiding whenever they heard someone coming.

At last, they reached his brother's home. Fortunately, the small bungalow overlooking the water seemed relatively unscathed. The front door was ajar, so they entered cautiously.

"Luca, Luca," Rocco called, but there was no response. They searched every room and although their belongings were still there, there was no sign of them. Evidently, they left in a hurry.

"Where could they be?" Ella asked.

"Maybe they've gone to our parents' house in Messina. We should go there now."

Tired, Ella collapsed on the sofa. "Can I get cleaned up first?"

Rocco realized she needed a break, and his demeanor softened. "Sure, I'll wash up too and keep an eye out in case someone comes."

Ella rushed into the bathroom, undressed, filled the tub with water, and stepped in. The cool bath was a relief from the heat of summer. She soaped up and scrubbed the dirt from her skin; it was a luxury to be clean again. To wash away the soap, she poured fresh water over herself, then got out of the tub and dried off.

Wrapping a towel around her, she headed to Bianca's room in search of clean clothes. Knowing her cousin would have something she could borrow, she rummaged through her wardrobe cabinet, found a simple green dress, and slipped it on.

When Ella returned to the living room, Rocco had changed into his brother's clean clothes. "I found fresh food!" He held up a platter with oranges, bread, and olive oil.

"*Bravo!*" she exclaimed, and they sat together and ate. After a diet of nothing but canned rations for weeks, the humble meal tasted incredible.

"We need to find Luca, Valentina, and Bianca. Are you ready to go now?" Rocco asked.

She nodded. "I'm ready."

"Nowhere in Sicily is safe, so we'll have to travel to Roma. A prisoner in the camp told me it's an open city now and the fighters on both sides have agreed to leave the civilians in peace."

"But Roma is so far away! Can we take your boat?"

"No, we can't sail out of Gela, but I have a plan. Luca's family is probably already in Messina. We can take our father's boat across the Strait to Villa San Giovanni and travel to Roma together."

"That sounds good. Should we pick some fruit for the journey?" She popped the last orange section in her mouth.

"Clever girl, always thinking ahead." Rocco grabbed a cloth bag hanging near the front door and they headed outside to Luca's citrus grove.

As they walked between the rows of trees, picking oranges, Ella noticed a cluster of large black birds at the far end of the orchard and pointed to the spot. "Why are there so many birds over there?"

Worried by what he might find, Rocco held her back. "Wait here," he said, then went to investigate.

The sound of screeching vultures and fluttering wings frightened Ella. She looked up and saw the scavengers scattering in all directions. A sick feeling welled up in her and she ran after her uncle. "*Zio!*"

Ella found Rocco on his knees, moaning mournfully in front of the dead bodies of Luca, Valentina, and Bianca. The vultures had been picking at their corpses and flew away when he arrived.

The remains told the story of their last moments. Someone shot them as they fled, and they were lying together in a final embrace. The sight was gruesome; decomposition had set in, making the family almost unrecognizable, but Ella could tell it was them. She screamed, sank to the ground next to Rocco, and broke down crying.

Chapter 37
Journey to Messina

Rocco dropped the last shovel of dirt on the grave he'd dug for his younger brother, Luca, his wife, Valentina, and their daughter, Bianca. Ella marked the spot with a handmade cross and they bowed their heads in prayer. No words could express the anguish they felt. Rocco wiped the sweat from his face, picked up the bag they'd filled with food, and headed north on the perilous journey to Messina.

Ella's mind was reeling. They were the only two still alive, and losing their entire family was a pain beyond belief. The weeks since the bombing in Gela seemed like an endless nightmare she couldn't wake up from.

"How could God let this happen?" Ella asked.

"We can't blame God for the evils of men," Rocco said.

Ella continued walking beside her uncle as they struggled through the rough terrain.

"*Zio*, when will we reach Messina?"

"I think we can make it in five days. We'll look for shelter in a couple of hours."

Keeping out of sight as best they could, they walked until

dark and finally reached the outskirts of Caltagirone. Before the war, the area was rich with fertile fields of grapevines and olive trees, but now they were neglected and withering.

The town, with its baroque architecture dating from the seventeenth century when Sicily was part of the Spanish Empire, seemed deserted, but to avoid detection, they stealthily made their way toward the city center. Ella noticed that the damaged buildings had flamboyant curves and flourishes with broken grinning masks and chubby winged cherubs. It reminded her of a sad fantasy land whose glory days had long passed.

Some of the ceramic shops that lined the main street had shattered windows and evidence of looting. As they walked along, looking for shelter, they selected an abandoned store with a broken sign hanging over the door that read, *Gino's Ceramica di Caltagirone*. Rocco pried open several boards covering the windows, and they slipped inside.

Slabs of marble, bags of clay, cans of paint, and assorted tools for making pottery and sculptures were scattered throughout the room. It seemed like a safe place to spend the night, so they found a corner spot and, using clay bags as pillows, they fell into an uneasy sleep.

Just before dawn, a light shining in their eyes awakened Ella and Rocco. An old man holding a flashlight aimed a pistol at them. "What are you doing in here?"

Rocco pressed his hands together in supplication. "We meant no harm, sir. We only needed a place to rest."

Deep-set brown eyes peered out from his wrinkled face, framed by a head of wild gray hair. "Why are you out here with a child? Don't you know there's a war going on?"

"She's my niece. We're trying to get to Messina."

"The Nazis bombed our home," Ella cried, the words

tumbling out between sobs. "And they killed our family . . . please help us."

"*Calma bambina.*" He lowered his weapon. "I didn't mean to frighten you. Come with me." He led Rocco and Ella upstairs to his residence above the store.

"This is my home." He held the door open for them to enter his modest apartment and they followed him to a large, covered outdoor terrace. "And this is my studio."

Morning sun filtered through the tall cypress trees that hid his private oasis, where chickens clucked contentedly in a roomy coop next to a small vegetable garden. There was a potter's wheel, a kiln, and dozens of gorgeous multicolored ceramics.

The pottery delighted Ella. She picked up a platter with an intricate floral design painted in dazzling blues and yellows. "It's so beautiful!"

"*Grazie,*" he said. "Caltagirone has been famous for ceramics since ancient times."

"Maybe someday I could become an artist too," Ella said.

"After the war, come visit me and I will teach you."

"I would love that!"

"Where are my manners? My name is Gino."

"I'm Rocco, and this is Ella."

Gino grasped his hand and shook it warmly. "There's so little light in the world; it's a pleasure to meet nice people."

"A pleasure to meet you too."

"Why would you travel to Messina?" Gino asked. "I hear it's dangerous."

"My father has a boat there. We plan to sail to the mainland and then make our way to Roma. It's supposed to be an open city now."

"I hope that's true. You can't be certain of anything these days."

"Well, we have to try. It seems like the best choice for us," Rocco said.

"I understand." Gino tossed some grain to his chickens. "In that case, I'll drive you to Messina."

"Is that even possible?" Rocco asked. "I was told the Fascists had mined the main roads."

"There are ways around their villainy."

"We would be most grateful, if it's not too much trouble."

"No trouble at all." Gino gestured to a door. "There's the washroom. You're welcome to freshen up if you like."

"That would be nice," Ella said.

"And please, join me for breakfast. I'd enjoy the company."

Rocco smiled gratefully. "We'd love to."

Gino put six fresh eggs in a basket. "We'll leave after we have a bite."

Ella hugged him. "Thank you, you're very kind."

"No need to thank me. The world has gone mad. We could all use some kindness right now."

After Ella and Rocco washed up, Gino served a breakfast of scrambled eggs and freshly baked bread. While they ate, he shared stories about his family who had been potters in Caltagirone for five generations. His wife passed away before the war and his son was fighting in the Italian resistance. Although most of his friends and relatives fled the island, he refused to allow anyone to force him out of his home and studio.

When they finished eating, Rocco and Ella got in the cab of his old Fiat pickup truck, and he drove them along narrow dirt roads through farmland toward Messina. They had formed an easy friendship in their short time together and talked about Ella's dream of becoming an artist and their shared hope of a brighter future for Italy after the war. In a few hours, they arrived at the periphery of the bomb-scarred city.

Rocco pointed at an unpaved gravel path that led up the hill to his parents' house. "It's over there."

Gino stopped the vehicle, and they got out. Rocco and Ella walked over to the driver's side window to say their goodbyes.

"I hope we can repay your generosity someday," Rocco said. "You saved our lives."

Ella stepped onto the running board. "I will never forget you." She leaned in and kissed him on the cheek.

"Good luck," Gino said. "May we meet again."

They waved goodbye as he drove away, then headed up the gravel path. The country house with burnt umber walls was still standing, but once inside, they discovered vandals had stripped the home of all its belongings. Fortunately, Rocco only needed to find one thing. He opened the back door, and Ella followed him into the yard.

Thankfully, except for a few broken windows, the glass greenhouse was untouched. They stepped inside and looked around. Some of the neglected carnations were wilting, and many had died, but several of the hardiest bushes bloomed with fragrant crimson and white flowers, in stark contrast to the war-torn community.

"I guess the thieves weren't interested in our plants." Rocco headed toward the far end of the conservatory. On top of a large wooden worktable rested his father's gloves and mother's sun hat. He held the gloves to his cheek. It was a heartbreaking reminder of his parents. "We have to be strong and stay alive to honor the family," he said, his voice shaking.

"I miss them all so much." Tears streamed down Ella's cheeks.

"Me too." Rocco hugged her, then reached under the table and pulled out an aluminum watering can. Inside were the keys to his father's boat, which he held in the air triumphantly. "Good fortune is smiling on us."

"Thank God. We could use some good fortune." It was the first time Ella felt hopeful since her home was bombed.

Chapter 38
Trial by Fire

After sheltering in the house until dark, Rocco and Ella walked warily toward the city to assess the situation. Axis anti-aircraft guns fired shells that streaked across the night sky, strafing the arriving Allied fighter planes. As they got closer, the explosions and wailing sirens intensified, and they hid on a hill overlooking the military encampment.

A scene of controlled chaos unfolded in front of them; commanders barked orders while German and Italian fighters marched in formation like rows of ants preparing for departure. Bright lights lit the shoreline where thousands of troops, along with hundreds of tanks, vehicles, artillery, and other weapons, were being loaded onto amphibious landing crafts. The boats sped the men and cargo out to massive warships anchored offshore. Between the sirens, constant announcements blared through loudspeakers, ordering German and Italian troops to evacuate Sicily.

"We should stay in Messina until they're gone," Rocco said.

"If they go, do we still have to leave?" Ella asked.

"Yes. They're retreating because the Allies are coming. If we're here, the Americans might imprison us again. Sanctuary in Roma is our only hope. Let's try and get some rest. We have a difficult voyage ahead of us."

After a sleepless night, they returned to the hill at sunrise and discovered the Axis soldiers had departed. "We must leave now, before the Allies arrive. Hopefully, Papa's boat has not been stolen," Rocco said.

They hurried down the hill, past countless damaged homes and buildings of the once vibrant city where dazed civilians wandered the mostly deserted streets. The residents picked through the rubble in stony silence, searching for loved ones and whatever possessions they could find, and barely noticed Rocco and Ella walking by on their way to the marina.

Much to their relief, the sailboat was in its slip, covered by a tarp and chained to the dock. "Incredible! It's still here and undamaged."

Ella hugged Rocco. "That's great, *Zio!*"

He unlocked the chain, and they climbed aboard. After hoisting the sail, the boat glided into the strait. The current was strong, but Rocco grew up sailing and knew the channel well. They only had two miles to traverse, and when they were nearly halfway across, Rocco smiled at his niece. "We're going to be fine, sweetheart."

"Can we go home when the war is over?" she asked.

"Absolutely."

In the distance, they saw a procession of U.S. Army vehicles roaring into the city. Unexpectedly, the deafening noise and shockwaves from exploding shells fired by Axis guns on the Italian mainland shook their boat. In retaliation, the arriving Allied forces unleashed a barrage of deadly shells.

Panic-stricken, Ella and Rocco realized they were caught in

the crossfire. He tried desperately to navigate the boat away from the flaming debris that rained from the sky, but it seemed impossible to avoid.

"Get down," he shouted.

Ella braced herself on the deck, desperately clinging to the rail. The boat rocked so wildly she thought it would overturn or break apart. She closed her eyes, trying to block out the terrifying pandemonium swirling around them.

"Hold on! I'll try to get us out of here." Rocco shielded her protectively as he attempted to steer the boat away from danger, but a moment later, deadly shrapnel struck him in the back, killing him instantly. He collapsed on top of her and the weight of his body was crushing as he became limp and lifeless. In shock and overcome with grief, she lay in the boat, covered with his blood. The projectiles had punctured their vessel, which was quickly sinking. Alone and clinging to his body, Ella sobbed as the cold water rose around her.

When I drown, I can be with my family again.

As she faced death with a sense of relief, Rocco's voice echoed in her mind. *We have to be strong and stay alive to honor the family.*

With monumental effort, Ella rolled his body off her and forced herself to get up. She gazed at Rocco with love and gratitude. "*Requiescat in pace, Zio.*" She kissed him on the forehead then jumped into the churning sea as the sailboat and her beloved uncle slipped silently under the water.

Turning away from the world she knew, Ella swam with all her might toward the mainland as the battle raged overhead. When she got closer to land, she let the waves push her ashore and crawled onto the beach, gasping for breath.

Miraculously, she had made it across the strait, but the effort had drained every ounce of her energy. She didn't know how she would get to Rome or how she'd survive alone. Her uncle had given his life for her, and she was determined not to allow his sacrifice to be in vain. As she lay on the sand, wondering what to do next, the sound of rowdy men's voices startled her, and she sat up.

Two young ruffians in shabby clothes emerged from the shadows of the cliffs. With catcalls and crude taunts, they surrounded her and kicked sand in her face. Ella curled up, trying to protect herself, but one of them grabbed her feet and began dragging her off the beach. Terrified, she screamed and fought back with what little energy she had left.

A gunshot rang out, and the assailants released her and froze. Delirious, Ella looked up from the sand and saw what appeared to be an angel. She couldn't make out her face, but the sun behind her glowed like a halo.

The radiant woman, dressed in white, pointed a rifle at the men. "Cowards! How dare you attack a child. Go now before I shoot you and leave your rotten bodies to sleep with the fishes!" Defeated, the scoundrels ran frantically toward the cliffs.

Ella blinked away her tears and saw a kind face surrounded by a luxuriant mane of shimmering auburn hair, looking down at her. The woman appeared to be in her forties and was tall and sturdy, with an olive complexion and large penetrating brown eyes. "Are you all right, *bambina?*" She helped Ella to her feet.

"I thought you were an angel."

The woman smiled. "Sadly, I'm only human. Why are you out here alone?"

"I'm trying to get to Roma."

"It's not safe. The Nazis have occupied the city. I left to escape from them. Do you have relatives in Villa San Giovanni?"

Ella found it difficult to speak, but finally said in a halting voice, "I have no family. They were all killed . . . and I'm alone."

"Poor child." She hugged her. "What is your name?"

"Ella."

"I'm Francesca. Come, you can stay with me."

"Thank you," Ella murmured gratefully, and they walked away from the beach, hand in hand.

Chapter 39
Full Circle

Rome, Italy—1978

Sofia and Ella sat together on the hotel balcony in silence, each feeling drained—Ella from reliving her childhood and Sofia from learning about the horrors her mother endured.

Sofia embraced her. "Thank you for telling me."

"I've buried those memories for so long," Ella said.

"Uncle Rocco would be proud that you survived for the family."

Sofia used to think there was nothing about Ella she admired, but now she was in awe and realized her mother was the most resilient person she'd ever known. "You're so strong. What you experienced would have destroyed most people."

"I had no choice."

"It's a miracle that Francesca found you."

"I miss her so much. I was heartbroken when she passed away."

"How did she die?" Sofia asked.

"It was sudden. She seemed fine until she came down with

what we thought was the flu, but it was a bacterial infection, and she died a week later."

"Did she ever meet Dad?"

"No. I met your father a short time after her memorial. Life is strange—if she'd been alive, I never would have left Roma." Ella squeezed Sofia's hand. "But it was worth it because of you and your brother."

"I'm sorry you've had to experience so much pain."

"It's been difficult, but after telling you, I feel like a weight has been lifted from my heart."

"I wish I'd known all this years ago."

Ella sighed. "I wanted to tell you, but Aidan thought it would raise fewer questions about his past if people thought we met in Boston."

"Was he still a priest when you met him?" Sofia asked.

"Honestly, I didn't know at first. He never dressed like a priest and only told me when we were on our way to America."

"That should have been a warning sign."

"I know that now, but I was blinded by love."

"We both were," Sofia said. "I idolized him and thought he was the most ethical man in the world. I was such a fool."

"Can you see why I didn't want you to search for your father?"

"Yes. But it would drive me nuts not to know the truth."

"All right, then," Ella said, exasperated. "You were born stubborn. Since I can't change your mind, I'll do whatever I can so you can finally let him go."

Sofia perceived the weariness in her eyes. "Mom, you must be exhausted. I'm sure you'd like to unpack and get settled."

"I am pretty tired, and I'd love a hot bath."

"The tub is nice. Have a relaxing soak. I'll wait for you here."

"I'd like that." She gave her daughter a kiss on the cheek and walked back into the room.

When Ella returned to the balcony, wearing a sleeveless burgundy dress, Sofia was studying a map of Rome. She put it aside and greeted her mother. "You look beautiful. Feeling rested?"

"Yes, I feel much better. There's a charming trattoria nearby. Would you like to go out for an early dinner?" Ella asked.

"I'd love to. But before we leave, I have something to show you." Sofia handed her a small envelope. "This is one of the reasons I wanted to come to Italy."

Ella sat down and opened it. She took a quick look at the photo of the Italian opera singer, Gemma Ricci, then silently read the message and grimaced. "I don't think he had an affair with her when we were together." She slid the note across the table to Sofia.

"The date's worn off, so I'm not sure when he got this. Did he ever mention her?" Sofia asked.

"No, but he played her records all the time," Ella said impatiently. "Now that you've shown me the note, can we please enjoy our evening and not talk about your father for a while?"

"Yes, but I'm going to Gemma's apartment tomorrow. Her address is in Rome, and I'd like to visit her."

"Do you have an appointment?" Ella asked.

Sofia shook her head. "I didn't want to give her a chance to say no. Besides, the element of surprise has been very effective for me."

"You can't go to a star's home uninvited."

"Welcome to my world. You wouldn't believe how many times I've shown up uninvited lately, and I'm still standing. Will you come with me?" Sofia asked.

"Of course, but it's probably a waste of time."

"That may be true, but they clearly had a relationship. I'm not sure if she still lives there, but if we find her, she might be able to help us. And from what I've learned, it's possible Dad has another family."

Ella buried her face in her hands. "After everything he's done, I wouldn't put it past him."

Chapter 40
The Eternal City

Early the next morning, Ella was already up, sitting on the balcony, admiring the spectacular view. A carafe of coffee, a pitcher of cream, and a basket of pastries rested on the small table. When Sofia arrived, they shared a laugh; both wore sky-blue summer dresses—Ella's flowing and loose, while Sofia's hugged her slim figure.

"We look like twins," Sofia said.

"Great minds think alike." Ella opened the basket and served the pastries.

Sofia sat across from her. "Are you ready for our adventure?"

"As ready as I'll ever be." Ella poured a cup of coffee from the silver carafe, added cream, and handed it to her daughter.

"Thanks!" She took a sip. "Just how I like it."

"A mother knows these things."

Sofia dug into the pastries. "I love these croissants. I've never had one filled with apricot jam before."

"They're called cornettos, which means little horn," Ella

explained and took a bite. "Italian pastries are much better than the French ones!"

"Of course they are." Sofia smiled, knowing her mother thought everything from Italy was better. "Is there anything you'd like to do before we go to Gemma's apartment?"

"I'd love to show you where I lived with Francesca after we came to Roma."

"I'd love to see it. Can we stop at Trevi Fountain first? I've always wanted to go there."

"Sure. It's right on the way," Ella said. "It's been ages since I've visited *Bella Trevi*."

As they savored the pastries, they looked out at the Eternal City, tinted golden in the light of the rising sun.

"Rome is so beautiful. The entire city is a work of art," Sofia said.

A wistful look crossed Ella's face. "It feels like coming home."

"Well, then it's a good thing you decided to join me. I can't wait to see your old stomping grounds!"

"What are stomping grounds?" Ella asked baffled.

Sofia chuckled. "It means where you used to live."

"Wonderful. Roma awaits us."

The morning was warm when they left the hotel and Sofia was already in love with Italy. The sights and sounds were unique, and every building was rich with history and centuries of stories to tell. As they headed down the street, Ella seemed invigorated by being back in Rome, and Sofia was excited to share the experience with her.

Trevi Fountain was a short stroll away, and the famous monument did not disappoint. People of all ages relaxed in the idyllic setting, eating and chatting as merchants hawked their goods, sweets, and trinkets, and a handsome busker, his case open for tips, played *Tarantella Napoletano* on a concertina.

Ella and Sofia sat on a stone bench and marveled at the majestic Baroque eighteenth-century masterpiece. The fountain was sublime with its statue of the god Oceanus, under a triumphal arch, riding his chariot pulled by sea horses.

"It's more magnificent than I ever imagined," Sofia said.

"This is where I met your father."

"Really? I'd love to hear about it."

Ella pointed to the left side of the fountain. "I had a little kiosk right over there, where I made a modest living selling flowers, like my grandparents."

"Wow. Did he buy flowers from you?"

"No. It was my tradition to give the last flower of the day to someone who needed cheering up," Ella said. "I saw him sitting alone by the fountain, looking sad, and gave him a red rose. When I looked into his eyes, my heart raced. It was as if I'd known him forever."

"Sounds like love at first sight," Sofia said.

"I thought it was. Time is so strange. Even though it was over twenty years ago, the memory is unforgettable."

Chapter 41
Fateful Encounter

Near the Trevi Fountain, Ella stood beside her wooden kiosk, decorated with vibrant hand-painted blossoms on every surface. Red, white, and green satin ribbons hanging from the cart danced in the breeze. At twenty-four, Ella had learned to value her independence and the humble blessings God had given her. She thought she understood what the future held but was unaware of the momentous turn her life was about to take.

It was the end of the day, and she had sold all her flowers except for a single red rose. Noticing a strikingly handsome man in a gray linen suit, sitting by the fountain and looking despondent, she approached him, and offered the flower. "*Ecco, signore, una rosa?*"

"*No, grazie, signorina.*" Aidan said dismissively.

"You speak good Italian for an American."

He looked up at her, impressed. "You have a good ear. Most people can't tell where I'm from."

"The Americans I've met only speak English," she said.

"Well, I was born in Ireland, so perhaps that saved me from the affliction." Aidan took the rose and reached for his wallet.

"No, it's a gift. No one should be sad at *bella* Trevi."

He examined the stem. "Lovely. Your roses have no thorns."

"Of course; I remove them. I wouldn't want anyone to prick their finger."

"How thoughtful." Aidan's dark mood lifted, and he slipped the flower through a buttonhole in his lapel. "*Bellissimo, grazie.*"

"Enjoy your evening." Ella walked away, leaving the scent of roses in her wake.

He followed her to the kiosk, which she was closing up for the night. "*Signorina*, I didn't catch your name."

She turned around and smiled. "Ella. And yours?"

"Aidan." He reached out and shook her hand. "I hope you won't think me forward, but I'd be honored if you'd join me for dinner."

She pulled her hand away. "No, sorry. We just met."

"Then come to dinner with me and we'll get to know each other. There's a lovely restaurant nearby. Will you be my guest?"

Ella searched his face, trying to read his intentions. "*Solo amici?*"

"Of course, only friends. What else? I'm almost old enough to be your father."

"Since when did that stop a man?" she asked.

"On my honor, *solo amici.*"

Ella was intrigued and could tell this sophisticated gentleman wasn't the typical brash American who only had one thing on his mind. Despite her apprehension, she accepted his offer. "All right, I believe you. A girl must be careful these days. There are a lot of rascals in Roma."

"Indeed, apes in trousers. A global blight. *Andiamo?*" Aidan gallantly offered his arm. She took it and they strolled down a lane lined with attractive boutiques and cafes.

"So . . . why are you so sad?" she asked.

"I make it a practice never to share my troubles. Most people don't care."

Concerned, she held his gaze. "I care, but if it's a matter of the heart I don't mean to pry."

"I don't have a heart, so that's not a problem," Aidan said.

"*Signore*, no one can speak Italian so beautifully without a heart."

"I've had plenty of practice. Rome has been my home since I came here as a student many years ago."

"Practically a native. What keeps you here?" she asked.

"My work."

"Oh, what do you do?"

He hesitated. "It's not particularly interesting. I wouldn't want to put you to sleep."

"Nothing puts me to sleep except empty-headed people and, if anything, yours is too full."

"That, my dear, is debatable," Aidan said.

"Let me guess . . . you're a poet."

"Unfortunately, my job is not that creative. I'm a scholar."

"Really? Where do you work?" she asked.

"Primarily Europe."

Ella found Aidan to be deep and mysterious. "I would love to hear more about it."

"It's merely dry historical research. I'm sure you'd find it boring." He gestured to an elegant restaurant with sidewalk dining lit by torchlight. "Well, here's Amalfi Cucina. Let's sit inside so we can listen to the music." Aidan held open the door for her and they entered.

Stylishly attired diners basked in the romantic atmosphere

as a quartet played soft and sultry jazz on a small stage. From the ceiling, an array of raffia-wrapped wine bottles hung like colorful icicles, and amber glass lamps cast a warm light on the intimate red booths that lined the walls. The formally dressed maître d' led Aiden and Ella to a comfortable booth by a crackling fire.

As they chatted, time passed quickly for Ella, and she felt strangely comfortable with Aidan. While sipping Chianti and relishing her pasta *cachio e pepe* with a black pepper and creamy Romano sauce, she glanced at him. His expressive steel-gray eyes were captivating and reminded her of storm clouds before a rain. "Is your family still in Ireland?"

"No, we moved to Boston when I was a child. What about you—does your family live in Rome?"

Ella's face dimmed. "I lost them during the War."

"That's dreadful. What happened?" Aidan asked.

Inundated with excruciating memories, she swirled her wine, eyes fixed on the eddies in her glass. Finally, she met his gaze. "Italy suffered terribly under Mussolini and the Fascists. We lived in a small village in Sicily, and tried to stay happy despite Il Duce, but . . ." She composed herself and dried her tears with her napkin. "I really don't want to talk about it."

"I understand. During our struggle for Irish independence, my brother was killed, so I know the pain of losing a loved one." He touched her hand gently.

Ella felt a deep connection with him and was confused by her growing feelings. "We have both lost too much."

"I'm sorry about your family," Aidan said.

"Roma is *mia famiglia* now. I'm blessed with good friends, and I meet new ones every day." A shy smile crossed her face. "Like you."

Aidan raised his wineglass. "To new friends."

They clinked glasses in a toast and sipped the wine, while

watching couples gracefully move to the music on the black and white tiled dance floor. When the band played the ballad "Body and Soul," he asked, "Would you care to dance? Fair warning, it's been a long time, so I may be pretty clumsy, but..."

"I'd love to," Ella said.

Encouraged by her acceptance, Aidan took her hand, and they merged into the sea of swaying men and women. Moving as if they'd danced together their entire lives, he pulled her body close. Ella found his touch irresistible and surrendered to the passion of the moment. When the song ended, they quickly separated, embarrassed by their impulsive intimacy, and applauded the musicians.

Aidan escorted Ella back to their booth. "Care for dessert, *signorina*? The crème brûlée is marvelous, or perhaps the chocolate soufflé?"

She was delighted by his second suggestion. "A little chocolate. We'll share."

Aidan flagged down their waiter. "Chocolate soufflé with two espressos, please."

Soon, the waiter arrived carrying the luscious cake, placed it in front of them, and left. Aidan slid the sweet over to her. "After you, my dear."

Ella slipped her spoon into the warm soufflé, and the delicacy slowly collapsed as the steam rushed out. Her face lit up as she enjoyed the rich smoothness of the chocolate. "This is so delicious it should be forbidden."

"They say forbidden fruit is the sweetest," he said and took a bite.

A burly man dressed in black with red hair and a pale complexion approached them, dashing the playful moment. He put his hand roughly on Aidan's shoulder and spoke to him in a language Ella didn't understand.

"*Cé hé an cailín?*" he asked.

Aidan's light-hearted mood turned to anger as he shoved his hand aside and replied testily, in the same dialect. *"Nach cuma dhuitse. Amach leat!"*

The man fixed his icy blue eyes on Ella and flashed a seductive grin. *"Buona notte, signorina,"* he said, then left before she could respond. Aiden glared at him as he walked away.

———

Rome, Italy—1978

"Wait!" Sofia said anxiously, interrupting her mother's story.

"What is it? Are you okay?" Ella asked.

"I think I met that guy who walked up to you in the restaurant. When I was in Ireland, a man who looked like that threatened me."

"Threatened you? Oh my God!"

"Was his name Jack?" Sofia asked.

"I don't know, and I couldn't understand what he was saying but your father told me he was speaking Irish."

"I bet it was him. Jack knew our names and where we live. He's a member of a secret society that Dad used to belong to called The Brotherhood of Archangels. Did he ever mention them?"

"No, but Aidan did have secrets. Several times, when you and your brother were young, he insisted we leave for the day so he could have private meetings at our house. I tried to make it an adventure so you and Liam would have fun."

"Oh yeah," Sofia said. "I remember all the times we'd go to Disneyland and SeaWorld without Dad. Was Jack one of the men he met with?"

"I have no idea. Aidan made sure we were gone before they

arrived and wouldn't tell me anything about them. But when we came home, I had to walk on eggshells and the slightest thing would set him off."

"What was he hiding?"

Ella shrugged. "We may never know. Sorry I wasn't honest about what I said in Yosemite. Those were the men I was referring to."

"That's okay. I understand the pressure you were under. What happened after the Irish man left the restaurant?" Sofia asked.

"Your father was so angry; I wanted to leave, but as you know, he's very persuasive."

Chapter 42
Solo Amici

As Ella and Aidan sat together in Amalfi Cucina, sipping espresso, an uneasy silence settled over them. His temper alarmed her, and she wanted to leave. Finally, she broke the tense mood. "*Grazie* for the lovely dinner," she said and stood.

"Forgive me. I didn't mean to be rude. Some of the people I work with can be infuriating."

"I understand. Life is difficult sometimes. *Buona notte, signore*," she said and walked away.

Aidan jumped to his feet and called out, "Ella, please wait."

She turned to him and looked into his hopeful eyes.

"Can't you stay a little longer?" he asked.

"Sorry. I need to go to *Campo dei Fiori*."

"But the night is still young. Please, allow me to accompany you."

Her resolve melted. "You remind me of a puppy that used to follow me around."

"Then perhaps I can follow you to the flower market?"

"*Va bene*, come with me. If you like flowers, it's paradise."

"I adore flowers. And I assure you, I'm housebroken." Grateful he had not lost this mesmerizing woman, Aidan tossed a wad of cash on the table, and they walked out.

Enthralled by each other's company, Aidan and Ella strolled down a moonlit street toward Piazza Campo de' Fiori, in the old center of Rome. The warm evening was enchanting; a breeze rustled the leaves on the trees and a heavenly feeling permeated the air.

Ella took his arm as they walked along in silence. She sensed he had an exciting life full of adventure, the kind of life she had always dreamed of. Being with this man felt so right. What had come over her? It made no sense; she'd only met him a few hours ago. "Please, tell me more about yourself."

Aidan smiled at her. "I'm an open book. Go ahead, ask me anything."

"Okay. What language were you and that man speaking?"

"Irish. It's my native tongue."

"I've never heard it before. How many other languages do you speak?" she asked.

"Only four I'm afraid. French, Spanish, German and Latin."

"Now I know you lied about being an American."

"It's no big accomplishment, really. Just more opportunities to create confusion."

"What other secret talents are you hiding?"

"If I told you, I'd have to kill you," he said playfully.

"Very funny!" She gestured to the fragrant outdoor market with flower stalls featuring a dazzling array of blooms in every color and variety. "Well, here we are . . . Isn't it magical?"

"Beautiful," he said. "Thanks for allowing me to join you."

Ella led Aidan through the historic piazza to a booth, where an enthusiastic young employee with eager eyes greeted her.

"*Ciao,* Ella! I see you've brought a friend."

"*Ciao,* Flavio. This is Aidan."

"*Benvenuto*! Nice to meet you. I'll be right back with your cart." He slipped behind a curtain and emerged with a rolling metal wagon.

As they ambled among the stalls, Ella selected her favorite flowers and Aidan insisted on paying for them. At the center of the piazza was a towering bronze statue of Giordano Bruno, the renowned Italian poet, philosopher, and scientist. They stopped and admired the cloaked and hooded friar, whose manacled hands clutched a book.

"Bruno is one of my heroes," Aidan said. "He was burned at the stake on this very spot while a bloodthirsty crowd jeered."

"I've always wondered why the Catholic Church would do such a cruel thing."

"They accused him of heresy for teaching that the earth and planets revolve around the sun. He refused to recant and sacrificed his life for the truth."

"His death was so sad, but that was long ago. At least he's being honored now." Ella took a white lily from her cart and placed it at the base of the statue.

"Unfortunately, man's inhumanity to man knows no bounds," Aidan said.

"Life is short. We must cherish every moment." She lifted a bunch of deep purple lavender flowers from her cart and held them up to his nose.

He inhaled the sweet herbal fragrance. "They're lovely, but not as lovely as you."

She swatted him teasingly. "I bet you say that to all the flower girls."

When they finished shopping, they left the market and headed toward a street branching off from the piazza. The moon cast a mesmerizing silver light as Aidan pushed her cart, piled high with roses, lavender, and an assortment of fragrant blossoms.

Ella smiled at him gratefully. "Thank you for buying my flowers and for all your help. I can take it from here."

"No. I want to help. Besides, this cart is heavy, and it's a perfect excuse to spend more time with you."

"You're very sweet, but it's unnecessary. I live nearby."

"Please, for your safety and my peace of mind, allow me to escort you to your home."

"I can see you don't like to take no for an answer."

"Guilty as charged," he said.

"All right, then. My flowers will appreciate it. But remember, *solo amici.*"

"Of course, only friends." He pushed the cart down the street.

A short time later, they arrived at Ella's residence. The old terra cotta building was full of character, with a red tile roof and green shutters framing the windows. Ella opened the door to her ground-floor apartment, turned on the lights, and Aidan rolled the wagon inside.

The cozy studio had a single bed. On the walls were paintings of flowers in vivid colors and displayed on the kitchen counter were ceramic platters and urns with floral patterns.

Aidan looked around, admiring the art. "The ceramics are beautiful. And the watercolors remind me of Georgia O'Keefe. Who's the artist?"

"Me," Ella said, shyly. "And I made the pottery too."

"You're the one with secret talents."

"Thank you. Art is my joy."

"You're an extremely gifted artist." He studied a painting

with sensually shaped lilies in vibrant shades of yellow, red and pink. "I'm sure your painted flowers will bring you more fortune than the real ones someday."

"That is my hope."

Aidan took her hand and gazed into her eyes. "Ella, I'll always treasure this glorious evening. Thanks so much for rescuing me from my ennui."

Puzzled, she wrinkled her nose. "I'm glad I could help with your ennui, whatever that is."

He laughed. "You're adorable. I've never met anyone like you."

"Of course, I'm one of a kind." She thought he was going to kiss her, and although she wanted to be kissed, she wasn't ready and stepped back. "Will I ever see you again?"

"You can count on it." With a supreme act of will, he separated from her like a magnet disengaging from metal. "*Buona notte.*"

She sighed. "*Buona notte.*"

When she closed the door behind him, Ella felt as if something of immense value had been ripped away. Attempting to bring herself back to reality, she collapsed on the bed and stared at the peeling paint on the ceiling as a lifetime of broken dreams weighed heavily on her.

Ella's reverie was interrupted by a knock at the door. She got up, looked through the peephole, and saw Aidan standing anxiously on the front step, then opened the door. "Did you leave something?"

He stared at her, his eyes wide with emotion. "Yes. I think I left my heart. May I please come in?"

"I'm not sure that's a good idea." Although inexplicably drawn to him, Ella wasn't certain she could trust him.

"I don't understand it either, but what we have is special," Aidan said. "I just want to talk with you."

"This is all happening too fast." Ella panicked, suddenly afraid of what might happen if she let him in. "Perhaps we will see each other another time."

"All right. I'm willing to wait for you as long as it takes." Aidan reluctantly turned, and Ella watched as he disappeared into the night.

Chapter 43
Leo

Rome, Italy—1978

Sofia hugged her mother, grateful to have one more piece of her family puzzle in place. "I knew so little about you and Dad. It's like I had blinders on."

"We deliberately kept you in the dark," Ella said. "It's a relief to speak honestly now."

"I'm glad you know you can trust me."

"You can trust me too." Ella took her hand.

"You seemed so much in love when you first met. What happened?"

"We were happy at first . . . I think your father never got over his guilt for leaving the priesthood and disappointing his parents. I tried my best, but it was impossible to hold our marriage together."

"You were right when you said that I didn't really know him."

"I'm not sure anyone can. Aidan pushes people away if they try to get too close."

"Enough about him," Sofia stood and reached out her hand. "I want to see where you used to live with Francesca."

"And I'd love to show you. *Andiamo.*"

As they walked from Trevi Fountain toward her old home, Ella shared stories about Francesca, who was a widow when she rescued her on the beach. Her husband, Vittorio, was her childhood sweetheart and the editor of a prominent Roman newspaper until the Mafia assassinated him as retribution for an exposé he published when he was only thirty. Sadly, they didn't have children, but she refused to remarry as she considered herself a monogamous woman who had mated for life.

Ella believed that her mother, Isabella, was watching over her from heaven and sent Francesca to care for her. After a year together in Villa San Giovanni, when she was thirteen, they moved to the Eternal City. From the day they arrived, the stunning art and architecture thrilled her. It was like nothing she had ever seen or imagined.

When they reached the legendary Roman Colosseum, an enormous elliptical amphitheater made of stone, they paused at the outer ring. Sofia read a plaque with information on the history of the arena. "Look at this, Mom. It says that four hundred thousand slaves, gladiators and prisoners were killed here and over a million animals were slaughtered in ritual hunts as entertainment."

"People can be so barbaric," Ella said.

"And never seem to learn from their mistakes." Sofia put her arm around her mother's shoulder. "Let's go." They left the Colosseum and continued on their way.

Before long, they arrived at Via Tasso, Ella's old neighborhood. Apartments from the 1930s flanked the narrow street. One building had a queue of people in front. The sign above the door read: *Museo Storico Della Liberazione Via Tasso.*

"What kind of museum is that?" Sofia asked.

"It's dedicated to the Allies' Liberation of Rome, but it used to be the Nazi headquarters."

A chill ran through Sofia. "That's terrifying."

"Francesca's family lived through the occupation and told us how vicious they were," Ella said. "It breaks my heart to think about all the innocent people the Nazis murdered."

Sofia felt sick to her stomach. "If there is a God, why would he allow such brutality?"

"My uncle Rocco always said, we can't blame God for the evils of men."

"Why not?" Sofia asked. "According to the Bible, God created humanity, so isn't he responsible for his creation?"

"I can't explain it," Ella said. "But we must have faith in God."

"Only if you believe he exists, and I'm not convinced."

Ella led her daughter down the street as she silently wrestled with the existential question. "Sometimes I lose faith too... We may never know for sure."

"Some things are unknowable, but it's important to question everything," Sofia said.

"Well, here it is." Ella pointed at a saffron-colored apartment building with white shutters. "This is where Francesca and I lived before I moved into my own place."

"Why did you leave, Mom?"

"After Francesca died, her younger brother needed more space for his family, so Matteo moved into the apartment with his wife and son."

"Is that when you moved into the studio apartment near the flower market?"

"Yes, and I had just settled in when I met Aidan."

At that moment, the front door opened, and a handsome man in his early thirties stepped out. He looked like he might be a model with pleasing symmetrical features, beautiful brown eyes and thick wavey hair. His impressive physique showed through his black T-shirt and tight jeans. He smiled at the women as he approached and asked, "*Posso aiutarla?*"

"*Si grazie,*" Ella said. "I lived here many years ago and brought my daughter to see my old home."

As the man looked at Ella closely, he recognized her. "Ella Bellini?"

Elated, he hugged her. "I am Leo!"

"Leonardo?" Ella's eyes widened in amazement. "When I left, you were such a cute *bambino.*"

"Yes, and the *bambino* has grown up."

"I'd like you to meet my daughter, Sofia."

"So nice to meet you," she said and held out her hand.

Instead of shaking it, Leo took her in his arms and hugged her as if he'd known her forever. "Sofia, you are as beautiful as your mamma. She was like a big sister to me."

"Do Matteo and Mia still live here?" Ella asked.

"No. They immigrated to Canada a few years ago. I stayed because of my work but I visit them often. We always wondered what happened to you after you left for America."

Ella took a deep breath. "It's very complicated."

"Complicated means interesting, and I want to hear all the details." He gave them an apologetic look. "Forgive me for not spending more time with you now. I'm a journalist, and my story is due today, so I have to run. Will you please join me for dinner tonight?"

"We'd love to!" Sofia said.

"I'll cook Francesca's *pasta nero a la frutti de mare*. How about seven?" Leo asked.

"That would be perfect," Ella said.

"*Perfetto.* See you then. *Ciao!*"

Leo kissed Ella and Sofia on both cheeks, then got into his shiny red Alfa Romeo parked in front and zoomed away.

Chapter 44
Dolce Diva

After leaving Leo's apartment, Ella suggested they stop for lunch at Botticelli Trattoria, which was nearby, before trying to meet with Gemma. Sofia agreed, and when they arrived, the hostess sat them in a leather booth with a marble-topped table.

"This is where Francesca used to take me for my birthday." Ella's eyes sparkled with delight. "After lunch, she'd surprise me with a present."

Sofia was pleased to see her mother happy. "I wish I could have met her."

"You would have loved her. Most people thought she was very stern, but once she let you into her circle, she was incredibly protective and would do anything for you."

"It's been a joy to learn about your family, and Leo seems like such a nice guy."

"He always has been," Ella said.

They scanned the menu. Pleased to see it was unchanged, Ella ordered all her old favorites to share; fritto misto, caprese salad, minestrone soup and rosemary focaccia bread.

"Francesca sounds like a wonderful person," Sofia said. "Tell me more about her."

"When we were still in Villa San Giovanni, she began my English lessons. She thought it was important for my future."

"No wonder you speak English so well."

"On my fourteenth birthday, she gave me painting classes and when I turned sixteen, she took me to Sicily to study ceramics with Gino."

"You're such a talented artist, Mom. Your pottery is beautiful and so are your paintings."

"I never should have stopped," Ella said. "Maybe I'll take it up again."

"I hope you do."

As the courses arrived, they savored each dish, and Ella prolonged the meal by ordering tiramisu and several cups of cappuccino. Sofia could tell she was stalling and getting increasingly nervous at the possibility of confronting the opera singer, or even worse, Aidan. "Don't worry, Mom. No matter what happens with Gemma, I'll be by your side."

"I've never been good at challenging your father. What if he's there?"

"It's highly unlikely, and we don't even know if it's still her address."

Resigned, Ella braced herself for the encounter. "Oh, all right, let's get it over with."

Sofia paid the check, then they walked outside and hailed a taxi.

On their way to the apartment, they drove through Rome's ancient *Esquilino* neighborhood, and exotic aromas from Asian and African food stalls filled the air from an outdoor market.

Ella pointed out the car window at the grand *Teatro dell'-Opera di Roma*. "Francesca took me to several operas there."

"Did you see Gemma perform?" Sofia asked.

"Yes. At the time, she was the most famous opera singer in Roma."

"Great! If she'll meet with us, let her know you've seen one of her shows. Stars have enormous egos. Maybe with a little flattery, she'll tell us what she knows about Dad."

Ella smiled. "You're a clever girl."

The taxi stopped in front of an impressive Art Nouveau apartment building. They paid and got out.

"Wow, I guess Italian opera singers make a lot of money," Sofia said.

"True. They're our national heroes."

When they entered the lobby and approached the front desk, Sofia informed the elderly tuxedoed concierge that they were here to see Ms. Ricci.

"Is she expecting you?" he asked haughtily.

"No, but my father, Aidan Malone, is an old friend of hers. My mother and I are visiting from America, and wanted to say hello," Sofia said with complete confidence.

"Wait here, please." He stepped to the counter behind him and made a call. A few minutes later, he returned. "Ms. Ricci will see you. She's in the penthouse. The lift is on the left."

As they got in the gilded elevator with a red paisley carpet, Ella stared at her daughter, impressed. "How did you get so bold?"

"After Dad abandoned me, I was forced to." She pressed the button labeled *Penthouse,* and the carriage glided up to the top floor. They stepped out and found themselves in an elegant foyer facing a frosted glass door etched with curving lotus flowers and a silver G. Ricci nameplate.

Sofia rang the bell, then squeezed her mother's hand reassuringly. "It's going to be all right."

"I hope he's not here," Ella whispered anxiously.

"If he is, we'll deal with it."

The door opened and Gemma, a barefoot diva dressed in a sleek white silk slip dress, with one of the spaghetti straps dangling alluringly off her shoulder, stood in the entryway. She was an astonishingly beautiful woman in her mid-fifties with short, exquisitely coiffed, platinum blonde hair. "*Ciao*, I'm Gemma."

"*Ciao*, I'm Sofia and this is my mother, Ella."

"How can I help you?" she asked.

"I think you know my father, Aidan Malone?"

"Aidan Malone! Yes, we used to be friends. Won't you come in?"

She led them into her luxurious living room. Original paintings of nude women by Tamara de Lempicka and iconic Art Nouveau pieces by Alphonse Mucha hung on the walls. Floor-to-ceiling windows offered a panoramic view of the city. Gemma gestured toward a plush white sofa that encircled a round glass coffee table with a vintage Belle Epoque Lady Absinthe Fountain displayed in the center. "Please, have a seat."

Settling on the sofa across from them, she tucked her long legs under her. "May I offer you a drink?"

"No, thanks. We just had lunch," Sofia said.

Gemma fixed her deep blue eyes on Ella. "Are you and Aidan still together?"

Embarrassed, she averted her gaze. "No, we're divorced."

"My father introduced us to your beautiful music. And when my mother lived in Rome, she saw you perform at the opera house," Sofia said.

Gemma smiled sweetly and turned to Ella. "So, you like opera? Which show did you see?"

"La Boheme," Ella said.

"Ah . . . Mimi is one of my favorite roles. I hope you will come and see me perform again, as my guests."

Ella's face flushed. Although she tried to conceal it, she felt a pang of jealousy, knowing that Aidan had been with this glamorous woman. "My daughter found a note you sent to her father."

Sofia reached into her purse. "And it seemed like you were close." She handed her the letter.

Gemma read it and took a deep breath. "Yes, he was one of my lovers many years ago. He called me his dolce diva." She gave the note back to Sofia. "When we were together, Aidan was a priest. Celibacy is an aphrodisiac, and he was very good in bed."

Ella blushed. "He left the Church for me, but our marriage failed."

"Don't take it personally." Gemma ran her fingers through her hair. "Men are never satisfied. They always want to put something in you or get something out of you. And when they tire of sex, they want money."

"We didn't have a lot of money, but we had a family, and I thought we had love," Ella said, her voice tinged with remorse.

Gemma leaned back on one of the aquamarine pillows scattered on the sofa. "Frankly, he never should have been a priest. It didn't suit him. The *coup de grâce* was when a bishop barged in one morning and threatened us."

"Was it Bishop O'Connor?" Sofia asked.

"I don't recall his name, but we were stunned he knew about us. To avoid a scandal, he gave Aidan an ultimatum; it was the Church or me. He couldn't have both, so he dropped me—how do you Americans say, like a hot tomato?"

Ella stifled a laugh. "It's hot potato, but I prefer tomato."

"Have you heard from my father recently?"

"Not for decades. I trust he's well?" Gemma asked.

"I wish I knew," Sofia said. "He recently disappeared, and we're trying to track him down."

"Oh my. I hope you find him."

"Sorry for barging in on you." Ella stood, eager to leave.

"No bother," Gemma said. "It was a lovely interruption from my daily routine."

Sofia got up. "Thank you so much for your time. It's been a pleasure meeting you."

The diva led them to the door. "When you speak with Aidan, tell him I said *ciao*." She gave them both a kiss, and they departed.

Gemma listened for the sound of the elevator descending, then sat on the sofa, picked up the phone and dialed. After a few rings, Aidan answered. "Pronto."

"I had a surprise visit from your ex-wife and daughter."

"What? They're in Rome?"

"Yes, and they're looking for you."

"How could they possibly know about us?" he asked.

"They had the note I sent you after our first weekend in Capri."

"Really?" Aidan paused. "I thought nothing was left behind."

"Well, it must have slipped through the cracks."

"I hope you didn't tell them anything."

"I told them exactly what they needed to hear, but I get the feeling they won't give up easily," she said.

"This could cause a problem. Make sure the documents are secure."

"They are. When you're ready, give me the word."

"Of course. I really appreciate what you're doing for me," he said.

"It's for me too. When this is over, we'll both have a lot to celebrate." Gemma picked up a crystal glass from the coffee table. "Are you coming for a visit?"

"Patience," Aidan said. "The wheels are in motion."

"I'm preparing our special drink."

"Have a Green Fairy for me," he said.

"As always, professor." Gemma hung up the phone, then placed her glass under the silver spigot of the absinthe fountain, put a sugar cube on the decorative spoon, and opened the tap. She watched as the green, anise infused spirit trickled into her glass. Sipping the hypnotic drink, she leaned back on her sofa, satisfied. The plan was in place.

Chapter 45
Gatekeepers

When they left Gemma's apartment building, Ella was visibly upset, and Sofia tried to comfort her. "Mom, I'm sorry you had to hear about their relationship."

They paused under the red awning at the entrance and faced each other. "I knew Aidan had a life before we met, but I never imagined he was having affairs while he was still a priest," Ella said. "Obviously, he was breaking his vows long before I came along."

"So, this is good news! You don't have to feel guilty anymore."

"You're right. It's time to let it go."

Sofia tried to lighten the mood. "Is it my imagination or are Italians better looking than Americans?"

"Of course they are. That's why you're so pretty."

Sofia smiled. "Thanks for the good genes."

"Only the best for my girl. What do you want to do next?"

"I think we should speak with Bishop O'Connor. Maybe he knows something. Finn mentioned him and you said he had a huge influence on Dad."

"He's a horrible man, but if you really want to talk with him, I'm willing to try."

"Thanks for helping me," Sofia said. "Let's catch a taxi."

They waved down a cab and after a bumper-to-bumper ride through Rome, arrived at the Vatican, the smallest country in the world, under the exclusive dominion of the Holy See. Sofia knew Vatican City would be impressive, but the mind-boggling grandeur of the gardens, statuary and majestic buildings awed her. Although she disliked pomp and pretension, she had to admit the hydra-headed Catholic Church was the eight-hundred-pound gorilla that made all other religions seem paltry by comparison.

After consulting a map, Sofia and Ella walked across St. Peter's Square on their way to the Governor's Palace. The seat of government for the Vatican City State was behind St. Peter's Basilica in the enormous palace complex. Standing at attention in front of the entrance gates were two tall Swiss Guards, whose ranks had served as the security force in Vatican City since the 1500s. Although their Renaissance style red, blue, and yellow striped garments with helmets topped by scarlet plumage suggested a merely ceremonial presence, the Swiss Guards were elite, highly trained fighters.

Sofia laughed at their comical appearance. "They look so silly!"

"Be respectful," Ella whispered. "They guard the Holy Father."

Sofia regained her composure, and they approached the steely-eyed sentries. "Hello, Swiss Guards. I love your outfits," she said mischievously. "We're here to speak with Bishop Brendan O'Connor."

The tallest guard stared at her as if beholding a strange and insignificant life form. "One moment, *signorina*." He consulted a directory, then looked down at her. "I'm sorry, but you cannot meet with the bishop here. He's retired. If you wish to contact him, you must send a formal request in care of *Palazzo del Governatorato in Vatiano.*"

"How long will it take them to respond?" Sofia asked.

"No telling. They are extremely busy."

"Is there another way to reach him?"

"Unfortunately, no," he said with finality.

"Thanks anyway," Sofia said. "I hope no ostriches died to feather your hats."

Unfazed, the guards were stone-faced as she walked away with her mother.

Ella chided her. "They don't kill birds for their feathers."

"Sorry, Mom, it was just a joke. There must be some other way to contact the bishop."

"Since Leo is a journalist, maybe he knows someone who can help us. We'll talk with him about it tonight."

"That's a good idea," Sofia said.

"We have some time before we need to be at Leo's. Would you like to look around?" Ella asked.

"Sure. We may never be here again." Sofia took her mother's arm. "Let's go."

The Vatican was home to some of the most extraordinary art and architecture in the world, but even a brief visit to St. Peter's Basilica, The Sistine Chapel, and the Vatican Museums was a revelation to Sofia. Inspired by the art of the immortal masters, including Michelangelo, Botticelli, and Raphael, she had an epiphany. The sublime masterpieces radiated a powerful and genuine spirituality that transcended religion. It was the beauty of the art, music, and rituals that attracted her mother to Catholicism, not the dogma. The religion was merely pointing to a truth greater than itself that couldn't be expressed in words.

After a whirlwind tour, Sofia realized they'd lost track of time and needed to leave for dinner. They ripped themselves away from the overwhelming cultural treasures, promising to return for a longer visit one day.

Chapter 46
Roman Allies

Sofia and Ella arrived at Leo's apartment right on time, and he greeted them on the porch with open arms. "Welcome to my home! Come inside."

They followed him into the kitchen, which was the hub of the charming two-bedroom flat with white walls and rich chestnut ceilings and floors.

Leo gestured to the bar stools at the marble island facing the kitchen. "Please, make yourselves comfortable."

They sat, and Ella looked around in amazement. "Everything looks the same except better."

"After I bought it, I began upgrading. And one of the best things about remodeling is the lost treasures you find." He beamed and reached under the counter, pulled out a large olive wood box, and placed it on the island in front of Ella.

She ran her fingers across the carved olive branches that encircled the top. "This is incredible!"

"Open it," he said, enthusiastically.

Ella unlatched the lid and opened the box Francesca gave her to collect milestones from her youth. Inside was her first painting, a miniature watercolor of a red rose, her first piece of pottery, a hand-painted olive oil dipping dish, and a necklace she made from shells they collected on the beach. She gingerly touched the cherished items.

"I have another present for you." Leo handed her a small-framed photo of Francesca and Ella in front of the house. "My father took this when you and my aunt returned to Rome. I know she'd want you to have it."

Ella got up and threw her arms around Leo. "You've given me my life back."

"It's been waiting for you. I always hoped you would return someday." He kissed her. "Are you ready for dinner?"

Sofia inhaled the spicy aroma. "Can't wait. I'm starving!"

Ella sat next to her daughter. "This pasta reminds me so much of Francesca. She taught me how to make it."

Leo winked. "And I haven't changed the recipe."

"Heaven forbid. That would be a sin."

He opened a bottle of chilled Pinot Grigio and poured them each a glass. "*Salute* Francesca!"

Ella and Sofia raised their glasses. "*Salute* Francesca!"

As they sipped the wine, Leo served the pasta. "*Buon appetito.* Please eat while it's hot."

They needed no convincing and ate with gusto. While Ella and Leo caught up on what had transpired since they last saw each other, Sofia listened, eager to hear their stories and learn more about her mother.

"I'm so happy you found each other again!" she said. "Leo, when Mom and Francesca were living in Villa San Giovanni, why did you and your parents stay in Rome?"

"Francesca wanted us to come with her, but my father was part of the Italian resistance, so he stayed to fight the Nazis, and my mother and I didn't want to be separated from him."

"It was my great fortune that she left Roma," Ella said. "If Francesca hadn't rescued me, I never would have survived."

"You were the daughter she always hoped for, and I'm grateful that neither of you were here. After she escaped, things got worse." A troubled look crossed Leo's face as he recalled the painful time. "Roma was declared an open city, but in reality, it was a prison, and the Nazis forced citizens to work in factories like slaves. There were curfews and other strict rules, and any infraction was punishable by a firing squad or public hanging. And to add to the intimidation, the victims' coworkers were forced to burn their bodies."

Sofia was appalled. "The Nazi occupation must have been hell."

"It was. They rounded up over a thousand Jews and sent them to their deaths in Auschwitz. The Gestapo controlled everything. Down the street, they took over an apartment building the locals called the place where Italians go to die."

Sofia teared up. "My mom showed it to me today."

Leo continued, haunted by the memory. "The boy's school I attended was right next door. Every day we could hear the screams of tortured prisoners through the walls."

The staggering horrors of the war felt very real to Sofia. "That's awful, Leo. I can't believe what you've been through. Since your family was in the resistance, how did you avoid getting captured?"

"When living in the city became too dangerous, my father hid us at Fatebenefratelli Hospital, on an island in the Tiber River, where patients with a deadly contagious disease known as Syndrome K were quarantined."

"What is Syndrome K?" Sofia asked.

"It wasn't real," Leo said. "It was a fake disease that my father and the other Italian doctors made up to protect the resistance. The Nazis were terrified of catching it."

"What a brilliant way to deceive them!"

"The lie protected many Italians and after nine months of occupation, the Allies liberated the city."

"And Francesca and I could finally return to her home," Ella said.

The doorbell rang, and Leo got up to answer it. When he opened the door, a smile lit his face. "Beppe! So nice to see you. Please, come in." He led a charming man in his thirties with horn-rimmed glasses and curly brown hair to the kitchen. "I want to introduce you to my long-lost family. Ella and Sofia, this is Beppe. He's one of our best investigative reporters at *Il Messaggero*. We've worked together for years."

"It's nice to meet you," Beppe said. "Sorry to interrupt your dinner. I dropped by to share some developments on our Vatican story, but it can wait until tomorrow."

"Nonsense, you must join us." Leo gestured to the platter of pasta. "Please, help yourself."

"*Grazie.* How could I refuse?" Beppe happily filled his plate and sat next to Leo.

"Hmm . . . You always seem to show up when I make pasta. Are you spying on me?"

"My eyes, ears, and nose are everywhere," Beppe said with a wry grin.

"So, what's the news?" Leo asked.

"From what we've learned, the Vatican Bank is being used by several prominent members of the Roman Curia to launder Mafia money."

Leo's mood darkened. "The Mafia killed my uncle. I'd love to take them and all their enablers down. Can we prove it?"

"We've got some strong leads. I'll keep you posted."

"What's the Roman Curia?" Sofia asked.

"It's the central body that administers the affairs of the

Church. The scandals at the Vatican Bank have been going on for years, and they're getting more egregious every day."

"But they're Catholics," Ella said. "How could they do such a thing?"

Beppe threw up his hands. "Because they can get away with it. There are a lot of greedy men and not enough oversight."

Sofia swirled her wine, then took a sip. "Hey, since you guys report on the Catholic Church, is there any way you can help us get a meeting with Bishop Brendan O'Connor?"

"Why would you want to meet with a retired bishop?" Leo asked.

"My dad has recently gone missing, and O'Connor was his godfather, so we thought he might know where he is."

"I'm sorry to hear about your father, Sofia. I'll see what I can do."

"Thanks, Leo," she said.

"We tried to schedule an appointment with the bishop at the Vatican today, and they were no help at all," Ella said.

Beppe rolled his eyes. "Not surprising. The Holy See is a monolithic bureaucracy."

"This is very important to Sofia." Ella touched Leo's arm. "Any advice you or Beppe can give us would be helpful."

"Sometimes, if we want to speak off the record to a big shot at the Vatican, we'll wait outside his residence and try to catch him when his limo arrives," Beppe said.

"That's true," Leo added. "It can be boring, but if you're up for it, I'll come with you,"

Sofia's face brightened. "That would be awesome! Do you know where he lives?"

"We can get his address, but it may take some time."

Ella kissed Leo on the cheek. "Thank you so much. We really appreciate it."

"We're glad to help. You're family."

Sofia was excited. At last, she was making progress and couldn't wait to talk with the bishop, who'd played such a dominant role in her father's life. "By the way, have you heard of a group called The Brotherhood of Archangels?"

Leo nodded as he twirled his pasta. "We investigated the society but couldn't confirm the reports about them, so the story was killed. Why do you ask?"

"When I was in Carndonagh, Ireland, I discovered a Brotherhood meeting place in a church. My father's portrait was on the wall with the date he was initiated."

"Are you sure? My understanding is that once someone joins the society, they're forbidden to leave," Beppe said.

"Yes, I'm positive. Could they have forced him to return?" she asked.

"It's anyone's guess. But given their reputation, he wouldn't want to be on their enemies' list."

Sofia drew a quick breath. "I hope he's okay."

Leo nudged Beppe. "Stop scaring her."

Ella waved it off. "She's a tough Italian girl and doesn't scare easily."

"I'm fine. Please, tell me more."

"It's been challenging to investigate them because they're so secretive, but we've learned they have ancient roots and worship the leader of God's Army, Michael the Archangel," Beppe said.

"How could my father be involved with such a fanatical group? He's extremely intelligent."

"In a battle between the mind and emotions, emotions almost always win," Leo said. "And unfortunately, religion has been used to manipulate people for millennia."

Sofia nodded. "You're right. I agree with Voltaire that religion began when the first scoundrel met the first fool."

"Enough philosophy. It's time for dessert! I've made Francesca's classic tiramisu." He took the cake from the refrigerator and served each guest a slice. "I'm so grateful to have all of you in my life."

Sofia held up her wineglass. "To Roman allies."

They all clinked glasses. "To Roman allies!"

Chapter 47
Answered Prayers

After returning to their hotel, Sofia and her mother showered and got ready to turn in. Francesca's olive wood box, containing Ella's childhood treasures, sat on their shared nightstand, where a table lamp illuminated the room with a soft glow. They plopped down on their twin beds and relaxed.

Ella turned onto her side and smiled blissfully at Sofia. "All my prayers have been answered. The two of us are together and I'm back in touch with Leo. What a fabulous day!"

Sofia fluffed her pillow and sat up. "I'm so happy for you, Mom."

"Coming to Roma is the best thing that's happened to me in years!"

"Same for me," Sofia said. "Do you think Leo and Beppe will find the bishop?"

"Yes, but don't get your hopes up, he may not be willing to speak with you."

"I know. All we can do is try," she said, sounding a bit discouraged.

Ella got up and began massaging her shoulders. "Don't worry. If he won't help us, we'll go home."

"Maybe. Let me think about it." Sofia closed her eyes, enjoying her mother's soothing touch.

"Tell me more about what you've been up to," Ella said. "Now that you've graduated from college, what's next?"

"I thought I wanted to be a teacher, but I'm not sure anymore."

"You have plenty of time to decide. You're such a smart girl, your options are unlimited."

"That's funny." Sofia chuckled. "Dad said the exact opposite. I tried my best, but it was impossible to live up to his expectations."

"He's always been too judgmental. I'm confident you'll succeed at whatever you decide to do."

"Thanks, Mom."

"Is there someone special in your life?" Ella asked.

"Not now. I had a few boyfriends in college, but all my relationships were emotional train wrecks."

"I'm sorry. But from my experience, it's better to be alone than with the wrong person," Ella said.

"Most men seem so possessive and needy."

"True, but there are a few good ones out there, like Leo and Beppe. Maybe one day you'll fall in love, but you're only twenty-one, so there's no rush."

"Mom, did you always want children?"

"Yes, after losing my family, it was very important to me. And in spite of everything, you and your brother are the greatest joys of my life."

"It's weird, but I have no desire to have kids."

"That's your choice," Ella said. "Marriage and children are not for everyone."

"After living through the divorce, I decided I never wanted to get married," Sofia said.

"Don't base your decision on my failed relationship. I was only three years older than you when I married your father and he was so overbearing, I lost myself."

"I hear you. If I'm ever tempted to get married, I'll make sure it's a real partnership."

"Good." Ella stroked her daughter's hair. "How was that?"

"Best massage ever," Sofia gave her a kiss.

"It's been a long day." Ella lay down on her bed. "Let's get some sleep now. Good night, darling."

"Good night." Sofia switched off the light and shut her eyes, but a moment later, they popped open, and she flicked the light back on. "So, what do you think really happened to Dad?"

"I'm not sure I want to know. Good riddance to bad rubbish." Ella pulled up the bedcovers and turned away from her daughter.

Realizing she was being annoying, Sofia said, "Sorry I don't mean to be such a blabbermouth."

Ella groaned. "You got it from your father. He could never stop talking, either."

"Okay. I'll try to control myself. Sweet dreams." Sofia switched off the light and took deep breaths, trying to quiet her restless mind.

Chapter 48
Sacred Vow

The afternoon sun in the cloudless sky beat down on Aidan mercilessly as he got out of a taxi at the *Piazza Cavalieri di Malta* at the top of Aventine Hill, one of the legendary seven hills of Rome, and approached *Via del Priorato di Malta*. It was one of his favorite places, and now that he had returned to Rome, he wanted to see it again before his meeting with Bishop O'Connor, who lived in the same exclusive neighborhood.

It had been years since he visited the illustrious property, on a rise overlooking the Tiber River. Once the fortified palace of Alberico II, who ruled Rome in the 10th century, it later became a Benedictine monastery, a Knights Templar stronghold and finally an institutional seat of the government of the Sovereign Military Order of Malta.

Aidan walked up to the monumental arched stone entrance and admired the architectural design of a ship ready to set sail for the Holy Land. The image was inspiring, as he was about to embark on his own epic journey. With keen anticipation, he peered through a keyhole in the ancient wooden door and beheld a perfectly framed view of the green-copper dome of St. Peter's Basilica. In the foreground was the grand cypress garden of the Magistral Villa. How foolish he was to think the small garden at El Encanto College held any resemblance to the majesty of this divine place. During his years, as a professor and family man, his ambitions had withered into a dry husk, but at last, he had found his *raison d'être*.

As Aidan walked down the peaceful, tree-lined street toward O'Connor's estate, he grew increasingly anxious. He'd forgotten how sweltering Rome was in the summer and although wearing a lightweight cream-colored linen suit, he felt overheated and wiped sweat from his brow with a handkerchief. Was it caused by the heat or his nerves? Disturbed by the news that Sofia and Ella were in Rome, he reasoned it was in his best interest to conceal this information from his godfather.

Behind the travertine walls that surrounded the property was a palatial, three-story Renaissance style residence. Open-sided loggias, with spiral shaped miniature cypress trees in huge terracotta pots, encircled the two upper levels. A tall wrought-iron gate embellished with gold guarded the long private driveway. Video surveillance cameras stood atop the pilasters on either side of the entrance. Aidan pressed the call button, and the pedestrian door swung open.

He walked to the entryway where an elderly butler in a black suit with a red silk ascot escorted him into the residence. Many years had passed since his last visit, and the furnishings were more luxurious than he remembered. The reception room included handmade wooden furniture from Sorrento with intricate inlaid marquetry, antique chandeliers, a polished ebony Bösendorfer grand piano and original paintings by Botticelli and Caravaggio.

The servant led Aidan to the central atrium, where he found the retired bishop, bent over his white roses, pruning the dead blooms. Aidan cleared his throat. "Excuse me, Your Grace, sorry to interrupt. Are we still meeting today?"

Bishop Brendan O'Connor, a commanding man in his early eighties with silver hair and mesmerizing blue eyes, looked up from his roses. He spoke in a deep, resonant voice with an Irish lilt. "Of course. I've been eagerly awaiting your arrival. Come, I want to show you something."

He led Aidan to a large, rectangular pond filled with iridescent koi swimming gracefully between pink and purple lotus flowers in full bloom. The striking fish had unique patterns of silver, gold, orange, and black.

"What do you think?" O'Connor asked.

"They're stunning. I've admired koi since my first visit to Japan."

"Did you know they represent good fortune and perseverance in the face of adversity?"

"Yes. An ideal symbol of our reunion." Aidan admired the serene pond with delicate streams of water arching into the pool from each of the four corners.

The bishop reached down and gently ran his fingers across the flowers, which swayed on their slender stems. "The lotus seed may remain dormant for decades. Then, if conditions are right, it rises from the mud to become a glorious flower. Like you, it is reborn from the darkness into the light. It's been a long road, but you've finally returned to your true path."

"Indeed. I feel like I've risen from the dead."

"I've known you since the day you were born, and it was never your destiny to be an ordinary man," he said, imbuing the word *ordinary* with disdain.

"When I met Ella, I was drowning in despair. I'd foolishly lost faith in our society and, she seemed like a life raft."

"If I hadn't demanded so much from you, things might have been different. Your fall from grace was my fault. I practically pushed you into the arms of that woman."

"It wasn't your fault. Although I'll always care for Ella and Sofia, I've realized my devotion to The Brotherhood is paramount."

"Your words warm my heart. Let's sit, shall we?" O'Connor gestured to a bench across from the pond and they sat together.

"I want to thank you again for your financial support over the years. And I'm forever grateful that you were willing to wait for my return until Sofia graduated."

"Well, you forced my hand, so I didn't really have a choice."

"I apologize for the difficult position I put you in," Aidan said.

"At first I was furious, but I understand your judgment was clouded by desperation, so I forgive you. Let's put all that behind us now."

Aidan unbuttoned his suit coat. "I hope I can prove myself worthy of your faith in me."

"We have never reinstated a fallen brother, but given the circumstances, I convinced the conclave to give you a second chance," O'Connor said.

"I promise I won't let you down again and will honor my word."

"I'm confident that's true."

"Is there any news from Ireland?" Aidan asked.

"We're on track with your mission, but there's some troubling news. Jack tells me your daughter has been inquiring about you in Derry."

"Sofia in Derry? That's hard to believe." Although he knew she was in Rome, he was surprised about Ireland. "She's a timid girl who's afraid of her own shadow. Jack is trying to cause trouble, as usual."

The bishop shook his head. "Unfortunately, it's true. Father Dolan confirmed his report."

"Well, she won't get far. She doesn't know I was a priest or even my real surname."

"It appears she knows a lot more than you think. Perhaps the mother revealed something?"

"I doubt it. Ella is aware of the consequences of breaking our agreement."

"Well, no harm done. Jack sent her away with a stern warning."

Aidan bristled. "I hope he's not involved with my assignment."

O'Connor gave him a stern look. "You need to get over your animosity toward him; he's had a hard life. Have you no compassion?"

"Please don't take offense. I know he's like a son to you," Aidan said. "It's just that after my brother's death, I can't seem to forgive him."

"Jack is one of our best foot soldiers and loyal to the grave, and there will be times when you'll need to work together."

"Forgive me, Your Divine Grace. I will do whatever you ask."

"In light of this, are you still resolved to go to Ireland?" the bishop asked.

"More than ever."

"Good. I've arranged for a flight this evening. You'll arrive early tomorrow morning in Derry."

"At last, I can fulfill my duty to William," Aidan said.

On a table beside them rested an ornate bottle embossed with the papal tiara above the crossed keys of Saint Peter, symbolizing the keys to the kingdom of heaven, and two crystal glasses. The bishop ceremoniously poured the wine and passed a goblet to Aidan. "This vintage from Chateauneuf-du-Pape is the covenant in the blood of Christ. All glories to Archangel Michael."

Aidan held up his glass. "*In vino veritas*. All glories to The Brotherhood."

The men held each other's gaze as they drank the sacred wine.

Chapter 49
Communion

Dawn tinged the clouds with a magenta hue as the sun rose over Derry Cemetery, where rows of gravestones dotted a lush green hill overlooking the town and the River Foyle. Aidan hadn't come to honor his brother's final resting place for many years, as the pain of losing William still tormented him, and the moment felt surreal. Although it had only been a few weeks since he left San Diego, it seemed like another lifetime.

Aidan walked among the neatly tended headstones and contemplated the significant events of his past. As in the Biblical story of Job, God taught him many agonizing lessons; he lost his son, his marriage failed, and he would never see his daughter again, but he had finally surrendered to his destiny, which was all that really mattered. The years of struggling to be a family man no longer existed for him and had vanished like a chimera.

Nothing could deter him from his mission, and he swore never to allow weakness to control him again. The enormous power of The Brotherhood was exhilarating, and he knew it was within his grasp to wield that power. With the wealth and global resources of the society, Aidan could destroy the depravity that had plagued humanity for millennia, and he was ready to join the fight against evil, whatever the cost.

When he arrived at his brother's monument, he stopped at the granite Celtic cross that rose above the tomb and read the inscription on the pedestal:

In Loving Memory of William Corin Malone
Born January 9, 1911—Died April 4, 1926
Murdered by the British on Easter Sunday
His Sacrifice Will Never Be Forgotten

Derry, Northern Ireland—1926

The angelic voices of a boys' choir soared above the sonorous tones of a pipe organ as young Aidan waited anxiously in the rectory for his older brother, William, and Father O'Connor to return. He was a sensitive boy with wavy blonde hair and blue eyes, brimming with intelligence and curiosity.

Standing next to him was his cousin, Finn, an enthusiastic lad with flowing golden locks and a charming smile. The eight-year-old boys, immaculately dressed in white suits, stared through the lancet windows overlooking the grounds of Saint Eugene's Cathedral. Today was their first Communion and as on most mornings in the historic city, fog shrouded the garden, which they found mysterious and delightful.

Aidan looked up at the Gothic Cathedral with its marvelous bell tower and spire rising above the fog, confident that the Roman Catholic Diocese of Derry was the most impor-tant place in the world. Butterflies flitted in his belly as he watched his friends and neighbors, dressed in Easter Sunday finery, parade up the stone steps and into the church. Now that the momentous day had finally arrived, he was becoming increasingly anxious.

"I'm a little nervous. Are you?" Aidan asked Finn.

"Nah. It's just a bunch of silly words. I'm doing it for Ma."

Aidan glanced at him. "Everything is so easy for you."

Finn gave him a playful punch on the arm. "You worry too much. We know what to do."

When Father O'Connor and William entered the room, Aidan and Finn turned to greet them. William was a mature fifteen-year-old who had somehow avoided the awkwardness of being a teenager. Enthusiasm was a quality he had in spades, and although he was seven years older than his brother, they were extremely close.

O'Connor, dressed in a white linen robe, with a green satin chasuble and red velvet stole embroidered with golden crosses, carried himself with practiced nobility. He scrutinized Aidan and Finn. "Are you boys spiritually ready to receive your first Holy Communion?"

"Sure. It's grand," Finn said.

"Aye, Father." Aidan fidgeted with the buttons on his coat.

Brendan regarded William. "You've been an outstanding example to your brother and cousin. I know you'll make a fine priest one day."

"Thank you," William said. "I'll serve the Church with all my heart and soul."

"I'm confident you will. Shall we go?" O'Connor started toward the door.

"Father, may I have a moment alone with Aidan?" William asked.

"Certainly. But have him in the Cathedral in five minutes. Come with me, Finn."

After they left, William handed an Irish friendship ring to his brother. "I want you to have this. I'm so very proud of you."

Aidan's face lit up with joy as he admired the special silver ring. "Thank you, brother. I don't know what I'd do without you." He slipped it on his finger. "Do you think Father O'Connor is proud of me, too?"

"Of course he is. Now stop fretting. We should go or you'll be late to your first communion." William took Aidan's hand, and they walked out the door.

Inside the Cathedral, multi-colored light from stained-glass windows illuminated the space with its towering red ceiling. The congregation, seated in polished wooden pews, observed the ceremony with reverence as Father O'Connor, assisted by two altar boys, prepared the Eucharist.

A parade of children between the ages of seven and eight marched ceremoniously down the aisle and kneeled on the steps in front of the altar. The girls wore lacy white dresses and veils, and the boys sported crisp white suits.

Aidan's parents, Clare and Gareth, in their thirties, sat with their daughter, Margaret Grace, a prim and proper twelve-year-old. Next to them were Finn's parents, Gareth's handsome younger brother, Seamus, and his beautiful wife, Nelda. Clare looked around anxiously for Aidan.

William arrived and sat next to his mother, who eyed him inquisitively. "Don't worry, Ma, he's on the way."

Clare pursed her lips in disapproval, but her anxiety vanished when she saw her son join the others at the altar.

Aidan was ready to fully embrace the Catholic faith by receiving the body, blood, and divinity of Christ in the Blessed Sacrament. Father O'Connor glided toward the children, golden chalice in hand. When he reached the initiates, he stopped and looked heavenward. "We beseech you, oh Lord, that being appeased, you may accept our humble offering. In the sacred words of our savior, Jesus Christ, this is my body . . . this is my blood . . . do this in remembrance of me."

Father O'Connor walked along the line of kneeling supplicants. Pausing at each child, he held up the host and intoned, "the body of Christ," then placed the Sacrament in their open mouths. He stepped up to Aidan, who took the Communion bread on his tongue and bowed his head. As the wafer slowly melted, he was overcome with profound feelings of love for the Holy Spirit and pledged to devote his life to serving God.

Chapter 50
Another Bloody Sunday

The tower bells rang as the congregation left the Cathedral after the Easter Sunday Mass. Aidan loved the music of the bells. Their deep resonance vibrated in his chest, which he found thrilling.

Clare tousled his hair. "You've done us proud, son."

"Thank you, Ma."

As Aidan and his family walked out of the Cathedral with Finn and his parents, they stopped to speak with Father O'Connor who stood at the exit, bidding the parishioners farewell.

Gareth shook his hand warmly. "I don't know how to thank you, Father, you are such a blessing to our family."

"It is I who am blessed," O'Connor said. "All the Malones are a treasure to our congregation."

Rising above the reverberating bells, angry voices interrupted their conversation.

"Look!" Finn said, pointing to the street where dozens of protesters had gathered in front of the Cathedral. Some waved the green, white, and orange Irish Free State flag and others held up signs that read:

RESIST BRITISH RULE
AVENGE THE EASTER RISING
IRELAND UNITED

Saint Eugene's was in the majority Catholic Cityside neighborhood and many citizens of religiously divided Derry supported the cause. Fervent parishioners hurried down the steps and joined the protest, adding their voices to the rousing chant: "Ireland United! Ireland United!"

Aidan felt afraid and confused. "What should we do?"

"Let's go back inside," Father O'Connor said. "While I agree with their goals, this public display will not accomplish them."

Aidan tugged on his brother's hand. "Come, let's go."

"No," William said. "Some of these lads are my friends and are part of our movement. I'll try to calm things down."

Clare grabbed his arm. "Please, son, don't get involved."

"But I am involved," William said, then vanished into the unruly crowd.

As the riot raged, Aidan and Finn tried to follow William, but Father O'Connor blocked them. "You must stay together. I'll bring him back."

Margaret Grace held Aidan protectively as O'Connor rushed off. Finn's father, Seamus, took his son's hand and led his family back into the safety of the Cathedral.

Before long, fights on the street broke out between Catholics and Protestants who had joined the fray. William ran up to his friend, a ginger-haired teenager named Jack McLoughlin, who was chanting through a bullhorn. "Resist British Rule! Avenge the Easter Rising!"

To quell the escalating passions, William seized the bull-horn and hurled it away. "Jack, stop inciting them!"

William's interference infuriated him. "Don't forget what they've done to us. They killed my parents, and the streets ran red with our blood. Let's overthrow these bastards, now!"

"I agree, but this is not the way. We must win the hearts and minds of our oppressors."

"That will take forever. The only way is to fight fire with fire!"

The sound of gunshots rang out. William and Jack turned to see two young Royal Ulster Constabulary police officers on horseback. The sergeant, a strapping giant, fired his rifle in the air to break up the rally. "Go home, you papist pigs!"

"It's the RUC, Jack. We must go," William said.

"Proddy dog traitors! May they rot in hell." Jack's eyes burned with fury.

Father O'Connor rushed through the demonstrators and approached the sergeant. "Please, sir, don't be rude to these good people. It's Easter."

The officer sized up the priest with contempt. "This is none of your goddam business, you bloated Catholic rabble rouser!" He knocked O'Connor down with the butt of his rifle, then shouted at the protestors, "Clear the streets or we'll shoot the lot of you!"

Some people dispersed, but many held their ground and continued chanting:

"Ireland United! Ireland United!"

Gareth, Clare, Aidan, and Margaret Grace rushed up to Father O'Connor. Clare kneeled by the priest, pressing her scarf against his bleeding head. "He's badly hurt!"

Looking around desperately, Gareth spotted his eldest son in the crowd. "There's William! Come, we'll get him away from that hooligan and then help Father O'Connor."

The jostling throng of protestors surrounding William blocked the Malones when they attempted to reach him. William struggled with Jack, who pulled out a pistol as his family watched, helpless and terrified.

"Put it away before the police see it!" William struggled to seize the gun.

"Let go! I'll kill the damn whoresons," Jack said, holding on tightly to the weapon.

"Our cause is bigger than you. Don't be a fool!" William shouted.

"If you're not man enough to fight for the blood of your countrymen, then get the hell out of my way!" Jack shoved William aside. "Death to the crown!" he yelled and pointed the gun at the RUC officers.

William grabbed the pistol, forcing it off target, but he was too late to stop the bullet. As the gunshot resounded, the constable and his sergeant looked for the gunman and saw the weapon fall from William's hand. The sergeant fired, shooting William in the chest, and the crowd scattered in all directions.

Aidan raced toward his brother, pushing his way through the turmoil, followed by Gareth, Clare, and Margaret Grace. William fell to the ground as his horrified family reached him. In anguish, Aidan slumped to his knees and cradled William's head in his lap as blood from the bullet wound soaked his white Communion suit. "Oh no! Please God, no!"

As his life slowly drained from him, William radiated a profound equanimity. He looked up at Aidan and said, "It's up to you now, brother," then took his last breath.

"Please, William, don't leave me." Aidan collapsed onto his brother's dead body and wept inconsolably over the unbearable loss.

After the shooting, the protest erupted into a full-scale riot. More police arrived on horseback, but enraged protesters continued to chant and resist arrest. To control the demonstrators, the officers created a barricade with their horses, using the animals as a battering ram to force the masses off the street. The stallions trampled some protestors; and the police officers beat others with their clubs or shot them. In the mayhem, many were killed or injured.

The Malones huddled around William, too numb to move, as Father O'Connor ran up to them. Blood from the gash on his forehead streamed down his face. "We need to get away now!"

Gareth, Clare, and Margaret Grace stood unsteadily, but Aidan wouldn't let go of his brother. O'Connor pulled him to his feet. "Come, lad, we must go."

"We can't leave William," Aidan cried out.

"Gareth and I will carry him. Hurry, your lives are in danger. You must leave Ireland immediately."

The men picked up William's lifeless body, and the family followed them, disappearing into the swirling madness of the crowd.

The next day, a bitter wind blew as the sun set on Londonderry Port, crowded with hundreds of passengers jostling for space while waiting in line to board the next ship bound for America. Desperate people, the economic depression etched on their faces, watched as a weathered steamship, the *Celtic Queen*, pulled away from the dock.

On the ship's deck, the Malone family peered overboard at their homeland shrinking in the distance. The turbulence of their lives mirrored the vast, roiling sea that carried them toward an unknown future. Wrestling with their thoughts and fears, the family struggled with the agonizing pain of losing

William, their home, their community, and the lives they had built in Ireland.

"Is Boston like Derry?" Margaret Grace asked.

"It's much better," Gareth said, with exaggerated confidence. "Father O'Connor has arranged a safe and comfortable place for us."

Aidan looked up at his father in desperation. "Will we ever go home again?"

"Not until the British are driven out of Ireland."

Clare stared blankly at the rolling waves that stretched across the endless horizon. "I know God will make them pay for what they've done."

"They murdered William!" Margaret Grace wailed.

"Hell is too good for them!" Gareth pounded his fists on the deck railing.

"Thank God Father O'Connor will give our son a proper Catholic burial," Clare said.

Gareth put his arm around her. "Don't worry, Ma. I'll avenge William's death. And if I don't, Aidan will."

Clare kneeled and clutched her son. "You must take care. We're counting on you now."

The boy nodded numbly. "I'll do my best. I don't want to let you down."

"God has special plans for you, son. Of that, I am sure." Gareth grasped his shoulder.

Aidan looked down at the ring William had given him, painfully aware that he was twisting it around and around, just like his world, which was spinning out of control.

William had been more than a brother; he was his best friend, and they shared everything. Without him, Aidan felt utterly lost and alone. Overcome by sorrow and confusion, he gazed at the shoreline as the lights from the port faded into darkness.

Chapter 51
The Reckoning

DERRY, NORTHERN IRELAND—1978

Aidan stood in front of William's grave, shaken by the memory of his murder, which was as vivid as the day it happened. He took a crystal rosary from his pocket and draped it over the Celtic cross above the tomb. Sunlight reflected on the crystals, casting rainbow colors on the headstone.

"Please accept this rosary as a token of my love and gratitude." He fell to his knees and wept. "Although I will never be as pure as you, I'll do my best to follow in your footsteps. I'm sorry I didn't come sooner, but I promise your death will not be in vain."

The loss had haunted him since he was a child, and he would punish the killer who stole his brother from him. After saying a silent prayer, he stood and walked with resolve down the cemetery hill and got in his car.

It was still early morning when Aidan arrived at the Loyalist Protestant neighborhood known as The Fountain. He parked his car and viewed the quiet well-manicured area with contempt. The enemy lived here, and most Catholics wouldn't step foot in this community. Thank God, justice would finally be done.

His feelings were as stormy as the ocean on the day his family fled from Ireland, and he tried to calm himself by praying to Saint Michael. He sat on a bus bench across the street from a row of brick terraced houses and pulled a newspaper out of his briefcase. While pretending to read, he monitored one of the flats.

A door opened and Sergeant Halifax, the ruthless man who viciously beat Bishop O'Connor and killed William, stepped out and headed down the stairs toward his car. Aidan discovered from the surveillance he ordered that the once intimidating police officer now spent his days feeding ducks in the park with his grandchildren. No longer a threatening man, he was bent, and his hair had thinned and turned gray. There was something pathetic about him; he was merely a disposable pawn on a much larger chessboard.

When Halifax got in his old silver Citroen, Aidan felt a pang of guilt, then crushed the momentary weakness, swatting it like a mosquito. The Sergeant cranked the ignition, and the vehicle exploded in a massive fireball.

Aidan had arranged for the assassination of his enemy, but it didn't give him satisfaction. However, it was a cruel world, and satisfaction was not what he craved, it was justice. He used to believe the ends could never justify the means, but now realized how quixotic he had been. To make a better world, there would be many times he'd have to kill to punish the leaders that made life miserable for the mindless sheep who followed them.

A crowd gathered around the burning automobile as Aidan slipped away unseen, got in his car, and headed to the airport.

Rome, Italy—1978

Bright stars shone in a cloudless sky as a Learjet made its descent and landed at a private airport in the Roman countryside. A white Mercedes-Benz limo waited on the tarmac. On the antenna, a magenta flag with the image of a golden lion crowned by stars fluttered in the breeze. The jet slowed to a stop and the aircraft door opened. Aidan walked down the stairs and into the waiting limo.

The limo sped away from the airport and glided along a winding road through the stark, rural landscape of Rome's legendary Appian Way. Aidan sat in the back seat, holding his gold rosary, a token given to him when he was first admitted as a brother into the society. For years, he'd hidden the beads away in a futile attempt to bury his past, but the masquerade had been a disaster and brought misery to all the people he loved.

As he watched the familiar landscape drift by, disquieting thoughts flooded his mind, and concentrating on his prayers was elusive. It had been a dark time when he left The Brotherhood, and the day was seared in his memory like a burning brand. He closed his eyes and recalled the fateful moment.

Chapter 52
Every Rose Has Its Thorn

Derry, Northern Ireland—1956

Aidan pulled up the collar of his dark blue wool overcoat. It was so chilly that he could see his breath. Hurrying down the footpath, wet from a winter downpour, he noticed lights from the Bishop's Gate Hotel reflected on the slick streets. As he approached the entrance, he thought about the strange way his life had unfolded. Although he still believed in what the society could achieve, given the right leadership, doubts plagued him, and he wondered if he was still serving God, because sometimes it didn't feel that way.

He stopped the revolving door with his briefcase and stepped inside the building. In the elegant walnut paneled lobby, a warm fire greeted him. He took off his coat and straightened his custom-tailored blue suit. Looking around to ensure that no one had followed him, he slipped into the hotel pub, The Tipsy Goat.

The intimate room had a polished wood bar accented with a gleaming brass rail. Wealthy patrons sat at cocktail tables as chic young men in red vests delivered their food and libations. Behind the counter, a flamboyant mixologist created a wide variety of drinks.

Aidan sat at the bar and Kate, a young brunette barmaid with a bob haircut, greeted him with familiarity.

"Looks like you've had a rough day, Mr. A." She ran her fingers through his damp hair.

"You know me well," he replied.

She placed a pint of Black and Tan in front of him. "This one's on the house."

"Much appreciated, Kate." He took a gulp.

"Anytime," she said, and turned to another customer.

Although late for his meeting, Aidan didn't care as his efforts seemed pointless, and nothing of substance ever changed. After downing the last drop of his drink, he grabbed his overcoat and briefcase and walked out of the bar.

The door to the lobby elevator opened, and he stepped inside.

"What floor, sir?" the uniformed liftman asked.

"Third, please."

The lift operator closed the gate, and the carriage delivered Aidan to his floor. He headed down the hallway and knocked on a door. A moment later, Mick, a brawny fellow with thick dark hair and a scruffy beard, opened it. "Welcome, sir. We were concerned you weren't coming."

He entered the room and closed the door. "Let's get on with it," Aidan said tersely.

Mick's colleague, Clive, a lean and sinewy young man with spikey red hair, motioned to a table with a bottle of Connemara whiskey and three shot glasses. "We have your preferred usque-baugh. Won't you take a moment to wet your whistle, sir?"

He glanced at the distinctive green bottle. "Very well."

The men sat at the table and Clive poured three shots.

Aidan took a sip of the revered single malt whiskey and gave Mick a hard stare. "It goes without saying that our arrangement is strictly confidential."

He nodded. "Don't you worry, sir, we understand."

"Here's the intelligence we've gathered." Aidan placed his briefcase on the table, opened it and handed him a file. "Commit it to memory, then burn it."

"Thank you, sir." Mick skimmed through the papers. "Your support for the Border Campaign is invaluable."

Clive lifted his shot glass. "To a free and Catholic Ireland!"

"A most worthy cause." Aidan toasted them and they downed their shots.

Mick wiped the whiskey from his beard and said, "Jack McLoughlin has given us a bit of trouble lately, and—"

Aidan cut him off. "Jack is your concern. I want nothing to do with him or any of his associates."

"As you wish. We'll deal with him," Clive said. "Our methods may differ, but our goals are the same."

"All roads lead to Rome," Mick chimed in.

"Indeed." Aidan stood. "Gentlemen, I have a plane to catch."

Clive and Mick rose to their feet, shook Aidan's hand, and he hurried out the door.

As a taxi drove Aidan through the streets of Derry toward the airport, he peered out the window and questioned his purpose in life. He had tried his best to be a positive force, but human nature was recalcitrant. Even his once beloved Catholic Church caused him nothing but distress. When he was part of its inner circle, he realized the institution was rife with corruption, petty jealousies, and cutthroat competition for power.

Since joining The Brotherhood over a decade ago, cynicism had replaced his youthful idealism. At first, he believed their efforts would change the world for the better, but every form of ignorance, cruelty, and hypocrisy continued unabated. Worst of all, many of his actions had caused death and despair, and there wasn't a single accomplishment he was truly proud of. He felt trapped in quicksand, but every attempt to escape only pulled him deeper into the muck. *I've made a mockery of everything I hold sacred.*

ROME, ITALY—1956

When Aidan returned home, he couldn't shake his despair. He checked into his favorite suite at the historic Hotel Hassler Roma, at the top of the Spanish Steps, and spent several days drinking himself into a stupor. One morning, when the newspaper was delivered to his room, he read a headline that made his blood run cold: *IRELAND BORDER CAMPAIGN KILLS FAMILY MAN.* His tears wet the page, and he ripped it to shreds. Once again, his actions had caused the death of an innocent man, and he had blood on his hands.

Later that day, Aidan arrived at O'Connor's estate, trying to conceal his inner torment as he headed down the hallway. He entered the bishop's spacious office with its floor-to-ceiling bookcases containing rare, handbound volumes and found his godfather sitting at an antique desk sipping espresso while studying a manuscript.

The bishop looked up and smiled. "Good work in Ireland. Although the Border Campaign has been a military failure thus far, it's an excellent propaganda coup for the IRA, so I think we should continue to support it."

Aidan faced him, his heart pounding. "We shouldn't be involved with political violence. Something went terribly wrong. I was told the building would be empty."

O'Connor walked over to a side table where a marble tray held a silver carafe and several gold-rimmed cups. "Would you care for an espresso? I've developed quite a taste for it." The bishop picked up the carafe and poured a demitasse for him while Aidan stood in tense silence. "The Italians do some things right," he said, handing him the cup.

He took a sip while gathering his courage. "I've searched my soul, and I no longer believe the ends justify the means. I can't do this anymore."

O'Connor gazed at him scornfully. "Don't be so weak; it's unbecoming of you. Our foot soldiers may make mistakes, but we must sacrifice to accomplish anything of value in this world. Sometimes we all wish to lay down our swords, however it is our duty to emulate Archangel Michael." He gestured to the open-air atrium. "Come, let's talk in the garden."

Aidan followed him to the courtyard, where an abundance of blooming flowers, including white roses, perfumed the air. A carved wooden bench sat in front of a marble fountain of the Virgin of Lourdes. The peaceful sound of water flowing from her urn did nothing to relieve the tension between the men.

The bishop picked up clippers from the bench, snipped a rose, inhaled its fragrance, and handed it to Aidan. "A touch of heaven, don't you agree?"

He took the rose and inadvertently pricked his finger on a thorn. "Heaven, with a bit of pain." Annoyed, he tossed the flower to the ground.

"Pain and beauty are eternal bedfellows. Every rose has its thorn."

Aidan pressed the wound to stop the blood, which trickled down his finger. "I'm sorry, but I can't continue to serve any longer."

"You don't mean that and as you know, it's not possible.

Once initiated, your commitment to The Brotherhood is eternal."

"No one was supposed to get killed," Aidan said.

"The innocent die every day. It's our mission to protect humanity from the forces of darkness, no matter how high the cost."

"Well, I'm not willing to sacrifice my soul."

His godfather stared at him condescendingly. "Don't be so naive. Consider our Savior's sacrifice; yours pales in comparison."

Unable to take the heat of his gaze, Aidan looked down. "I need to get away from all this. My heart isn't in it anymore . . . and I'm struggling with my faith."

"I see we've been working you too hard," O'Connor said. "Take some time off and I'm sure your well of faith will be restored."

Aidan turned to him, dispirited. "I doubt it."

"Pray to our patron saint, who lifts all souls from darkness." The bishop held out his hand adorned with an ecclesiastical gold ring set with a large amethyst encircled by diamonds. "All glories to Archangel Michael."

For the first time, Aidan refused to kiss the sacred ring. He shook his head, then walked away as his godfather watched him with icy incredulity.

With no idea of what to do or where to go, Aidan left the estate, and wandered down the street in a daze, convinced he'd wasted his life as a priest and a member of the society. Hurrying blindly through the Aventine Hill neighborhood, he followed the Tiber River past the Roman Forum, spinning in a cyclone of disturbing thoughts and feelings as he tried to figure out a path forward. He'd lost his way and was drifting aimlessly like human plankton, motorless and blown by the elements, alienated, and ensnared in a world he no longer believed in.

Before he knew it, Aidan arrived at Trevi Fountain, a mile and a half from the bishop's home. He stopped in his tracks and beheld the breathtaking work of art. It was as if someone had removed a blindfold from his eyes and he perceived its true beauty for the first time. As a student, he came here often to admire the inspiring fountain, but after becoming a priest and member of the society, he stopped doing things purely for the joy of it and his life had become repressed and stifling.

Aidan sat on a bench and observed people enjoying simple pleasures. Life would be much easier if he could be like them. A luminous young lady at a flower stand caught his eye. Her golden-brown hair and vivid green eyes glistened as she chatted with her customers. She seemed joyous and carefree, and he envied her humble life. Perhaps the key to happiness wasn't in trying to save the world or humanity, but merely appreciating the beauty of the moment. To his surprise, the beguiling woman approached him. As he would soon learn, her name was Ella Bellini and meeting her would change his life.

Chapter 53
The Solitude

The memory of meeting Ella at Trevi Fountain over two decades ago disturbed Aidan. In his weakened emotional state, she was irresistible. It wasn't her fault; his craven desire to run away from his destiny blinded him and he lost the opportunity to use the resources of The Brotherhood for the good of humanity. Fortunately, he had another chance.

As the limo made a sharp turn on the Appian Way, Aidan opened his eyes and looked out the window. It was dawn and pink clouds streaked across the sky. He clutched his gold rosary beads and quietly recited a prayer.

Blessed Michael, Archangel . . .
Be our safeguard against the wickedness and snares of the Devil.
By the power of God, thrust Satan down to Hell.
And with him those other wicked spirits
Who wander through the world for the ruin of souls.
Amen.

The vehicle slowed and the chauffeur, a young man in a dark suit, aimed a search light at an unmarked turnoff, then veered onto a private dirt lane leading toward a steep mountain.

After a short drive, the limo arrived at a high stone wall and stopped at the entrance. An armed guard stepped out of the gatehouse and signaled to the driver who lowered the backseat window. The man peered inside. "Hello, Mr. Malone. His Divine Grace is expecting you." He opened the gate, and they drove in.

Once inside the compound, Aidan felt elated when the stone Temple of Venus came into view. It was even more beautiful than he remembered. Carved into the mountainside in 200 BCE, the structure was not visible from the road. The Brotherhood had transformed the pagan site into their shrine in 1312 and it was now the exclusive temple complex for the society's leadership. Although not openly acknowledged by the Church, their fates had been entwined for centuries. Every year, the group surreptitiously selected four exceptional priests to pledge unconditional fealty to them. The candidates were carefully vetted and, if chosen, were released from their priestly duties. To be considered, nominees needed extremely high intelligence and multilingual skills. Above all, they must be fearless and willing to do whatever the mission requires.

Aidan was grateful to serve again in such a meaningful way. He knew what the forces of evil had done to his brother and other innocent people throughout history. It was unrealistic to think that meaningful change could be achieved through purely peaceful means. They were impotent weapons against Satan and would never lead to victory. While he hated to give him credit, Jack's mantra about the need to fight fire with fire was right.

As they got closer, Aidan could see light from inside the

temple shining through a massive stained-glass window embedded in the stone. At its center was a magnificent, golden-winged lion with a crown of silver stars, which he contemplated with reverence. Saint Michael had revealed the sacred path to him years ago, but he had forsaken his mission. Unlike Jesus, the Archangel didn't turn the other cheek, and neither did his warriors. Although emotional entanglements were forbidden, pleasures of the flesh were encouraged to increase their passion for the fight. Finally, without a shadow of doubt, he knew he must sacrifice everything to achieve his goals.

The limo headed into a tunnel under the temple. Overhead lights created a strobe effect as they drove down a steep road into the recesses of the cavern. The driver stopped and opened the backseat door. Aidan got out and surveyed the craggy stone walls and ceiling of the subterranean garage. Not much had changed; dozens of vehicles and storage vaults filled the space.

Gesturing to the entrance, the chauffer said, "Please wait inside, sir," then got into the Mercedes and drove away.

When Aidan entered the vestibule, there wasn't a soul in sight and the only sound was the ethereal refrain of Gregorian Chant playing softly through speakers mounted on the walls. Spectacular Renaissance tapestries depicting scenes from the Book of Revelation hung above blue pearl granite floors. He sat on a plush gold velvet sofa in the elegantly furnished space.

While waiting, flickering light beckoned from the end of a hallway, and Aidan walked toward the amber flames. He entered an octagonal room, symbolizing eternal life with a quartet of blazing fireplaces facing north, south, east, and west and basked in the warmth of the fire.

"Good morning. It's a joy to see you in the sacred chamber again," Bishop O'Connor said.

Aidan turned to greet his godfather, who was wearing his

bishop's vestments, with one new embellishment—a large silver ring with ornamental keys hanging from his magenta silk sash.

"Good morning, Your Grace. It's an honor to be here."

"I had no doubt that you would pass your first trial and join me today."

"It was gratifying to send William's killer to Hell."

"Divine vengeance is sweet," O'Connor said. "Come, let's get started."

The bishop led Aidan to a gilded bronze elevator and opened it. Once inside, he turned the intricate dial, adorned with Christian symbols, to an icon of the cross keys of Saint Peter, and the elevator descended.

"Where are we going?" Aidan asked.

"The catacombs."

"In all my years of service, I've never seen them."

"You wouldn't have. We reserve them for penitents."

The lift stopped, and the bishop opened the elevator gate. They stepped out into a vast cavern lit with oil lanterns suspended from the natural stone ceiling. Made of fossilized travertine, the walls, floors, and curving pathways shimmered in the dim light.

"These are the oldest catacombs in Rome. Over one hundred thousand bodies are buried in the ossuary, including many saints and martyrs. Of course, we've done a bit of remodeling over the centuries."

"It's extraordinary," Aidan said.

The bishop picked up a torch from a table on the landing and lit it with a wooden match. He held up the torch to illuminate a rough-hewn stone stairway descending into an abyss. "The grottos of solitude are below."

Aidan peered into the dark chasm. "Is there electricity?"

"No, we've chosen to keep the grottos as our founders created them. Shall we?"

Determined to endure his penance, Aidan followed the bishop's wavering torch down the treacherous steps into the inky darkness. As they descended, the air became increasingly moist and cold, and the walls seemed to weep. At the bottom of the stairwell, they reached the grottos, which had several gated cells chiseled out of the rock walls. The flame from the torch cast eerie shadows in the dark, claustrophobic cavern.

O'Connor swung open the heavy iron door on one cell. "Many eminent men have atoned for their sins on this hallowed ground."

The cramped enclosure had a low ceiling and was empty except for a large metal bowl. "But there's no bed or toilet," Aidan said.

"The floor is your bed, and the bowl is your toilet. Are you up to the sacrifice?" the bishop asked.

"I pray that I am."

"An attendant will bring bread and water every morning and empty your waste, but I forbid you to speak with him. During your solitude, it will become clear if you are worthy. If not, you must return to your life as an ordinary man."

"I'd rather die," Aidan said.

"Then remove your clothing and enter the solitude as you were born . . . with nothing."

Aidan stripped and placed his clothes in a box outside the cell, then stepped inside.

"When you complete your trial, I will return." He closed the iron gate and locked it. "All glories to Archangel Michael."

"All glories to The Brotherhood." Aidan bowed his head in submission.

Chapter 54
Penance

Gripping the bars of his cell, Aidan listened to the bishop's footsteps as he ascended the stone stairs and watched his glowing torch recede in the distance. Before long, the sound vanished, the light winked out, and he was left in utter darkness and silence.

Naked, alone, and shivering with cold, Aidan sank to the floor, but the stones were rough and frigid, and the damp air penetrated deep into his bones. To get warm, he stood and paced like a caged animal, counting his laps, five steps forward and five steps back, ten times, a hundred times, a thousand times.

His energy spent, he sat and tried in vain to transcend the discomfort, but the beating of his heart and the rush of his breath became deafening. He was angry at himself for his lack of fortitude but couldn't banish the feelings of dread surging through his body. Attempting to regain self-control, he got on his knees and prayed with all the fervor he could muster.

Our Father who art in heaven, hallowed be thy name.
Thy kingdom come, thy will be done, on earth, as it is in heaven.
Give us this day our daily bread, and forgive us our trespasses, as
we forgive those who trespass against us, and lead us not into
temptation, but deliver us from evil. Amen.

After reciting the Lord's Prayer for hours, Aidan was too hoarse to speak. He continued repeating the invocation silently, but the words gave him no solace. Overcome with vertigo, his knees buckled, and he fell to the ground as a cacophony of phantasmagoric sounds and images tortured him until he passed out.

Aidan awoke to the clattering sound of the hooded attendant pushing metal bowls through a narrow opening in his cell. As the man departed, his torch revealed three containers: one with water, another with a small round of unleavened bread, and an empty receptacle for his waste. When the attendant's light faded away, the bleak embrace of isolation surrounded Aidan once again, and he fell to his knees and prayed.

Blessed Archangel Michael, as you lead the glorious Army of
God, lead me, your unworthy servant, through this trial so that I
may fight for you to defeat the forces of Satan.

To keep track of the passing days, he counted the servant's visits. He knew the only way to endure the isolation, and sensory deprivation was through complete submission to his routine of pacing, praying, and carefully rationing the bowls of food and water until he completed his trial.

Lying prostrate on the cold floor, with his arms stretched out, Aidan tried to steady his mind, but despite his efforts to count the days, his sense of time faltered, and he became increasingly disoriented. His bruised ribs ached from being pressed against the hard stones, his head pounded, and the gnawing pain of starvation tormented him.

Suddenly, the seductive aroma of roasting meat wafted through the air. Aidan opened his eyes and saw an angel with a glowing body the color of golden topaz, flowing silver locks, and eyes that flashed like lightning, relaxing by a bonfire just outside his cell. The androgynous spirit was eating a sumptuous feast and had transformed the dark grotto into a lush garden filled with fruit trees. With a wave of the angel's hand, Aidan's door opened.

"You've suffered long enough, my friend," the seraph said in a honeyed tone. "Please, come break bread with me and warm yourself by the fire."

Aidan stepped out of his enclosure and sat next to the radiant being, who draped a warm blanket over his shoulders and offered him a slice of apple.

"Divine one, thank you for your kindness," Aidan said. As he took a bite of the sweet fruit, the blanket morphed into an ebony serpent that coiled around his body, slowly squeezing the life out of him.

As Aidan desperately gasped for breath, the demon taunted him. "You have failed the ultimate test, and now your soul is mine!"

Aidan spat out the fruit, which had turned black and bitter. The viper slithered away, the malevolent spirit and garden vanished, and he found himself back in his dank cell. He gripped the bars and screamed, his voice sounding like the wail of a wounded beast. Inundated with intense visions, he closed his eyes, lay down, and tried to sleep, but his thoughts were a raging maelstrom.

From out of the darkness, a voice called out. "Dad, can you

hear me? I've been looking everywhere for you!" Sofia's anguished plea echoed through the cavern and pierced his heart.

"Sofia, I'm here!" He leapt to his feet and peered into the impenetrable blackness. When the only response was his voice ricocheting back at him, he realized it was yet another hallucination. The memory of their life together was filled with joy and sorrow, and he collapsed on the floor and wept.

Although he loved Sofia with all his heart, he knew that losing her was the ultimate price he must pay. Resigned to his excruciating sacrifice, he held his hands together in prayer. "Archangel Michael, I surrender my life to you," he chanted, repeating the refrain over and over until his tears finally subsided.

The sound of footsteps broke the silence. Aidan looked up as Bishop O'Connor approached his cell and placed the torch in its holder. He took a red woolen robe from a box outside the cell, then unlocked the door and opened it. Aidan stood stiffly, his body emaciated, and searched his godfather's face for approval.

"My son, you have completed your solitude." He handed the robe to Aidan. "Have you made peace with your decision?"

"Yes, my past is dead to me."

"Do you have any doubts?" O'Connor looked deep into his eyes.

"None at all." Aidan exited the cell and put on the robe.

"Has God revealed his plans for you?"

"Yes. He has freed me from fear and delusion, and I know it's my destiny to serve The Brotherhood eternally."

"Blessed be. Let's get you shaved and cleaned up."

"I won't stray from the path again," Aidan said.

"Our patron saint has accepted your sacrifice, and you are

now reborn in the Army of God. As an exalted holy warrior, the rules governing ordinary men no longer apply to you." Relishing his victory, the bishop held out his hand. "All glories to Archangel Michael."

"All glories to The Brotherhood." Aidan bowed down and kissed his ring.

Chapter 55
Trapped

Comfortably dressed in T-shirts and jeans, Sofia, Ella, and Leo sat on a bench in Rome's Municipal Rose Garden, drinking espresso, surrounded by a profusion of multicolored, fragrant flowers. The women shared a blanket to ward off the morning chill. Their location had a view of the city and the tranquil Tiber River, which reflected the light of the rising sun, but they weren't there for the scenery. The reason for their daily pilgrimage was that they had discovered Bishop O'Connor's estate was directly across from this spot in the Rose Garden.

"Leo, it's so thoughtful of you to come with us, but we hate to waste your time," Sofia said.

"Nonsense, we're family. I wouldn't have it any other way."

"Do you know how long he'll be out of town?" she asked.

"Our source didn't know for sure, but he's expected to return this week."

"At least it's a lovely place to enjoy the day," Ella said.

Leo winked and refilled their cups from a thermos. "Especially with the two most beautiful women in Italy."

Ella smiled. "You're such a charmer."

"Is there any news on The Brotherhood?" Sofia asked.

"We've continued investigating but have hit a brick wall. It's a covert society and the only person willing to speak with us said that no one knows about their inner workings except the members. According to him, they're supported by a group of wealthy ultra-orthodox Catholics, but we don't know if he's credible and can't verify his claims."

"They can't be Catholics," Ella said.

"Well, there's no evidence The Brotherhood is affiliated with the Church."

"But the meeting place I found in Ireland was in a Catholic Church."

"I know. However, other than that, we haven't been able to confirm any direct connection between them. Our source also told us that as followers of Michael the Archangel, they consider themselves the intelligentsia of the faith, destined to shape the future of humanity."

Sofia shook her head in disbelief. "They sound like megalomaniacs!"

He shrugged. "What they mean by that wild claim is unknown, but we'll keep digging. When I sink my teeth into a story, I'm like a dog with a bone."

"Thanks so much for looking into them," Ella said.

"I'll keep you posted if there's any news." Leo held up his cup. "*In bocca al lupo!*"

"*Crepi il lupo,*" Ella responded.

Sofia looked at them curiously. "What are you guys talking about?"

"It's an old Italian saying to wish someone good luck before they start a challenging endeavor," Leo explained. "It means *in the wolf's mouth,* and the response is *let the wolf die.*"

"Some Italian sayings are really odd," Sofia said. "But I'm all for avoiding wolves."

Ella laughed. "We can only hope."

Sofia heard an idling motor and jumped to her feet. "His car is here."

A white Mercedes was stopped in front of O'Connor's estate. The gate swung open, and the limo pulled in.

They abandoned their drinks and blanket, dashed out of the Rose Garden, and ran across the street. Not wanting to miss her chance, Sofia rushed onto the property with Ella and Leo close behind. The gate slowly closed, then slammed shut, trapping them inside.

A driver in a gray suit and sunglasses got out of the vehicle and opened the passenger door. Brendan O'Connor, dressed in a casual black cassock with purple piping, and a purple zucchetto covering the bald spot on his head, stepped out.

His bodyguard, a tall, muscular man, in a black military-style uniform and beret, spotted the intruders and stood in front of the bishop defensively. "What are you doing here?"

"Sorry, we didn't mean to disturb you," Ella said.

The chauffeur rushed to his boss's side. "Who are you, and what do you want?"

"I'm Sofia, Aidan Malone's daughter, and this is Leo and my mother, Ella."

"This is private property," the bishop said, bristling with indignation.

"My father is missing, and we need your help," Sofia said.

"How could I possibly help you? Your problem sounds like a personal matter."

"Well, since you're his godfather, we thought you might know where he is."

"Seems to me you didn't think this through at all."

O'Connor turned to his chauffeur. "Call the Carabinieri," he said, then walked into his house.

The driver dialed the police using a cell phone the size of a brick as the bishop's bodyguard pulled out a pistol from his belt and trained it on Sofia, Ella, and Leo.

"You're making a big mistake!" Leo said. "I'm with the press."

"Shut up," the guard snapped. "You can tell your story to the authorities."

They huddled together nervously until a police car screeched to a stop, sirens blaring, and two officers rushed up to the gate which the driver opened. Despite Leo's protests, the police put them into the back of their car and drove toward the *Arma dei Carabinieri* headquarters.

On the drive, Ella sat between Sofia and Leo, her eyes closed. Overcome with stress, she buried her face in her hands. "The last time I was arrested, Rocco and I were forced into a detention camp. I can't believe this is happening."

Leo rubbed her back soothingly. "It's not the same, Ella. I'll explain everything to the police, and we'll straighten this out."

"Please forgive me for putting you in this situation." Sofia stroked her mother's hair.

Ella looked up and took a deep breath. "I'll be fine. Just a terrible memory."

"How long can they hold us, Leo?" Sofia asked.

"It depends on the charges."

Distraught, Sofia stared out the window. "This is a disaster."

"You did nothing wrong," he said. "Besides, it was my idea to confront him."

"But I went too far when I ran onto his property."

"Worst case, they will fine us for trespassing," Leo said.

When they arrived at the Carabinieri General Command

center, a fortified building in central Rome, a police officer took their identification and locked them in a small white interrogation room with a linoleum table and four plastic chairs. The sparse, windowless space was lit by a row of flickering fluorescent light tubes overhead. Silence engulfed the room as Ella and Sofia sat next to each other, dreading what was to come.

Restless, Leo stood and stretched. "They claimed someone would give us an update soon. But being Italy, that could take forever, so we might as well relax."

"I feel so bad, Leo. You haven't seen me in decades, and I immediately get you in trouble."

"This is not your fault, Mom. You both trusted me, and I got us into this mess."

They looked up as the door opened, and Bishop O'Connor entered with his bodyguard. To their surprise, his mood had changed dramatically, and he seemed sincere and contrite. "I apologize for your arrest, but we needed to confirm your identities." He returned their documents. "There are fanatics who would do me harm, and we have security protocols. Let's attribute this unfortunate situation to poor communication." The bishop turned to Leo. "Mr. Moretti, I respect your contributions to journalism. You may go now."

"Apology accepted, but I'm not leaving unless you free them, too."

"They are free to leave as well." He faced Ella and Sofia. "I'm sorry for what you've gone through, but I have good news. I spoke to Aidan, who just arrived in Rome, and mentioned you're looking for him. He's agreed to see you this afternoon."

Sofia was amazed. "That's wonderful!"

"Although Aidan didn't explain why he's been out of touch, I suggested he meet with you in person to sort out your differences. It would be my pleasure to take you to him."

"We'd really appreciate it," Ella said.

"It's the least I can do."

Leo shook the bishop's hand. "Thank you for facilitating their reunion."

"Of course," O'Connor said. "Nothing is more important than family."

As Leo left, accompanied by a police officer, Ella turned to O'Connor. "What you're doing for us is so thoughtful. Sofia misses her father and needs to speak with him."

"Certainly. We'll leave in half an hour or so. My car is quite comfortable—you can wait there. Please come with me."

Sofia and Ella followed him and his guard out of the interrogation room to the parking lot. His attendant unlocked the limo, and they got in. O'Connor peered at them through the open door. "I brought some refreshments for the drive." He gestured to a platter with tomato and cheese finger sandwiches. "And there are chilled beverages in the refrigerator. Enjoy." The bishop closed the door, and the men walked back into the building.

Sofia opened two bottles of Pellegrino and handed one to Ella. As they waited, they ate the food and drank the sparkling water.

"He's being so nice to us," Ella said. "I guess a leopard really can change his spots."

"I'm so grateful for all you've done." Sofia gave her a kiss on the cheek. "Without you, I'd still be spinning my wheels and getting nowhere."

Ella looked out the window, pensively. "I'm glad it worked out for you."

"Mom, I know this isn't what you wanted. Are you going to be all right?"

"I really don't want to face your father, but I probably need to."

"I'll be by your side, and we'll do it together. Hopefully, he'll explain why he left, and we can put all this behind us."

"Don't count on it. Aidan can be very deceitful."

"That's for sure, but I think I can get the truth out of him," Sofia said.

Ella yawned and leaned back. "I can hardly keep my eyes open."

"Me too, it's been a rough day. We could both use some rest." Sofia sighed. At last, her search was almost over, but she felt conflicted about confronting her father. Although relieved to have found him, she was furious about what he'd done. She closed her eyes and instantly fell into a deep sleep.

When the bishop and his bodyguard returned, O'Connor got into the limo next to the driver and gazed at the sleeping women through the open glass partition. He closed the privacy panel, and they pulled away from the police headquarters. After an hour's drive through the Roman countryside, the limo stopped. The bishop slid open the partition and announced, "Ladies, we've arrived. I hope you had a pleasant nap."

Groggy and disoriented, Sofia and Ella slowly came to consciousness. Their vision was blurred but they could see the limo had stopped at the entrance to an enormous walled compound. They looked at each other, blinking to clear their eyes.

"I think he drugged us," Ella whispered.

"Trusting the bishop was a big mistake," Sofia said quietly. They tried to open their doors but were locked in and held each other in fear.

"Sorry, Sofia. I should've known better."

An armed guard swung open the steel gate, and they drove into the complex, through a wooded area toward an ancient stone temple carved into the mountainside.

Sofia recognized the image of the winged lion embedded in

the shrine and pointed at the stained-glass window. "That's The Brotherhood's crest. This must be their headquarters."

They passed through a long tunnel and parked in a vast underground garage. The driver opened their door, and they got out, greeted by more armed guards.

"Why all the guards?" Sofia asked.

"As with all organizations, our society requires maximum security. You're safer here than on the streets of Rome or Derry or Boston," O'Connor flashed a disarming smile.

Sofia's heart sank, realizing The Brotherhood had been tracking her every move.

Chapter 56
Ties That Bind

Bishop O'Connor led Sofia and Ella through The Brotherhood's temple, which was unlike any church they had ever seen. The immense space had no pews, and the red-veined granite floor was polished to a mirror shine. High ceilings, accented with gold, featured elaborate frescoes of Michael the Archangel weighing souls on his perfectly calibrated scales, engaging in battle with rebel angels, and casting Satan out of Heaven.

The altar, with a channel of fire in front, ran the length of one wall. Towering above the flames was a white marble sculpture of Saint Michael, his mighty wings unfurled as he impaled Satan with his sword. Light shining through the stained-glass image of the golden-winged lion bathed the statue in vibrant colors.

As they walked out of the temple and through a maze of travertine hallways, Sofia and Ella looked around for ways to escape, but it seemed impossible. At the end of a long corridor, they reached a wooden door carved with images of the Four Horsemen of the Apocalypse, who symbolized death, famine, war, and conquest. The bishop opened the heavy door, and they entered a narrow passageway which led into a natural stone cavern.

In the center of the circular space was a ring of curved stone benches, smooth from centuries of use. Encircling the bleak chamber, tall beeswax candles stood in alcoves like flaming sentinels reflecting their light on the chiseled rock walls. A shaft of stark sunlight shone through an opening in the ceiling, hundreds of feet above. When Sofia and Ella walked in, the frigid air enveloped them, clinging to their skin like frost on a window.

"Have a seat." The bishop motioned to the benches, his expression inscrutable. "I'll let Aidan know you're here." He left them alone, and they heard the click of the door locking behind him.

"This place is a fortress," Ella said, shivering with cold and despair. "We couldn't leave if we wanted to. We're at his mercy now."

"The bishop fooled us into believing he'd help, but he made it clear they've been tracking me the entire time I've been searching for Dad."

"He tricked me too, and I knew how devious he was."

"I never should have asked you to join me in Rome."

Ella put her arms around Sofia. "Don't blame yourself. No matter what happens, I'm not sorry I came."

The sound of footsteps on the stone floor startled them as a tall man in a hooded red robe emerged from the passageway. In the dim light, they couldn't make out his face, but when he stepped into the stream of sunlight from above, they gasped. It was Aidan, transformed into an almost unrecognizable shell of his former self. He looked gaunt and frail, with sunken eyes that were wild and haunted.

"Oh my God, it's Dad," Sofia whispered to her mother.

"He looks like he's been through a war," Ella said.

Aidan stopped in front of them and pulled back his hood. "I see you two have finally reconciled. It's a pity you bring out the worst in each other."

Sofia ran up to her father and tried to hug him, but he stopped her.

"Dad, what's happened to you?"

"God has shown me the way."

"It looks like you've lost your way!"

"Sofia, stop clinging to the past! You have always been weak, but it's not a trait you should continue to cultivate."

"Weak? Hardly. I found you, didn't I?" she asked, incensed.

"Disobeying my wishes reveals your lack of character, not strength. I instructed you not to search for me. How did you find me?"

"I saved your journal from being burned, and after a lot of searching, I figured it out."

He shook his head in disappointment. "So, besides being self-centered and invading my privacy, you're a thief. Are those the values I taught you?"

Anger shot through Sofia's body. "You taught me not to be a hypocrite, and you seem to have failed that lesson spectacularly!"

Aidan studied her as if she'd lost her mind. "There's nothing hypocritical about my actions. As I told you, you're not welcome in my new life and I can no longer be your father."

Sofia fought back her tears; she would not let him break her, but his words were like a knife in her heart.

Ella jumped up and stood between them. "How dare you reject your own daughter!" She slapped him in the face. "You can deny it, but you'll always be her father!"

"What else do you want from me?" he asked. "You've both been well provided for."

"If you think that's all we care about, you're delusional," Sofia said.

"How can you be so ungrateful after all I've sacrificed for you? You're extremely selfish!"

"We're not selfish. I didn't ask to be born, and you broke your marriage vows to Mom without a second thought. You can't just walk away from your family."

"My earthly family, and I've done my duty as a husband and father." Agitated, he paced back and forth. "I have a higher calling now and I must serve my heavenly master."

"Who . . . Your imaginary deity, Michael the Archangel?" Sofia asked.

"Don't be blasphemous! God wants me to serve Him above all else."

His words infuriated Sofia. "That's bullshit. You don't know what God wants. And a benevolent deity, if there was one, wouldn't want you to abandon your family!"

"She's right," Ella said. "I was a fool to blame myself for our problems. It had nothing to do with me. Now I understand that your fanaticism destroyed our marriage."

He stopped pacing and fixed his gaze on Ella. "You don't have the intelligence to understand me. This conversation is over!"

"That's fine. It's never been a conversation with us anyway," Ella said. "It's always about you and what you want."

"You said the unexamined life is not worth living and now you've become a blind follower. What happened to your intelligence?" Sofia asked.

"This is pointless," Aidan said. "Your perception is clouded by ignorance."

Sofia realized she would never get through to him. "All right, since you've made your choice, please let us go."

Aidan looked away, his breathing labored as he fidgeted

with the sash of his robe. After a prolonged silence, he turned to them and said, "I think that can be arranged . . . under certain conditions."

"Good," Ella said. "We're ready to leave now."

"I'm sorry to lose you, Dad, but it's clear you've swallowed the cult's poison."

Jack's voice rang out. "Poison is not our style, little lady."

They turned and saw him approaching with the bishop and two brutish guards who glared at them.

"Aidan, I'm afraid this meeting needs to end," O'Connor said. "We can't trust them; they know too much about our society."

"The boss is right," Jack said. "We're going to hold them in the catacombs indefinitely."

Aidan stood in front of Ella and Sofia, protectively. "No, we should release them as long as they promise not to speak about us."

The bishop threw up his hands. "I'm sorry, Aidan but it must be done. We have too much to lose. They need to stay here for the rest of their lives and atone for their sins."

"They would never survive here. For my sake, please let them go."

"His Grace has done more than enough for you!" Jack said. "And unlike you, I've never let him down."

O'Connor scowled at Aidan. "Our mission is more important than your emotional entanglements with these women!"

Jack nodded to the guards, who grabbed Sofia and Ella, holding them immobile as they awaited their next orders.

"Stop," Aidan shouted, then turned to his godfather. "Please, I'm begging you."

"Don't forget your vows. I gave you a second chance, and it's time to sacrifice everything for Saint Michael. Was I wrong to believe you were up to the challenge?" O'Connor asked.

Aidan's shoulders slumped and he lowered his head. "No, Your Divine Grace. I will do as you wish."

Her father's sycophantic behavior appalled Sofia. "I feel sorry for you. Your life is a tale told by an idiot, full of sound and fury, signifying nothing!"

"You're quoting Shakespeare to me? You have no concept of what that means."

"Quite the contrary. It's a perfect description of who you've become."

Aidan turned to O'Connor. "Please forgive them. They're just foolish women," he said, then prostrated himself in front of his mentor.

Ella stared in disgust at the man she once loved. "You're pathetic!"

"Now, now, ladies, don't be rude." The bishop patted Aidan on the head like a cowering dog.

Their situation seemed hopeless, but Sofia had an idea. She gave her mother a downward glance and Ella read her mind. With blinding speed, they stomped on the guards' feet causing the men to yelp in pain and momentarily release them. Freed from their grip, they ran frantically toward the passageway leading out of the cavern, but were quickly overtaken by the guards, who wrestled them to the ground, then handcuffed them.

"It's time to show you to your room," Jack smirked and led the way as Sofia and Ella were dragged kicking and screaming out of the cavern.

Chapter 57
No Way Out

Deep in the catacombs of The Brotherhood's headquarters, Ella and her daughter stood trembling in front of a dank cell in the grottos of solitude. Sofia chastised herself for being so stubborn. The culmination of her search was a fate worse than death. They would rot in a cage until their bones were tossed into a mass grave, never to be identified. How could Aidan let this happen to them? It was as if the man she once called her father was dead and a crazed zealot had taken over his mind. If she'd known about his descent into madness, she never would have pursued him or invited her mother to come along.

"Welcome to your forever home," Jack crooned in a cloying voice, as he held up his torch to illuminate their cell.

One of the guards, who resembled a troglodyte with long arms and squat legs, removed their shackles, then shoved the women into the cramped enclosure and locked the door. He turned to Jack, awaiting instructions.

"Go tell the attendant to bring their rations."

"Yes, sir!" He grabbed a torch, and the guards headed up the stone steps.

Sofia clutched the bars of their cell. "You won't get away with this."

"Really, who's going to stop me? No one knows where you are."

"You can't keep us here forever!" Ella shouted.

Jack held out his arms wide and gestured to the vast subterranean space. "Tell that to the thousands of skeletons that have rested here for centuries."

"I'll destroy you if it's the last thing I do!" Sofia threatened.

"I'd love to see you try." Jack chuckled, stepped up to the cell, and scanned his captives sadistically. "You should be grateful. I'll provide everything you need."

"We need our freedom," Ella said.

"Well, that's not going to happen, but I'll make sure you receive bread and water and an empty bowl for your waste every day. What more could a lady want?"

"To see you dead." Sofia seethed with fury.

Jack leered at them. "As a special treat, once a week you'll have a nice cold shower, which I'll supervise."

"You pretend to serve God, but you're a criminal and a pervert," Ella said.

"Not at all. Have you read the Bible lately? To quote Peter 2:18, '*Slaves, in reverent fear of God, submit yourselves to your masters, not only to those who are good and considerate but also to those who are harsh.*'" He eyed them lustfully. "I'll tell you what, if you'd prefer warm showers, clean clothes, and delicious meals, old Jack will provide them . . . in exchange for a little carnal pleasure."

"Not a chance, you freak!" Sofia spat at him through the bars.

He wiped the saliva off his face, unfazed. "In time, you'll see I can be your best friend or your worst enemy."

"Leave us alone," Ella said.

"You'll have plenty of alone time, but eventually, you'll crave my company. I've always dreamed of having a mother and daughter as lovers, and I'm more than man enough for both of you."

"Spoken like a scumbag with a big mouth and a tiny prick," Sofia said.

"Just the opposite, little lady. I'll be back soon, so meditate on the wisdom of my words. You're going to need me." Jack licked his lips salaciously and strutted away with his torch, leaving Sofia and Ella in increasing darkness with each step.

"He's despicable," Ella said. "What are we going to do?"

"I don't know, but there's got to be a way out of here," Sofia replied, trying to convince herself as she sank onto the damp stone floor.

"How?" Ella asked, sitting next to her. "It's impossible. We should pray for a miracle."

"You can try, but I don't see any gods handing out miracles right now."

As they clung to each other in the pitch-black silence, tears of desperation streamed down their cheeks. After what seemed like hours, the light of a torch pierced the darkness.

"Here he comes," Ella whispered.

To their relief, instead of Jack, it was a robed attendant approaching. Without speaking, he slid a tray of food and water under the bars of their cell.

"Could you please leave a torch?" Sofia asked.

The man avoided eye contact and didn't respond.

"Please. Have you no compassion?" Ella asked.

Ignoring them, he left the cavern. Once again, they were alone in the darkness.

"This is a nightmare. How are your prayers going, Mom?"

"Not good. I don't think God can hear me anymore."

"You always said that God helps those who help themselves. Praying isn't the solution. We need to do something."

"But what can we do?" Ella wrapped her arms around her legs protectively. "I think we've died and gone to hell!"

Sofia put her arms around her. "We're not dead and there's no one left in hell; all the demons are on Earth. But I think I have a plan that might get us out of here."

"Really?" Ella asked. "What is it?"

"When Jack returns, we'll agree to his sexual advances and—"

"I would never do that!" Ella said, cutting her off.

"Of course, not. We'll only pretend to. After he unlocks the cell, we'll attack him, gouge out his eyes, steal his keys, and try to escape."

"Brilliant plan. Do you think it will work?"

"I don't know, but we have nothing to lose," Sofia said.

A scuffling noise grabbed their attention. It sounded like an altercation was occurring in the catacombs. Then there was silence, and the sound of footsteps.

"Oh, no! It must be Jack." Ella shuddered in fear.

"I'll take the lead. Once he thinks he's getting his way, I'll kick him in the balls. When he doubles over, you grab the keys."

Terrified, they watched a shadowy figure with a torch approach them. As the man got closer, the light reflected on his intense face. To their shock, it was Aidan.

Sofia's blood boiled. "Have you come to gloat?"

"Trust me," he said, then unlocked their cell and stared at them beseechingly. "I couldn't help you earlier because we were outnumbered. There's a way out, but it's precarious. Stay close to me and be quiet."

When they stepped out of the cage, Aidan led them up the rough stone stairway, which was dimly lit by his flickering torchlight. Sofia took her mother's hand, and they began the arduous trek out of the catacombs. As they reached the entrance to the landing, Aidan motioned for them to wait, then peered around to make sure they weren't being observed.

He waved for them to come, and they followed him onto the landing, which was lit by oil lanterns. Aidan tamped out his torch and set it in a copper tub filled with extinguished torches. Instead of heading for the elevator, he led them through a side door to a modern steel staircase that ascended steeply through the cavern. The space was illuminated by huge electric bulbs, suspended on cables dangling hundreds of feet from the craggy stone ceiling. As they walked, deep rumbling sounds reverberated in the chamber, shaking the stairs and making the lights sway, casting strange shadows on the stone walls.

"Please, I need to rest." Ella stopped, trying to catch her breath.

"There's no time for that," Aidan said. "You must be off the property before anyone realizes you're gone. We're taking a service route to the exit. Hopefully, no one will see us."

Ella was flushed, and her legs ached. Sofia hugged her. "I know you can do it, Mom. Take my arm. I'll help you."

"All right." Ella pushed herself to continue hiking the seemingly endless stairs that zigzagged upwards through the bowels of The Brotherhood's subterranean complex. The stairway led to a series of landings that branched off into enormous rooms. The first was an emergency living quarters with cots and rations for hundreds of people.

"This looks like a bomb shelter," Sofia said.

Aidan nodded. "It's engineered to withstand a nuclear attack."

He prodded them up the stairs, past an electrical substation with generators, transformers, and pipes branching in all directions. The next landing housed massive water tanks, and the one above it contained what appeared to be bank vaults and archives.

Exhausted, Ella and Sofia were slowing down. Aidan turned around, impatiently. "Hurry, we've almost reached the loading area where I can drive you off the compound." Relieved, they forced themselves to pick up the pace and trailed him through a passageway that led to the parking garage. When they entered, Aidan stopped in front of a black sedan. "Wait here. I'll get the keys and be right back." He rushed into the building.

Suddenly, they heard the ominous wail of a predator closing in on its prey. Sofia and Ella turned toward the sound. From across the garage, Jack howled like a wolf and the bishop grinned triumphantly as they rapidly approached them.

Jack's taunting voice called out. "Hey ladies, going for a joy ride?"

Sofia and her mother broke down, unable to contain their distress. Their hopes of freedom were dashed. They were so close, but it was all over now.

"We're going to die here," Ella said, her voice barely above a whisper. For once, Sofia was speechless. They'd reached the end of the end, and nothing could save them.

Chapter 58
Double Crossed

Hearing the commotion in The Brotherhood's underground garage, Aidan rushed up to Sofia and Ella, shielding them as Jack and the bishop arrived. "The catacombs are for penitents. They don't belong here, so I freed them, and you must honor my decision."

"Quite the contrary," O'Connor said. "It's not your decision; it's mine."

"Don't do this. I'm warning you!" Aidan stepped toward them threateningly.

"Warning me? How dare you disobey my orders!" The bishop signaled for Jack to proceed.

Jack sauntered up to Sofia and Ella, pointing a handgun at them. "It's time to go back to your cage."

O'Connor gave Aidan a hard look. "I'm disappointed in you."

Jack waved his gun at him. "If you'd taught your daughter obedience, she would have listened to me in Derry and none of this would have happened."

Aidan faced him. "You've caused enough damage. My brother took the bullet that was meant for you!"

"Get it through your thick skull; the British killed William, not me." He aimed his weapon at Ella and Sofia. "Follow me, ladies, or you'll be hogtied and dragged to your cell."

"I won't allow you to harm them. You must set them free," Aidan demanded.

"Dad, please stop him. Jack threatened to rape us!"

"It's true," Ella said.

Infuriated, Aidan lashed out at Jack. "I've always known you're a despicable abuser of women, but I told you to stay away from my family."

"She's a liar!" Jack shouted.

"Unlike you, they don't lie. Go to hell!" Aidan whipped a pistol out of his pocket and shot Jack in the head.

As he collapsed from the mortal wound, his gun skittered across the floor and O'Connor went after it. Aidan called out a warning. "Sofia!"

She sprinted with catlike grace and grabbed the weapon an instant before he could reach it. Aidan and Sofia trained their pistols on him. The bishop had lost control of the situation and glowered at them.

Aidan turned to Sofia and Ella. "There's only one condition you must agree to. Never speak about me, The Brotherhood or what happened here to anyone."

"I promise," Sofia said.

Ella nodded. "You have my word."

"I'm sorry for all the pain I've put you through, and I'd like to make amends," Aidan said. "I was about to sell the ranch, but since I know how much you love it, I'll put the property in your names."

His offer surprised Sofia. "Would you really do that for us?"

"You can count on it."

Ella was moved. "Thank you."

"But you must leave Italy as soon as possible," Aidan said.

The bishop shook his head. "I can't allow it."

"It's the only way that's acceptable to me." Aidan pointed the gun at his godfather. "And you have no choice, unless you want to end up like old Jack."

O'Connor eyed the body lying on the floor in a pool of blood. "You would never . . ."

"I've done worse."

"Have you lost your mind? I'm your superior!"

Aidan scoffed. "You may outrank me in the hierarchy at the moment, but I have all I need to destroy you."

The bishop was taken aback. "That's unconscionable. We agreed you'd burn the documents if I allowed you to rejoin the society."

"Well, it was in my best interest to keep them, along with all the recordings, as proof of your crimes."

"This is outrageous!" O'Conner said. "How could you stab me in the back this way after all I've done for you?"

"Under your leadership, the society has become corrupt. I'm going to purge the rot and guide us to glory."

The bishop's eyes burned with rage. "What do you want from me?"

"Absolute loyalty and submission."

"You won't get away with this."

"Oh, but I will. I've instructed a trusted associate to take the evidence to the press if anything ever happens to me, Ella, or Sofia. It will all be public, and you'll die in prison. I swear it on my brother's grave."

"My people will stop you."

"Actually, the majority of the brothers support me."

"That's impossible. You just returned."

"Not really. You were blinded by arrogance," Aidan said

with the ghost of a smile. "The plan has been in the works for years, and you're the last piece to fall into place."

Unblinking, the bishop and his protege faced off. Beads of perspiration trickled down O'Connor's brow. After a moment of tense silence, he spoke in a low growl. "I see . . . I've taught you well."

"I learned from a master. Now, you must show me the respect I've always deserved."

"No one has ever done more for you or cherished you more than I have," O'Connor said, his voice quavering. "And when I choose to retire you will inherit my mantle of leadership. Surely that's fair."

Aidan held the pistol to his godfather's head. "Nice try. Do what I say, or you'll retire eternally right now. The choice is yours." He cocked the gun.

The bishop stared at him pleadingly for a moment, opened his mouth to speak, then, realizing it was futile, wilted like a dying rose, collapsed on the floor and bowed at Aidan's feet. "I'm at your service," he said, his voice tinged with the bitter taste of betrayal and resignation.

"Good. Arrange for them to be driven to their hotel immediately."

Realizing Aidan had outmaneuvered him, O'Connor stood and walked dejectedly to the entrance. As he summoned two servants on the intercom system, Aidan lowered his weapon and took the gun from his daughter.

Seconds later, two guards in black suits arrived and removed Jack's corpse. Aidan led Ella and Sofia to an elevator that took them out of the parking garage, and they ascended in stunned silence.

When they stepped outside, Ella and Sofia burst into tears and held each other, traumatized but grateful to be alive, free, and breathing fresh air again. They squinted at Aidan in the light of the setting sun. Although they had seen him be a fanatic and a killer, they pitied him. He was still capable of kindness, and they saw that side too. Aidan was infinitely more complex and troubled than they ever imagined; a conflicted man who, despite his intelligence, was lost beyond all hope.

He spoke quietly, as if he were fading away. "I will always value the time we had together, but you must forget me now. Erase me from your memory."

"Sorry, Dad, I don't think that's possible." Sofia gazed at him sadly.

The bishop's white limo pulled up, and they got in. Ella looked wistfully at Aidan. "*Solo amici,*" she whispered.

"Yes, forever friends," he said under his breath and closed the car door.

When the vehicle pulled away, Sofia and Ella watched as Aidan slipped into the temple without glancing back. Sofia's heart sank, knowing she would never see him again. The loss of someone who was so connected to her was gut wrenching. It had been a transformative experience, and she realized her father was far from the man she thought he was. Although it would be hard, she was determined to put him out of her mind and move forward with her life.

Sofia glanced at Ella; her face had softened as if she had finally let Aidan go. It was a blessing to be close to her mother and she felt intense love for her. "Mom, when we get home, I hope you'll move in with me at the ranch."

Ella leaned over and kissed her daughter. "Nothing could make me happier."

As the limo drove through the open gates and headed down the road, Sofia and Ella saw Leo's red Alfa Romeo parked on the shoulder, several hundred feet away.

Sofia knocked on the glass partition. "Stop the car!"

The chauffeur pulled over and lowered the panel. "What's wrong?"

"You can drop us off here. We don't need you to take us to the hotel."

"That's not what I was told to do, miss," he said.

"I don't care what you were told. Open the doors, now!" she commanded.

The driver released the locks, they got out, and he sped away.

"I can't believe you're here!" Sofia said, as they ran up to Leo and Beppe who got out of the car to greet them.

"We've been inside the compound for hours. How on earth did you find us?" Ella asked.

"I drove Leo's car to the police station and arrived just before you left so we were able to follow you," Beppe said.

"I really didn't trust that bishop," Leo added. "And there was no way I was going to leave until I could confirm you were okay."

Sofia and Ella threw their arms around them and held on as if their lives depended on it.

"I'm really loving the hug, but I think we should get the hell out of here," Beppe said.

They all hopped in the car and pulled away.

"I can tell you went through something really terrible. What happened?" Leo asked.

"We've been sworn to secrecy," Sofia said. "And for your safety and ours, we can never talk about it."

"And you must promise not to mention us in any story you publish about The Brotherhood," Ella said, resting her head on Sofia's shoulder.

Leo studied their troubled faces in the rearview mirror. "Of course. We would never betray your confidence."

"You can count on us," Beppe said.

"Thanks. If you don't mind, Ella and I would love to get some rest." They closed their eyes and leaned back, desperately trying to calm their frayed nerves. As her breathing slowed, Sofia thought about what had transpired. Nothing turned out the way she planned, and she pondered what the future would hold for her and her mother. They had endured a perilous journey through a labyrinth of lies, and just as steel becomes tempered in fire, she knew they had become stronger. If they lived through this, surely they could survive anything.

Chapter 59
No Regrets

After seizing power at The Brotherhood's headquarters, Aidan drove to Rome. It was late at night by the time he arrived at Gemma's apartment and unlocked the front door. From inside, he heard the classic Edith Piaf song "Non, Je Ne Regrette Rien" with Gemma's incandescent voice singing along with the recording. When he entered, he found the diva lounging on her white sofa, wearing green silk pajamas, in front of the glass table with the Lady Absinthe Fountain.

She looked at him with concern. "You're much thinner than the last time I saw you."

"The ordeal was rough, but worth it. I'm on the inside now." He walked over to the phonograph and picked up the album cover. "You've chosen the perfect song."

"So, you have no regrets?"

"Absolutely none."

Gemma got up, turned down the volume, and embraced him. "Did everything go as planned?"

"Not at all. I had to improvise and accelerate our timeline when the bishop brought Sofia and Ella to the compound."

"Are they all right?" she asked.

"They're safe, but they were locked in the catacombs, and I had to kill Jack to get them out."

"Oh my God. Did you kill the bishop too?"

"He's more useful alive. For now, he'll be the face of The Brotherhood, but I'll be pulling the strings." Aidan took her hand, and they settled on the circular sofa together.

"I'm glad that arrogant asshole is finally in his place."

"After abusing you, and so many other young girls, he's getting exactly what he deserves."

"Do you think he even knows why you took him down?" she asked.

"Well, he molested children and embezzled millions from the Vatican Bank, so I think he has a pretty good idea."

"I'll bet you never expected an atheist soprano would be your most valuable asset." She sang a crystal-clear trill, swooping up to a high C.

Aidan smiled in delight. "You, my dear, are much more than an asset. You've reignited my passion and taught me that what people believe is irrelevant; it's their actions that count."

"We make a divine team."

"Yes, we do, my dolce diva. You're an incomparable woman and this is only the beginning."

"What's next, professor?"

"We'll use the resources of the society to further my agenda."

"Can you give me a hint?"

"It's a long list, but I intend to tackle the glaring inequities in the world."

"That's quite an ambitious goal! How will you keep the donors on your side if you give away their money?"

"There are ways to placate the wealthy with fame, power, and the promise of an afterlife. I already have some key politicians in my pocket, and influential leaders in the United States and Europe have pledged their loyalty."

"Nicely done. Let's have a Green Fairy to celebrate." Gemma placed sugar cubes on the spoons, opened the absinthe spigots, filled two glasses with the green, anise-flavored spirit, and handed one to him. They sipped the hypnotic elixir.

"I couldn't have done it without you," Aidan said and kissed her.

Chapter 60
Jiggety Jog

"Home again, home again, jiggety jog!" The sound of Aidan's voice wafted through Sofia's mind as she swayed on the hammock under the shade of the old oak at the ranch in San Diego. He used to recite the nursery rhyme about a farmer coming home from the market every time they returned to the ranch, and it reminded her of how quirky and playful her father once was. She agreed with the sentiment; it was awesome being home again but also a little strange. In many ways, she felt like a new person in a world that looked the same yet was entirely different.

Aidan was right about change being hard, but she learned to embrace it. The cyclone of change that swept her into its vortex had been terrifying and life-changing, but now all she wanted was to slow down, relax and enjoy her life.

Sofia gazed at the initials she and Liam had carved into the trunk of the majestic tree. Nothing could ever replace her brother, and he would always be a part of her, but now instead of sorrow, she was grateful for the brief time they had together.

A flash of light from a crystal perched on the table beside

her caught her eye and she picked up the stone, which sparkled in the sun. As she held the good luck charm Kieran Kelly gave her at Mystic River, she remembered his words: *The purity of this crystal destroys all negative energy around it and will lighten your journey.*

It seemed to have worked. Her search had more negative energy than she ever could have imagined, but she reconciled with her mother, and though still a work in progress, made peace with her father's decision. As a bonus, she met special new friends like Kieran, Finn, and Leo, along the way, so it was all worthwhile.

Sofia inhaled the fresh morning air and listened to the sweet, serenading song of a mockingbird high in the tree. When she first returned to the ranch with Ella, she wondered if her childhood memories would haunt her, but that wasn't the case. It was impossible to forget her father after all they'd been through, but it turned out his absence was a blessing in disguise. Without his overbearing presence, she could finally be herself, and it felt liberating.

Since returning to California three months ago, Sofia and her mother had made amazing progress. Aidan honored his promise to put the ranch in their names and even had his car delivered to them. She found a renter for the beach house, and Ella moved in along with Luna, her beloved calico cat. They got along famously and were more like best friends than mother and daughter.

Furnishing the empty ranch house seemed like a daunting process. Fortunately, after a few days of searching, Sofia discovered Aidan had donated most of their belongings to a local Catholic charity, Saint Vincent de Paul, and she bought back the pieces she treasured. By adding items from her cottage and Ella's apartment, they had everything they needed and after some personal touches, the house became their home.

One of the first things Sofia wanted to do was bring Gaia back to the ranch. At Hilltop Stables, Maria and Gusmaro were pleased to see them and inquired about Aidan. Sofia told them he was working on a series of research projects that might keep him in Europe indefinitely, so her mother had moved in with her. They were relieved the story they made up to explain Aidan's absence worked flawlessly and resolved to use it with anyone who asked about him.

When Maria led them to Gaia's stable, they discovered that Sofia's faithful companion had become bonded with another gorgeous palomino named Gabi and the horses didn't want to be separated. Ella fell in love with Gabi, and Sofia purchased the horse on the spot. Gusmaro brought both mares to the ranch, where Sofia and Ella spent many joyful hours riding together.

Shortly after they had settled in, Kieran stopped by for a visit and brought the wedding painting of Ella and Aidan. It was an expressive piece of modern art, but they weren't sure if they should keep it and considered tossing it in the trash. Both were concerned that seeing Aidan's image might be disturbing, but although things ended badly, the portrait reminded them there were good times as well. Instead of focusing on his duplicity, they chose forgiveness and hung the art in the barn where Aidan left his goodbye note.

Over the course of her journey, Sofia learned a lot about her parents and herself, and her point of view shifted dramatically, as if she were seeing life through a new lens. The parents she thought she knew were a fiction. Her simplistic conception of them bore little resemblance to the multi-dimensional people they actually were.

At the start of the summer, which seemed like a lifetime ago, Sofia naively idolized Aidan. But after he abandoned her, she had to find her own way. Now she understood her mother loved her unconditionally, unlike her father who was a tragic figure, lost in his delusions. Life could be a roller coaster and although it had been a rough ride, she was eager to see what was around the next bend.

Sofia also realized she'd been intolerant about many things, including religion. If worship and ceremonies made people happy and harmed no one, she decided to quit being so judgmental. It was a luxury having time to think about the meaning of life, and she concluded that since a finite human brain couldn't possibly comprehend an infinite expanding universe, she happily surrendered to living in a state of wonder which gave her the freedom to have new realizations. And because it was her personal path, she had no desire to talk about it or convince others to agree with her.

Since Ella received comfort and peace by attending Mass at her church in Little Italy, Sofia started going with her and sharing the experience. Every Sunday, they would go to Our Lady of the Rosary, followed by a luscious Italian lunch and a visit to the farmer's market. Best of all, it brought her even closer to her mother.

Sunlight filtering through the branches warmed Sofia, and she knew it must be close to noon. She'd whiled away the morning ruminating and relaxing, but now the sun had reached its zenith, so she jumped out of the hammock, picked fresh zucchini, tomatoes, basil, and parsley from the garden, and hurried toward the house.

She stepped inside and was delighted to hear Ella singing "Volare." How different the home was now, filled with good cheer and no pressure from her father to be perfect. Her mother stood at an easel by the window that overlooked the garden. The subject of her new watercolor was Luna, who posed contentedly in the bay window, curled up in the sunlight next to a vase of purple and yellow wildflowers.

Sofia spotted the cat lounging on the windowsill. "How do you get her to pose like that?"

"I don't have to. She always finds a sunny spot to show off how pretty she is," Ella said.

"I love it!" Sofia said, admiring the canvas.

Ella set down her brush. "Beautiful subjects make beautiful art."

"Ready for lunch?" Sofia held up the basket of fresh vegetables.

"Sounds great. Can I help?" Ella asked.

"No. I'll take care of it. It's nice to see you painting again."

"Thank you, darling."

She headed for the kitchen and Ella resumed singing the popular Italian tune.

As Sofia cut vegetables for the pasta primavera, the crystal butterfly that hung in the window cast rainbow prisms across the counter and reminded her of the good times she shared with her father. When she began to sauté the garlic, Ella joined Sofia in the kitchen. "Smells good. You're a fantastic cook. I'll grate the Romano."

"Thanks, Mom."

Sofia finished up the pasta while Ella grated the cheese and set the table. Soon, they were savoring the home-cooked meal.

"Cooking and eating are much more enjoyable when I'm with you," Ella said.

"It's more fun for me too. Hey, do you want to ride to the pond after lunch?"

"I'd love to. It's so wonderful having horses and living in the country again. I feel like I've died and gone to heaven."

"But I'm glad we got to skip the dying part." Sofia smiled and twirled the pasta primavera on her fork.

Ella laughed. "It's been a whirlwind but look at us now."

Chapter 61
Special Delivery

It was a warm Indian Summer afternoon as Sofia and Ella rode Gaia and Gabi along the banks of the stream that wound through the ranch, ending up at a large pond. They dismounted and the mares whinnied, then headed to the water for a drink. The tranquil refuge was one of their favorite places.

After they settled on a blanket shaded by a canopy of coast live oaks, Sofia said, "Mom, I have a surprise for you from the Italian market."

Ella was delighted when Sofia pulled out a blue box of Perugina Italia Dark Chocolate Baci Balls out of her bag. "What a treat! These remind me of my childhood."

Sofia opened the chocolates and handed her mother one of the sweets wrapped in silver foil. "I thought you might like them."

"I love them! Francesca would buy these at Christmas time. I was always so excited to read the secret note inside." Ella unwrapped the chocolate ball and read the enclosed message. "*True happiness comes from creating something new.*" She took a bite. "What does yours say?"

Sofia opened her message. "*Even the stones placed in one's path can be made into something beautiful.*" She popped the sweet into her mouth.

"Wisdom from a chocolate," Ella said.

"How do the Baci Balls know what happened to us?" Sofia smiled.

"They're magic."

They stretched out on the blanket and watched the horses eating grass at the water's edge. "Sometimes I can't believe we got out of the catacombs alive." Sofia turned to her mother. "Do you think Dad will ever come to his senses?"

Ella brushed a lock of hair from her daughter's eyes. "You really need to let him go."

"I'm trying, but it's not easy. Despite everything, I think he still loves us, or he wouldn't have helped us escape."

"Maybe it was love or maybe it was something else. We'll never know and that's okay, because having him out of our lives is the best thing that ever happened to us."

"Sorry I brought it up," Sofia said.

"There's no need to be sorry, but we shouldn't dwell on the past."

"You're right. Life is short, and we should be grateful for all our blessings . . . like art, chocolate . . . and skinny dipping."

"What dipping?" Ella asked.

"You know, when you swim naked. Kieran said he used to go skinny dipping with you and Dad. Is that true?"

Ella blushed. "Yes, but I was very young."

"I'd love a swim right now."

"But we didn't bring bathing suits," Ella said.

Sofia pulled off her shirt. "So, we'll swim in our birthday suits. What do you say?"

"Well, I'm not young anymore, but what the heck."

Giggling like teenagers, they stripped and jumped into the

clear pond, splashing each other, and romping in the cool water. A short time later, they got out, dressed, and relaxed on the blanket.

"That was exhilarating," Ella said. "I feel younger already."

"And I feel older. I guess I'm finally growing up."

"You've always been an old soul. You just didn't know it."

Sofia turned on her side and faced her mother. "I've been thinking a lot about what to do with my life, and Leo really inspired me."

"I'm sure he inspires a lot of women," Ella said with a gleam in her eye. "He's so handsome."

"Not that way, Mom. I admit he's attractive, but I want to become a journalist like him."

"That's an excellent idea. You've always loved writing and research."

"I thought I'd be a journalist when I graduated, but after a big controversy, I gave up that dream."

"Why? What happened?" Ella asked.

"In an article I wrote for the college newspaper, I revealed there was plagiarism in a research study by a prominent faculty member. He was popular, and a lot of people blamed me for getting him in trouble."

"No one should have blamed you for telling the truth."

"They did. And I couldn't stand to face that kind of criticism ever again, so I quit. But after what we went through in Italy, I've grown a rhinoceros hide."

"You can do anything you put your mind to."

"Thanks for believing in me," Sofia said. "Are you ready to head back?"

"Can we stay a little longer?" Ella asked.

"Sure. There's nowhere I'd rather be."

Sofia and Ella lay down, closed their eyes, and enjoyed the

serene music of nature as the warm breeze rustled the leaves of the tree that sheltered them.

Soon, they dozed off but were awakened by Gaia nuzzling them. Sofia opened her eyes. "Hey, baby, are you hungry for a snack?" She stroked the horse's mane, then opened her backpack and pulled out the carrots she brought for them. "Here you go, sweetheart."

Ella sat up, waved a carrot, and Gabi sauntered over for her treat. "I think the girls are ready to go home."

"The horses are in charge, so we better get going," Sofia said.

They packed up, mounted Gaia and Gabi and rode back to the house as the setting sun painted the sky with crimson clouds.

After a hot shower, they relaxed in the living room, where Ella continued with her watercolor. Sofia sat at her desk, piled high with books, and logged on to her new Apple II personal computer to make a list of topics she was interested in writing about, as well as newspapers and magazines she could submit them to. At long last, she had settled on a career path and was eager to embark on her new challenge.

As they worked in silence, lost in concentration, the doorbell chimed, and Sofia got up to answer it. A postal worker handed her a large envelope from Boston that required her signature. She signed and brought it inside.

"Who was that?" Ella asked.

"The mailman."

"This late?"

"It's from Kieran." Sofia held up the envelope.

"That's nice," Ella said. "Maybe he's coming for another visit."

"I hope so, but if it's just a letter it seems strange he'd send it by special delivery."

Ella walked over to her, and they sat on the sofa together. Sofia ripped open the envelope and took out a letter and a newspaper clipping. As she scanned the obituary from the *Boston Herald*, her face turned ashen, and she was gripped by a numbing chill. "Dad had a heart attack, and he's dead!" She burst into tears, and Ella hugged her. "It's hard to believe he's gone."

"After what he did, maybe the bishop killed him," Ella said.

"Could be. I think he's capable of anything." Shaken, Sofia picked up the handwritten letter and read it to her mother.

Dear Sofia and Ella,
I'm sorry to be the bearer of such sad news, but I was
stunned to find Aidan's obituary in the paper this morn-
ing. I know his family has treated you badly, and
assumed they wouldn't tell you, so I'm sending this
letter special delivery in case you want to attend his
memorial service. Unfortunately, I can't be there as I'll
be teaching at a yoga retreat in Sedona. Aidan will
always be my brother from another mother. I love you
both and promise to visit the next time I'm in California.
Namaste,
Kieran

Dazed, Sofia set the letter down and dried her eyes with a tissue. "I shouldn't cry. He put us through hell, but I still love him." She paused, trying to hold back a wave of conflicting emotions then looked at the obituary. "His funeral is this Saturday. It says he's survived by his parents and sister."

Ella drew a quick breath. "But I thought you said his parents were dead."

"Well, his horrible sister must have lied about that, too." Sofia continued reading. "There's no mention of us."

Disgusted, Ella pushed the newspaper away. "To them, we don't exist."

Sofia's grief turned to outrage, and she squeezed her mother's hand. "We need to be there, Mom."

"We shouldn't get involved. Let it go, Sofia."

"No, I can't. And I'm going to make damn sure they all know we exist!"

Chapter 62
Requiescat In Pace

Sofia and Ella parked their rental car at Sacred Heart Cemetery in Boston and got out. It was a frigid, blustery morning, and the service was scheduled to begin in a few minutes. As they headed toward the outdoor ceremony, a fire engine red Lincoln Continental Town Car raced through the lot and screeched to a stop at a parking space in front of Ella and Sofia, almost hitting them.

A tall, aggressive woman wearing a full-length fur coat with matching hat and mittens, jumped out then slammed her door, flashing them a condescending look as she bustled past. Abruptly stopping in her tracks, she whirled around and stared at them in disbelief. Sofia recognized her instantly. It was Aidan's sister, Margaret Grace.

"What the hell are you two doing here?" she demanded. "You weren't invited."

"We have every right to be here," Sofia said.

The imperious woman gaped at Sofia and Ella. "Over my dead body!" Before they could respond, Margaret Grace spewed a barrage of venom. "Aiden explicitly stated in his will that you were not to attend his memorial service as it would be offensive to the Church and his loved ones. I thought I made myself abundantly clear—we don't consider you members of our family, so leave and do not contact us again."

Undaunted, Sofia stepped up to her challengingly. "I don't believe you and we never received my father's will."

"I was waiting until after the service to send it. And just so you know, you won't receive any additional money from his estate. The rest of his assets are being left to my sons and the Church."

"We didn't come here for his money." Ella gave her a scathing look.

"We came to pay our last respects," Sofia said.

"I don't have time for your nonsense. I'm late. Now, respect Aidan's wishes and go," she commanded, then turned and left in a huff.

Ella shook her head in disgust. "I told you we shouldn't have come."

"Don't worry, Mom. She's just a bully and we're not going to back down." Sofia took her arm, and they walked out of the parking lot. A restless wind stung their faces as they trudged across the damp grass between the gravestones toward the funeral. Despite being bundled in a heavy coat, Sofia couldn't stop shivering. It seemed as though the bleak and miserable weather magnified the cold reality of her father's passing.

"He was always troubled," Ella said. "But they destroyed him."

Aidan's memorial service had already begun and the poignant sound of bagpipes playing "Amazing Grace" filled the air. The piper, standing under a tree, wore an orange and green County Derry tartan kilt, and matching Glengarry hat with an eagle feather. As Sofia and Ella approached the service, they saw a small group of mourners facing the grave.

Next to the casket, a large, framed photo of young Aidan, dressed in priestly vestments, rested on a wooden easel with bouquets of white calla lilies on either side. Below his image were the words:

AIDAN MATTHEW MALONE 1918—1978
FOREVER A PRIEST
REJOICE FOR HE IS IN THE ARMS OF THE LORD

Her father's intense steel-gray eyes stared back at Sofia, reminding her of how brilliant and handsome he was; it was a face she missed and would never forget. While contemplating the photo, she heard the unmistakable deep voice of Bishop Brendan O'Connor beginning the eulogy.

"I have known Monsignor Malone since the day he was born in Derry, Ireland, sixty years ago." O'Connor, dressed in his bishop's regalia, had a gold chain and large cross hanging from his neck. "I officiated at his baptism and helped him grow into a fine young man and a treasure to his family and the Church. It is with deep sadness that we lay him to rest today."

Sofia and Ella made their way toward the grave, each holding a red rose. Noticing their arrival, the bishop paused, disconcerted by their transgression. He quickly regained his composure, looked away from them, and continued speaking. Sofia tuned him out, but as hard as she tried, she couldn't forgive him for his role in breaking up their family. As they reached the coffin, all heads turned, radiating an intense wave of disapproval at them. Ella cast her eyes down, not wanting to meet their hostile stares, but Sofia held her head high, carrying herself with defiance and dignity.

Sitting in chairs in front of Aidan's coffin, Clare and Gareth glared at them with contempt. Now in their eighties, they were doddering and frail, their dour faces frozen in permanent frowns.

"Those are his parents," Ella whispered to Sofia.

She glanced at them. "I've never seen such sour faces. Do you think they ever smile?"

"I doubt it."

Next to Gareth and Clare were Margaret Grace, and her husband, Declan, who scowled at the intruders. Their four adult sons sat beside them in stiff black suits, mirroring their parents' disdain. Although lasting only seconds, the enmity felt like an eternity.

In the row behind Aidan's family, a gathering of priests, nuns, and parishioners listened somberly. The mourners were strangers to Sofia, a part of Aidan's past that was a mystery to her. But he had another life they knew nothing about. Were any of them truly close to her father? And did they even know about The Brotherhood and the crimes the organization was involved with? Her cheeks flushed with anger. The memorial was a sham, another show of false piety.

When they reached the polished mahogany casket inlaid with a silver cross, Ella placed her rose on top and whispered, "*Solo amici.*"

Sofia took Kieran's quartz crystal out of her coat pocket and placed it on the coffin along with her rose. "I hope this will lighten your journey. I'll always love you." Her eyes uncontrollably filled with tears, and she wiped them away.

The bishop pivoted to confront Ella and Sofia. "Aidan was an exemplary priest. Why should such a great man die? The Bible affirms that death is a consequence of original sin." He stared at them accusingly.

Unable to stay silent any longer, Sofia fired back. "Don't preach to us, you hypocrite. My father loved me and my mother. You took him away from us and now you claim we don't exist? You know perfectly well we do. And we know your secrets."

Shocked by Sofia's blasphemous confrontation with their beloved bishop, an audible gasp arose from the onlookers who murmured and squirmed uncomfortably in their seats.

Bishop O'Connor grimaced, then addressed the mourners. "Please ignore these poor lost souls. Monsignor Malone is with his heavenly father now, along with his brother, William, whom we lost so long ago. May they both rest in peace. Let us pray."

The flock obediently lowered their heads in silent prayer and the bagpiper began playing a plaintive dirge. While the funeral workers cranked the straps that guided the casket into the ground, it began to drizzle, and the crowd slowly dispersed.

As Ella and Sofia left the memorial hand in hand, there was a clap of thunder, the sky darkened, and they were drenched by a sudden downpour. Anxious to get out of the rain, they dashed along the path and took refuge under a covered gazebo in front of a rustic stone chapel.

Sofia pulled two handkerchiefs from her purse, handed one to Ella and they dried their faces. "I guess we should have packed umbrellas."

"Don't worry, we'll wait here until there's a break." Ella gestured to a bench.

They sat in silence as lightning streaked across the dark gray sky and peals of thunder rumbled, each feeling the heaviness of Aidan's demise in their own way.

Sofia turned to her mother. "Death seems so final, but maybe the people we love are never really gone."

"I've always believed the soul is eternal," Ella said. "So, our relationships must be too."

"It's weird, but sometimes it feels like he's still alive."

"Of course. He'll always be a part of your life—and mine."

They embraced and Sofia rested her head on her mother's shoulder.

In the top-floor window of the stone chapel, a face gazed through the distorted rain-soaked glass. It was Aidan, surreptitiously watching Ella and Sofia comfort each other in the gazebo across from him. He picked up a phone and dialed.

"Pronto," Gemma answered, from her penthouse in Rome.

"It's done. Sofia and Ella will never search for me again."

"Music to my ears. I'm glad they're safe."

"After all our hard work, I think we deserve a vacation," Aidan said.

"Fabulous! Lucia and I are going to the villa in Capri. You should join us."

"Splendid. I'll leave as soon as my funeral is over."

Gemma laughed. "How does it feel to be dead?"

"Thrilling! I may be dead to the world, but I feel more alive than ever."

"Just as we planned. See you soon. Ciao!"

When he hung up the phone, the rain had abated, and Aidan looked out the window. He watched inscrutably as his daughter and former wife left the shelter, walked away from the cemetery, and out of his life, forever.

Sofia and Ella got in the rental car and drove toward the airport, relieved to be heading home. After a marathon of chasing shadows, a weight had been lifted from their hearts and minds.

"What a tragic end to his life." Sofia glanced at her mother, sitting in the passenger seat.

"Ashes to ashes, dust to dust," Ella said. "Don't worry, darling. We're going to be all right."

"Of course we are. As you said, Italian women are tough."

About the Author

Photo by Jenna Gilmer

A.C. Adams is the nom de plume of co-authors Anthony Leigh Adams and Christina Adams, who have written, produced, and developed film and television projects for many studios, including Disney, ABC, and CBS.

Christina is a producer of the Emmy Award-winning series, *The Amazing Race* and multiple programs for Oprah Winfrey. Anthony composed the music and co-wrote the book and lyrics for their most recent theatrical project, *Sideways: The Musical,* which is based on the Oscar-winning film and is in development as a Broadway musical.

The Adamses also wrote and produced the original musicals *Love-In: A Musical Celebration* and *Primal Twang: The Legacy of The Guitar.* Both shows were filmed and aired nationally on PBS. *Primal Twang* won Best Documentary Feature at the Rome International Film Festival.

Adams Entertainment, Anthony and Christina's production company, is based in La Jolla, California, where they work and live with their two calico rescue cats. *Chasing Shadows,* their debut novel, is inspired by true events. For more information visit: www.adamsentertainment.com